LISA HELEN GRAY

FAITH

A NEXT GENERATION CARTER BROTHER NOVEL
BOOK ONE

LIVE, LAUGH, LOVE.

FAITH

PROLOGUE

FOUR MONTHS AGO

SOMEONE, SOMEWHERE, IS ALWAYS LOOKING for something more in life. They don't want some cheap hook-up in a pub. They don't want to have some meaningless encounter. And for others, like me, they don't want to be the girl who lost their virginity whilst still at school, still learning how to survive in the world we live.

I'm the girl who wanted more.

I'm the girl who knew love didn't bring instant happiness. It was the people you surrounded yourself with, the situations you put yourself in, and the happiness you felt within that defined your contentment.

I've experienced happiness every day of my life.

But ever since I was a little girl, I'd had a dream I'd believed, treasured and worshipped. I'd wanted to find my Prince Charming. Someone who would love me irrevocably, who was my other half. *The one*. And I wouldn't settle for anything less.

Now, however, at the age of twenty-five, I've given up on that dream. The wait had become depressing.

Maybe I'd set my hopes too high, my dreams too big.

You see, I have some very inspirational men in my life, and I want the best of all of them in my other half.

When I found a man, he would be as protective as my dad.

Loyal as my uncle Mason.

Strong like my uncle Malik.

Kind as my uncle Myles.

And make me laugh harder than my uncle Max.

But in the world we live, those traits just don't exist within one man. No one is that lucky.

My perfect man isn't out there.

I'm a hopeless romantic, though, so deep down, I do keep believing, which is why I'd let my best friend and co-worker talk me into a dating site called One Love. If there's any chance of me finding my perfect man, I guess it's not the worst place to start.

We'd had some prospects to look over, but the more I spoke to them, the more I found them all lacking in something. It could be the fact that we were all hiding behind a screen. Just how much could you get to know someone online? Words just weren't enough. You needed to see facial expressions, possible triggers, annoying habits and so on.

Let's face it, you aren't going to admit to someone you chew with your mouth open and snore louder than a fog horn, or tell them you hate strong women. No, you have to experience that stuff and, well, tonight was the time for me to do that.

The man I'm going to meet is called Noah Anderson, a bank manager from a town an hour away. He likes animals, has a German Shepard, and loves travelling when he has time off work.

It was the German Shepard that had persuaded me to agree with my best friend Nina and go out on this date.

I was still having second thoughts about meeting him though. Still ready to give up completely. He could be a real creeper, you just never know nowadays.

Roxy, my own German Shepard, who I'd taken in when she was a puppy after being left in a shoe box at the vets I own, is why Noah had been picked out of the top five we chose. Roxy's my pride and joy, and anyone else who freely shares their love for animals is good in my eyes.

My thoughts drift to my outfit, wondering if it's suitable for a first date and not too sexy.

I'm wearing a LBD, the material fitting snug to my body, with a split up my right leg and a dip between my breasts, showing off more cleavage than I've ever shown in my life. It actually makes my pale complexion glow a little.

Nina had brought over some accessories, so I'm wearing a diamond necklace that dips between my breasts, instantly drawing your gaze there, with matching earrings and bracelet. Even my bag—which took me a decade to find in my closet—was sparkling like diamonds. And thanks to my sister Lily, who has a thing for shoes she doesn't even wear, I managed to get some black, tied around the ankle, stilettos that have a glittering heel.

I've kept my hair simple, not wanting to overdo it since I have so much of it. So, I'd put my waist-length auburn hair in a fishtail, letting it fall to one side and down my shoulder.

"You look hot, babe. Seriously, I bet half the men tonight will be picturing you naked."

I look at Nina through the mirror and laugh, shaking my head at her dramatics. One thing's for sure: you can't be self-conscious around Nina; she'd knock that shit out of you.

Literally.

"Are you sure this isn't too much?"

Waving a hand at me, she walks over, before moving my boobs—can you believe it—to give more cleavage. Like they weren't already out there. I slap her hands, moving them back and giving her a glare.

I'm already nervous as hell, I don't need her to make things worse. I'm debating if it's too late to bail, but I know she won't let me. Plus, what can one date hurt?

"All right, but if I had them, I'd totally have them D's on display. He's taking you to that fancy Italian restaurant, isn't he?" I nod, even though she knows exactly where we're going because she'll be there too. "Then, no, it's not too much. Have you seen what some of those bitches wear?"

"If you're sure. I'm still pissed they couldn't get you a table. Are you sure you'll be okay across the street?"

Because of the demand, they don't give tables to singles on busy nights. Being that it's a Saturday, Nina had no chance of getting one. We even tried to get her someone to go with, so she could watch out for me, but when the time came to make the booking, there were no tables available.

So, across the street at The Duck Inn she'll wait, until I either give her the call or the text to meet me out front, so we can ride home together. Only because I didn't want him driving me home and knowing where I lived if things went wrong. This was our first time meeting face-to-face, after all. We'd been talking for nearly a month before I'd agreed to meet him for a date. Even as unsure as I'd been, Nina talked me into it, saying I needed to get out there.

"Yes, Laurie said she'll meet me for a few."

Laurie was Nina's cousin, and like her, was all blonde and long-legged. Both were model gorgeous.

Making sure I have everything I need, I grab my jacket and umbrella before leaving my flat.

My flat is situated above a hairdresser's. It was the only space I'd been able to find within my budget after opening the vets with Susan. But it works for me. It has an open-plan kitchen/living room. The only doors lead to the two bedrooms and bathroom. It's cosy. And the landlords let me keep Roxy—after I agreed to put down a pet deposit.

It may not look like much, but to me, it was everything.

"Come on, girl. Let's go meet Mr. Tall, Dark and Handsome."

EVEN WITH AN umbrella I managed to get wet. My shoes feel squishy as I walk into the famous Italian restaurant.

I haven't even met Noah yet and already this is becoming a disaster. I feel miserable.

"Welcome to Rosa's. May I take your name?"

My gaze drifts to the older gentlemen. He's wearing an expensive-looking three-piece suit, his heavy stomach on show, and a red tie. A black, thick moustache covers his entire upper lip, and his eyebrows meet above his long nose.

And currently, I can't tell if he is frowning at me or eyeing me up. There just aren't any facial expressions.

Yeah, this date isn't going to plan.

"I'm Faith Carter. I have a table booked under the name Anderson?"

He lifts his nose at me before grunting from the back of his throat and looks down at his tablet, his eyes running across the screen.

"If you could just take a seat in the bar area, a waitress will call you when your table is ready."

I don't get a chance to reply because he looks behind me, smiling to greet the next customer. A flutter of panic tightens my stomach as I wonder if Noah is already here. The host didn't say.

We'd agreed to meet here at half-eight and that the table would be booked under the name Anderson.

I didn't factor in the bar.

With wet, squishy feet, I move over to the bar area as directed, smiling happily when I see a large fire roaring in the exquisite fireplace, sparks snapping playfully from the burning wood. Two vacant, elegant, leather sofas face each other in front of it.

I eagerly make my way over, my shoes squelching with every step, not even bothering to look for Noah. My goal in life, at this moment, is to get my feet warm and my sister's shoes dry, so she doesn't kill me.

Sue me.

As soon as I sit down, I slyly slip off my heels, making sure they're facing the flames.

Since I have nothing to do, and not seeing Noah anywhere, I take out my phone and check for any messages on the website we met on. There are none.

ME: He's not here. What do I do?

NINA: Has he texted you? Maybe the weather has slowed him down? There is quite a bit of traffic.

ME: We can only talk through the app. I didn't give him my number. And no, he didn't message me. My feet are wet. :-(

NINA: Lily is so going to kill you if you've wrecked them shoes.

ME: Thanks for your support.

NINA: You love me.

And I did—love her. Even though I'm the oldest sibling in my family, you'd think I was the baby. I was grateful to have Nina in my life, who just treated me as a friend.

I have two younger brothers and a younger sister. Along with them, I have six male cousins, five uncles, and a dad. Doesn't matter that I have five aunties, a mum, and five kickass female cousins. They all have a part of my heart, but sometimes it's frustrating to be treated like the baby when I'm not. Nina doesn't do that with me. It's why I haven't told anyone about coming out on my date tonight.

That said, they can all be a little overwhelming, especially at family gatherings. We are all tight—more like brothers and sisters—but there's a time in a girl's life when she wants something for herself.

Insert Nina at the age of eleven. We had just started high school—both coming from different primary schools—and met during our lunch break...

"Holy Moses, is that your lunch balance?" Nina had asked, all blonde-haired and blue-eyed.

I'd instantly been drawn to her, been somewhat quiet and a bit of a daydreamer. I'd been reading since I was old enough to pick up a book. Fairy tales were my favourite, and the minute I'd laid eyes on Nina, she'd reminded me of a Disney Princess.

"My mum was worried I was going to miss out on something." I shrug, feeling shy. My mum had deposited one-fifty into my lunch account for the school term.

"I got, like, ten pounds. Want to be friends?"

And from there, we were friends. Always laughing at how ridiculous my mum could be. But she was the best mum in the world, so I never judged her over-protective or nurturing behaviour. I revelled in it.

"Anderson, table for two?" a brunette waitress calls, bringing me out of a fond memory.

I put my hand up to show her I heard her, before slipping my shoes back on. I follow behind her at a slower pace, my shoes feeling worse than they did before. When the empty table comes into view, my heart sinks a little more. I'm enduring all of this and he isn't even here.

He's ten minutes late.

I'm about to place my clutch down on the table when I'm suddenly knocked off course. I stumble into the chair and drop my bag and its contents all over the floor.

"Shoot!" I squeak out, righting myself before I fall and make a bigger tit out of myself. I'm embarrassed and immediately drop to the floor, my poor dress stretching to its limits.

"I'm so sorry. I didn't see you."

My head snaps up to the deep, masculine voice, startled when dark brown eyes stare back at me, almost black and void of emotion. If it wasn't for the fact he sounded sorry, I wouldn't have believed him.

"It's okay."

I try to keep one eye on him as he bends down to help me pick up my bag and everything that has rolled across the floor.

"It's not. I'm sorry. Can I get you a drink as an apology?" he asks as we rise.

Flustered, and somewhat flattered, I shake my head. "I'm meeting with a friend, but thank you."

He smiles, finally showing some kind of facial expression, and I relax. "Shame. Well, sorry again for… well, knocking you over. Enjoy your date."

It isn't until he walks out the door that I realise he'd said 'date', when I had told him I was meeting a friend.

It seems odd he would say it, but after looking around once again for any signs of Noah, he's forgotten. I just want this date to be over with now and to go home.

I shouldn't have agreed to come, especially when I had been wanting to cancel all day. I've had a uneasy feeling in the pit of my stomach since I woke up, and it still hasn't gone. I'd thought it was just down to the nerves of going on a date. One I hadn't told my family about because I knew they wouldn't be pleased.

ANOTHER FORTY-FIVE minutes have passed. I can feel the heat of embarrassment on my face from being stood up.

Not only is it embarrassing, but I feel so ashamed, like I'm not good enough. There might be a simple explanation, I'm sure, but I'm done with it. I might be picky when it comes to men, but I've never led one on, or stood one up. Not that there have been many dates in the past.

Customers have been eyeing me with pitiful looks. A girl all dressed up and no one to tell her she looks beautiful. I'm tired of waiting.

The same waitress who has popped over to my table continuously to see when I was expecting company or if I wanted anything, walks over again. This time she has a sheepish expression, like she's about to tell me something I'm not going to like.

She doesn't even open her mouth before I know what's coming, and I don't blame her. I just hate the look she is giving me. I don't want her pity or for her to feel sorry for me.

"I'm sorry, Miss, but we're going to have to ask you to leave. We have paying customers who are waiting for a table."

"It's fine, I'll go."

Fumbling with my purse, I get up from the table before grabbing my jacket and umbrella. And to make matters worse, I trip over the leg of my chair, knocking into the couple seated behind me.

"Gosh, I'm so sorry. I'm sorry." I turn back to the waitress and wave my hand at her when she tries to help me.

On shaky legs, I stand up straight and square my shoulders, my eyes burning with unshed tears.

I've been stood up.

Completely, utterly and embarrassingly, stood up.

What a complete fucking jerk.

When I get home, I'm so going to send him an email to end all emails. I'm going to give him what for and make him regret ever standing me up.

Quickly sending off a message to Nina to meet me outside, I put my phone back in my purse and make my way outside.

She's already in the smoking area when I step out. Her head is bent over her phone. She raises it when she's finished reading and gives me a questioning look.

I walk over, glad Laurie isn't with her. There's only so much humiliation a girl can take—being a virgin at twenty-five staying at the top for a long as I live. People don't understand why I choose to keep it that way and explaining it does nothing to enlighten them. They just think I'm a naïve girl with her head in a fairy-tale. I'm not. I just don't want to give the one thing I can never get back to someone I'll never truly love.

The next item on the humiliation list is being a rare virgin and having to find a man on a dating website, only to then get stood up. That's totally up there on every woman's top ten embarrassing things.

"That was quick. What's wrong?" Her voice is full of concern when she gets a good look at me.

"He didn't bother to turn up. I kept getting pitying stares from the waitresses, and then to make things worse, I was asked to leave, then tripped and fell on a couple behind me. I just want to go home, get into bed, and forget about this fudging night altogether."

Anger sparks behind her eyes. She nods her head with determination, and I know she's searching for a way to fix this. She's always been that way; always there for me no matter what.

"Then we will. Let me grab a bottle of wine or two and we can make a night of it. Did you at least eat?"

That's another thing that pissed me off. I've been wanting to eat at Rosa's for years. I'd waited to go because I wanted the experience to be romantic, not family related. Not that they would let my cousins in. All the males in my family eat like every meal will be their last. And they can be loud and downright disturbing sometimes.

"No," I whine, throwing my hands up in a fit. "It sucks. I should have just texted you to come over but I didn't want to make a bigger scene. Go grab a bottle… actually three. I'll order a Chinese now and by the time we get back, it should be there."

"Good on ya, girl. Then we can email the fucker and tell him he has little balls and wasn't worth it anyway."

I laugh, loving my bestie to pieces. Besides my family, she is the only person in the world I've become close with. Not even Susan, my business partner, knows much about me. We're friends and go out from time to time, but we mostly keep it professional.

BY THE TIME we get back, I'm ready to put on some pyjamas, get into bed and watch a horror movie with plenty of gore and blood. Romance is not going to be watched for a while in my house. And the people who truly knew me would understand what a rarity that is. I'm a sappy, hopeless romantic.

Romance novels.

Romance movies.

Romance TV shows.

I loved them all.

That stuff, apart from animals, who were my kindred spirit, were my all-time favourite things in the world.

Oh, and cooking.

I loved baking.

Heading up the stairs, I grab my bag and rummage for my keys.

"Shit, where are they," I grumble, wondering how they could get lost in such a small bag.

"Um, Faith… you won't be needing your keys."

The wariness in her voice has me looking up. I see her frightened eyes on my door. Dread fills my stomach and I turn, finding the door to my flat open a notch.

"Oh, no," I gasp, looking around the hallway for any other signs of intruders, but there are none. The flat across from mine is currently empty, and its door is perfectly in place.

"I'm gonna call the police."

"What if he's still in there?" I whisper-hiss at her. My eyes drift back to the door again, finding no forced entry, and the tension in my shoulders loosens. "Relax, it's one of my cousins. They have a key. They're probably raiding my fridge."

Nina relaxes, shaking her head and smiling. "One day, we need to get those fuckers back for always scaring us. Remember the time Maddox—Oh, my god."

"No!" I gasp, looking around my near-empty flat and trashed belongings.

Pictures upon pictures I'd hung with pride on every inch of my walls were now torn down, smashed on the carpeted floor.

My sofa has been flipped over, but even from this angle I can tell it's been slashed open, the brown suede completely shredded, no longer useable.

My TV is gone. My Xbox One, my Wii, my DVD player, all of my boxsets, and pretty much anything of value is missing.

My knees threaten to give out, but Roxy's barking has me running to her, pinpointing her in the bathroom. I open the door and let her out, dropping to the floor to pull her into my arms. They locked her in there. They locked my poor baby in the toilet. I run my fingers over her, looking for any signs of injury, but feel none. I sag with relief, not knowing what I would have done if they'd hurt her.

"Poor baby. It's okay, it's okay," I coo, cuddling her close and letting her lick the tears from my face. She leaves me, sniffing around the room in array, seemingly unperturbed by what's happened.

The mess is still as startling as the first time I saw it. Then my eyes widen.

"What—what is it?" Nina asks, her phone to her ear.

I'm not sure whether she's talking to me or to whoever she's on the phone to, but I ignore her and run to my bedroom. I push through the door, stepping over torn clothes and broken pictures and make my way over to my dressing table. All my costume jewellery is there, and I carelessly throw it to the side as I search for the necklace my dad gave me the day he adopted me.

It's gone.

A pained scream leaves my throat and tears fall down my cheeks as I fall haplessly to the floor. Everything in the flat is replaceable with time. I can get more pictures from Facebook, or from my family. I can buy new furniture and clothes. Hell, I can even replace the presents bought for me and the books that I'd noticed were shredded and all over the place.

But the necklace… It's irreplaceable. My dad could get another one made as my uncle Malik designed it, but it wouldn't be the same. It wouldn't hold the same sentiment. It held high significance to me—meant everything to me. It was symbolic of a beginning for me, for the start of our family.

It was a heart pendant with a crown on top, and it had mine, my mum's, and my dad's initials carved into the back. When you opened it, it had a picture of me, Mum and Dad on the right, and on the left it read, *Family is a gift, and you're mine.*

It was the day Maverick Carter became more than my mum's boyfriend.

More than our landlord.

More than my friend.

He became everything to me on the day he gave me that necklace.

He became more than just a father, a protector, and loved one.

He became my hope.

"No!" I wail, feeling my world crumble around me.

Why would someone do this?

Who would do this?

It doesn't make sense.

My phone chimes in my hand, and I'm prepared to ignore it, but when I see my bank's name flash across the screen, warning bells start ringing in my head.

I don't bother reading the message, already having a gut-feeling of what it will say. Instead, I access my account and feel my heart sink further.

My entire savings are gone.

All gone.

"Faith?" Nina croaks out.

I look to my best friend, hoping, somehow, this is all some joke, but the sorrow in her expression is enough to confirm this is real. This isn't my cousins coming in and turning my furniture and pictures upside down and telling me I have a ghost. This is real. "It's all gone," I whisper, feeling so lost and alone that I don't think I'll ever be able to recover.

And one thing is clear as I empty my bag out in front of me, finding my cards, keys and ID missing.

This was planned.

This was Noah.

And he's going to pay for it. One way or another.

ONE

B AD LUCK ALWAYS COMES IN THREES.

It's the way of life.

And for four months, I've been on edge, waiting for the third to kick me right in the arse.

Because four months ago, I was robbed. My identity, my money, my belongings, and my trust in the world taken from me in the blink of an eye.

And a week later at one our family Sunday barbeques… I lost both my great-grandparents. On the same day. On the day I'd made myself sick with worry about telling my parents what had happened to me.

I'd spent the week hiding from my family, blocking their calls and turning them away at the door. I didn't want them to see what had happened, how stupid I had become.

Plus, I was worried what their reactions would be.

You see, when you mess with a Carter, you mess with us all. It's always been that way and always will be. We grew up close. If one of us had a problem, we all helped. If one of us were sad, we were all there to cheer you up. If someone fucked you over, we made them pay. All of us.

But today, I know I'm going to have to tell them. My mum has been worried sick, demanding to come see me, asking me why they weren't allowed to visit me at my home.

It's been hell having to lie to them, especially when we are all still grieving my great-grandparents. They were the best anyone could ask for, and Sundays aren't the same without them.

Nina promised to keep my secret and had even stayed with me until the landlords came and replaced the locks and added security in the hallway. They weren't happy to find that one of their buildings were broken into, but they were more worried about my safety. They were a great couple, even going so far as to invite me to stay with them.

A knock on my door jerks me out of my daydream and my nerves resurface. I'm hoping, after this, I will have more to tell my parents, to give them some peace of mind.

I open the door and smile when I see the officer working on my case. PC Collings came on the scene after police came to take fingerprints and whatever else they needed. He also took the list of belongings that were stolen.

Money wise, I'm going to have to wait for the bank to refund me my stolen money.

"Hi, Collings. Come on in. Can I get you a cup of tea?"

He smiles as he shakes my hand. "It's okay. I can't stay long. I just wanted to get you up to date on the case."

From there, I know it's not going to be good. It never is. We've had this conversation a few times, and it always leads to him telling me they have nothing.

"I'd offer you a seat but the garden chair broke last night when I tried to fix the lightbulb." Thanks to Nina's mum, I was able to scrounge an old TV, a sleeping bag, a garden chair and a few blankets. Nina gave me some clothes and a bit of money to tide myself over. After four months, they're still my only possessions.

My wages have gone straight on bills, rent, food, toiletries and other essentials that were broken in the burglary.

He chuckles. "It's fine. I'll stand. It won't take me long." He leans against the kitchen counter before facing me. "As you know, we have alerts out for your necklace and other items they might want to sell, but so far, nothing has come up. The profile for Noah has been deleted and we are no closer to finding him."

"But you still think it was a bogus account?"

"We do. It's what most internet trolls do. Today, I just wanted to let you know we spoke to your bank again and they will be issuing a refund on the money taken. We also have a private investigator/officer coming in soon to go over everything once again with you. There may be something you missed, something small that could help us."

"Someone new?" I interrupt. "Why?"

"We're afraid, after doing a wider search, that you aren't the only person this has happened to. Johnson has been working on the case for a while, following this person's steps in his own time, but so far, no luck. Whoever this person is, they're a professional. Johnson's agreed to come on payroll since the latest victims have all been around this area. Either the offender has ties here and needs to stay, or something has happened and he can't travel as far as he had been before."

"Oh, God," I gasp, my hand going to my chest.

"I have to go, but I'll be in touch and keep you updated if any new information comes to light. You'll be getting a phone call or a visit off Johnson in a few days. Don't worry, he'll have identification, and I might be with him— if I'm not put on another case."

"Wait. Before you go, did they *all* happen around here?"

He grimaces. "No. All over actually."

It sickens me that someone has got away with this for so long. Hope for getting my necklace back has just flown out the window.

"Okay, thank you for keeping me up-to-date."

"My job, Faith. Stay safe," he tells me, before leaving my flat.

I deflate against the door. I thought for sure I'd finally have some good news to share with my parents—when I tell them. Now I have nothing. They're already going to be disappointed in me.

Knowing I need to face the music, I grab my bag and coat, and clip Roxy's chain on her before heading out the door. I'm on the stairs when I bump into someone carrying a cardboard box. Stuck in my own little world, I pay no attention, calling a quick apology over my shoulder.

WALKING INTO MY childhood home, I feel sick. I'd made sure to call ahead and tell my mum to keep my brothers, sister and cousins away.

I should have amended that to include my uncles, because when I walk in, my stomach sinks at seeing all five of them. No Mum or Dad.

Malik is sitting in the chair, looking bored; Max is talking to Myles about someone he thinks is sniffing around his daughter; and Mason is chatting to Evan.

But when I walk in, all eyes turn to me, questions lurking behind them.

"Um… where's Mum and Dad?"

Uncle Max steps forward, a frown on his face. "I'm telling you now, girl, if you're pregnant, you're going to be a single mum, because I'm going to fucking kill him for touching you."

"Max," Myles scolds, coming over to place a warm hand on my shoulder. "It's okay, baby. We've got you. You've got support from your family."

"I'm with Max." My uncle Malik stands up next to Max, showing him his support. I'd roll my eyes, but I'm too confused and embarrassed. This is worse than when Max tried to give all us girls the sex talk.

With diagrams.

And pictures.

It was one of the most humiliating days of my life. All the other girls in my family agreed, and we'd begged our mums to warn him away from ever giving us one again. And if that wasn't bad enough, he always seemed to know if one of us started our period. He took us to Boots and bought us everything a girl could ask for.

At the time, all I'd wanted was a hot water bottle, my mum, and my bed—okay, and chocolate. I didn't need my uncle buying my sanitary towels for me, and then proceeding to let everyone he spoke to know that I had just turned into a woman.

Yeah, it sucked.

"Me too," Evan pipes up.

"Leave her alone, guys." My mum's voice carries warning as she steps into the living room.

"Mum, I said alone," I whine. She walks over and hugs me, and I hold her a little longer, needing her comfort. I've stayed away for so long, even when they'd needed me after my great-grandparents' passing.

"Whatever you're gonna tell us can be said in front of your uncles. We need to know who we gotta kill."

My dad, handsome as ever, walks in the room, all intimidating. I can see the worry around his eyes, and I know I've been putting them through the wringer.

I sigh, giving in to my fate. They're going to find out eventually, if not straight after I tell my parents, so I might as well get it out the way and tell them all together.

"Alright. I need you all to sit down."

"Oh, God, she's pregnant," Max yells, throwing his hands up dramatically.

"Max!" I shout, wanting to die right there.

"No, she's not," Dad shouts back, before turning to me. "Right?"

"I'm gonna fucking kill him." That from Malik.

"Just let her talk," Myles puts in. "She needs to know we support her."

"Jesus-fucking-Christ, sit down and let her fucking talk," Mason yells, grabbing everyone's attention.

They all listen, and as they take their seats, leaving me standing there like I'm on stage, I clam up, wondering how to begin.

"I—I don't know how to tell you."

"Please, just tell us," Max pleads, sitting on the edge of the chair. "Your dad is gonna get a hernia if you don't spit it out."

More like he is.

"I just don't know where to start," I say softly, already feeling tears beginning to burn the back of my eyes.

"How about from the beginning, darling." My mum reaches out, squeezing my hand, and that's all I need to begin.

"I'm twenty-five, I'm single——"

"Thank fuck," Max mutters.

"Max," Myles warns.

"Just wait until this is Charlotte standing there, telling us *she's* pregnant. Let's see how calm you stay then."

At that, Myles goes deathly pale and glares at Max.

"Did you really need to bring them in? I can't say what I need to," I tell my mum, frustrated.

"Just ignore them. Go on."

"Okay, well, I was getting fed up——"

"Sexually frustrated," Max puts in, and I glare.

"So, I let Nina talk me into signing up for a dating site."

"Please tell me you didn't get married to some old, hairy bastard?" my dad yells, standing up. Mum shoves him back down, glaring at him.

I keep going, needing to just get it out. "I ended up picking a date, just one, to see what it would be like and… well——"

"You got pregnant?" Max interrupts.

"No," I yell. "I'm not pregnant!"

"Hallelujah," Max roars, falling back on the sofa.

"What happened?" my dad asks, his jaw hard.

I gulp as I watch his hands fold into fists. "I went on this date and he didn't turn up."

He relaxes, but then squints at me, clearly confused. "And that is why you've been avoiding your family for months?"

I shuffle on my feet, eyeing the floor. The minute I look up, tears are spilling down my cheeks and it all comes out in a massive ramble. "I got home, and it was gone. It was all gone. Roxy was locked in the bathroom and my necklace——

our necklace, the one you got me the day you adopted me—had been taken. He took all my money and savings and trashed everything. I'm behind on bills, student fees and loans. I have nothing. I've been sleeping in a sleeping bag for months and have a garden chair for a sofa—had; it's broken now. I've lost everything. And I'm so sorry I didn't tell you but I've been so ashamed. I know it was the man I was meant to meet. Somehow, someone took my keys from my bag, cards from my purse, and I didn't even notice. And all because I was embarrassed about been a twenty-five-year-old virgin."

I end the rant on a shout, breathing hard. They all look stunned, my mum the only one with the ability of motion as she comes to hold me.

"And stay a virgin," Max tells me before giving Myles a look I can't read. I don't see anything else because I fall into my mum, sobbing.

"I'm so sorry. I didn't want you to be disappointed in me. And I knew when you found out you'd want to replace everything, but my necklace was irreplaceable. I failed you. I let you down. You've told me, throughout most of my life, never to talk to people I didn't know on the internet. I'm just sorry, Mum."

"It's okay. This isn't your fault, girl. You did nothing wrong, nothing at all. You have nothing to be sorry for. But you got one thing right: we would have replaced your shit. And we *will* be doing that too. I don't want excuses. You have a business that you love and have worked hard to run. There is no way I'm letting you lose that as well because of some predator."

"I let you down." I look up from her shoulder, eyeing my dad, who's barely keeping it together. "I'm sorry I got my necklace stolen, Dad."

He snaps out of it, looking at me. His eyes soften, and when he holds his arms out for me, I run into them like I did when I was a kid. And the minute he envelops me in a hug, the weight I've been bearing, lifts. I feel safe for the first time in months.

Not even when my landlords put locks on the windows, changed the ones on the front door, or when they put cameras in the hallway and entrance, did I feel safe.

But my dad… he's made me feel safe from day one.

"Liam is already looking into it. He's hacked into her file at the police station. He'll call when he has something," Myles says.

I pull away, but still hold on to my dad as I shake my head. "No. You have to let the police deal with this. He's done it before and I don't want you getting into trouble."

"We won't get caught." Malik shrugs, like it's no big deal.

"But he knows where I live," I whisper.

"Trust me, after we've finished with him, baby, he won't even remember your name," my dad growls, hugging me tighter.

"Can we eat now? I'm—" Max starts.

"Hungry?" Mum interrupts, rolling her eyes. "Come on, everyone is waiting round Harlow's for us."

We all head out, walking down the street to Harlow's. My gaze shifts to my great-grandparents' house, feeling a pang of grief hit me, like it does every time I think of them.

The house is empty now. Harlow, my mum and other aunties cleaned it out a few months back, keeping everything of importance and taking the rest to a local charity shop.

Mum has plans of letting Hope, Madison and Maddox move in there, since, after me, they are the eldest, until the time comes when one of them wants to start a family. But Maddox has other plans and the rest are waiting for it to be redecorated.

As happy as it makes them to remember our great-grandparents, it's hard to live in their home—with reminders everywhere. They decided to update everything and give the place a new look, so we don't feel like they're going to walk around the corner any second.

"Come on," Mum coos softly, rubbing my back as she steers me up Harlow's path and around the back, into the garden.

Everyone is gathered around the picnic tables. Mason walks over to his son Ashton who is manning the barbeque.

"Hey, you okay?" my sister Lily greets.

Lily is a rare creature. She's quiet, incredibly kind and so intuitive of others around her it's uncanny. She's also soft-spoken and easily intimidated. How she survives in a classroom teaching English still amazes me.

"I guess you'll all find out in a second. I think they're going to want to tell everyone."

"What?" she asks, her brows pinching together.

"Come on. I need a drink if I have to listen to these guys yell at each other over who will be the first to beat him."

She stops me, her beautiful, delicate features scrunching up in confusion and hurt. "What do you mean? What haven't you told me?"

Seeing the hurt flash in her eyes, I drag her over to the tables and proceed to listen to my mum and dad fill everyone in; Max butting in every few seconds to remind everyone I'm not pregnant.

I'm still shocked he didn't demand I pee in a cup.

"Does this mean you'll bake me some cakes if I buy all the shit you need?" Aiden, my youngest brother at seventeen, says. "And thank fuck you're not pregnant."

Giving him a small smile, I nod. "Yeah, but you'll have to buy new pots and pans. Everything was destroyed."

His jaw ticks. "I'm still pissed you didn't tell me."

"I'm sorry. I didn't want anyone to know," I tell them.

Lily stands suddenly, her fork clattering on her plate. "I need to go. I'll see you all later."

Everyone watches for a split second before they try to call her back. Mum goes to follow her, but I shake my head, standing up.

"I'll go. Be right back."

"Bring her back too. This is family time," Dad warns.

I nod before rushing off after her, finding her opening her car door. "Lily, wait." She stops but doesn't turn, giving me her back. "Lil, please, look at me."

She turns slowly to face me, tears running down her cheeks. "Why didn't you tell me?"

I didn't realise she would be this hurt. Since Maverick brought her home to us, she's been my best friend. She wasn't just my sister, she was the greatest friend a girl could have.

"I didn't want you to be worried. I knew you'd want to help in some way and I couldn't have that. You've got your own life to live. You didn't need to worry about mine."

"I thought we were sisters who told each other everything," she tells me, her words choked.

Tears spring to my eyes. "We are. We're best friends. I didn't know you'd be this hurt. I'm so sorry."

"You didn't think I'd be strong enough to handle this. I'm not weak. I might be quiet, I may find certain things hard to cope with, but I'm not weak."

Lily had a rough upbringing before she came to live with us. Some of it she's shared with me, some I can only guess. But whatever her psycho mum and her boyfriends put her through, still gives Lily nightmares.

She can't be around alcohol unless it's with family, so it stopped her going out and having fun with friends who did drink, and she still suffers with night terrors. But she's never let that bring her down or scare her from living.

It's why she moved out as soon as she turned nineteen.

"You're the strongest person I know, Lily. I didn't not tell you because I think you're weak. I was ashamed—ashamed I had to use a dating site to try and find my Prince Charming," I admit, using the term I've used since I was five. Yep, Prince Charming has been someone I've been searching for, for a long time.

Her eyes soften as she steps close and pulls me into her arms. "I love you. Don't ever keep stuff from me again. Now, I have a double bed at home with a new bed frame, and a bunch of other stuff you can have."

"No—" I start, but she puts her hands up, stopping me.

"The only people to ever crash at mine is Maddox when he's been out on a bender and doesn't want to get a taxi home, or Aiden when he's too full from eating all my food. I don't actually use any of it, so it's yours. I haven't gotten rid of my sofa yet either. It's still in my garage if you want that too."

She really is the best sister anyone could ask for. "Thank you," I tell her, hugging her hard. "I love you."

"I love you too."

"Now come back in before Dad comes out to get you."

She pulls back and rolls her eyes, ready to deny it, but then a booming voice startles me. "Too late, you took too long to get my girl back. Now come on, it's family time."

We both turn to face Dad, finding him smiling, a soft expression on his face. As hard as he looks and as badass as he is, when it comes to me and Lily, he's a huge softy.

Holding hands, we both rush up to him and give him a hug.

"We love you, Dad."

He clears his throat, holding us closer. "Not as much as I love you pair. Now come on, your mother's going grey."

We laugh, and each tucked under a shoulder, the three of us walk back into the garden together.

TWO

WITH A FILE IN HAND, I WALK INTO Nina's office, diverting her attention from her computer. She smiles brightly at me.

"Hey, chirpy. What's up?"

She's commenting on the fact I've been in a foul mood all day. I have valid reasons. With a new neighbour living across the hall, our bedrooms connected, I've heard every movement they've made. It's made me jump out of my skin, causing me to lose sleep. And, well, me and no sleep… not a good combination.

I couldn't even complain to my landlord because, apparently, he's their nephew. Being evicted right now would just be a kick in the teeth. I'm not sure I'd be able to cope if anything else were to happen.

It sucks because I don't know how much more banging and drilling I can take.

"Did you go over Sir Fancy Pants' file?" I ask her.

Sir Fancy Pants is a spotted, tabby-coloured cat that belongs to an eleven-year-old girl. It was brought in early this morning by her mother.

"No. Isn't that the cat who belongs to that frantic young girl?"

"Yeah. I'm just a little confused. On his file it says he was brought in because he's been humping their neighbour's cat and they wanted him castrated."

"Oh, that's why she was saying he was hurting the other cats?" She laughs, her eyes twinkling in amusement.

"That's the thing, after going over Haylee's notes, I'm confused. She's put him down for a castration tomorrow morning. But he's a she and is around four weeks pregnant."

"What?" She laughs, throwing her head back. "How the hell did she get that mixed up?"

"I know, right? This is her second mishap since she started two months ago. She should be able to tell the difference."

"Maybe she didn't look and just booked him in?"

This time I give her a 'are you for real' stare. "You know the rules. All animals brought in are supposed to be given a full examination. I'm going to have to have another sit down with her. Anyway, can you call the owners, explain Sir Fancy Pants is actually Lady Fancy Pants and is currently up the duff?"

"Okay, so let them know it's their cat that's the hussy. Got'cha."

Laughing, I turn towards the door. "I'm finished. I'll see you Thursday," I call over my shoulder. Tomorrow is my day off and I plan to use it to get my flat back together.

Dad insisted on having everything new delivered. I reluctantly agreed, knowing it would be easier to let him win than to keep arguing. When he started insisting on me staying with them until he'd done some of his own security checks, I put my foot down. There were some battles worth fighting for.

Tomorrow is when everything arrives, the first delivery due at seven. I also have paint waiting for me at home, ready for me to give the place a proper makeover. It hasn't felt like home since the robbery. I read an article online which stated that making changes around your home will help you with your way of life. I'm hoping that decorating will make the place feel brand new. It won't feel like the broken mess I found it in four months ago.

"See ya, wench."

I leave a note on my desk to remind myself to have a word with Haylee when I'm back, before leaving for the night. I only live down the road from the vets, so my tired feet only have a short walk ahead of them. Starving and too tired to cook, I stop at my local Chinese takeaway on the way home.

When I get back to my building the outside light is off, along with the hairdresser's sign, which is usually blinding in neon pink.

"Great," I whisper to myself, juggling my Chinese and bag to get my keys from my pocket. The inside is pitch black. I swallow audibly, my heart racing as I head up the stairs.

This is just perfect.

I've got three tubs of paint waiting for me and no electricity to even see it.

Just great.

I'm about to take the last step when a large, looming figure walks out from the right. A scream screeches from my mouth as I drop the bag of food and try to take a step back.

I realise my mistake too late and twist my ankle on the step below when I land on it too hard and off balance. Strong hands grip my biceps, stopping me from falling and probably crushing my skull in the process.

"Please, no. Don't. You can have everything in my purse, just please don't hurt me," I scream, wishing I had listened to my dad when he'd told me to stay with him and Mum. Hell, I should have taken up my brother Mark's offer to come stay with me. But because I'm too stubborn for my own good, I freaking declined.

"Please."

"Jesus Christ," a deep, husky voice says, as hands lift me a little to place me between mine and my neighbour's doors.

"Ow!" I gasp, falling against my door when a sharp pain shoots up my leg. I forget about my potential mugger in front of me and focus on the pain.

"You okay?"

"Do you ask all the girls you're about to attack if they're okay?" I snap. With no lights on, I can't see him, but I do feel him take a step back. "I wasn't going to fucking attack you. I was walking out of my flat to check on the fuse box."

"Yeah right," I reply sarcastically, but then what he says registers. "Shit, you're the new tenant?"

"Yeah," he growls, seeming annoyed. And he has every right to be. I just accused him of attempting to attack me.

"Why didn't you say that?" I snap, feeling defensive.

"You didn't really give me much of a chance before you started screaming." *Oh, well, shit. He has a point.*

"I'm sorry. I'm just… I'm jumpy, I guess."

"Yeah, the, um… landlord said you were robbed or something a while back."

I'll have to thank Gina and Martin for sharing when I next see them. It doesn't pass my notice that he didn't call them his aunt and uncle. I guess he doesn't want me to think he has special privileges and all that.

"Yeah. Um, *why* are none of the lights working?"

I hear him move, something open, and the flick of a switch, before buzzing echoes around the room and the lights turn on.

I'm stunned for a split second, blinking away the brightness. I'm about to ask what happened when the words get stuck in the back of my throat. My mouth gapes and I have to tip my head back to get a good look at him.

I have to be imagining him. I have to be. He's so ruggedly handsome I could only have dreamt him up.

I stumble against the door in shock, wincing when I press down on my bad foot.

He's… God, he's really freaking handsome, and having grown up around a lot of good-looking men, that's saying something.

He's got ash-blonde, messy, unkept hair, and a strong, chiselled jaw covered in a weeks' worth of scruff—a look I find particularly appealing. But it's his emerald-green eyes, flecked with white, that leave me breathless. Thick black eyelashes frame them, making them seem even brighter.

I blink rapidly, feeling like my eyes must be deceiving me as I take him in.

Hands down, he has to be the sexiest man I've ever laid eyes on. I've never understood the term, 'come to bed eyes', until now. Would they melt when he kissed someone, or would they brighten? My breath falters at the thought, picturing him kissing me.

Okay, where did that come from?

He's got a strong build, muscles bulging in his white T-shirt, but not over the top like my cousin Trent, who works at a local gym. My mind wanders to how hard his chest would feel under my fingertips.

Even though you can clearly see he keeps in shape, it's not from spending hours upon hours at a gym. He's just that fit.

His tattoos snake up his arms and peek out through the collar of his T-shirt, making him look even sexier. Even his hands have tattoos on them.

His black tracksuit bottoms fit snug on his hips—and around his large thighs that look like they could snap someone's neck.

I don't even know where that image came from. But thanks to every male in my family always watching fights on TV, I've seen plenty of them to know that if the man in front of me ever wrapped those around someone's neck, they would pass out.

He just excludes power.

"Are you okay?" he asks me.

My cheeks heat when I realise I've been standing there staring at him. He can't hold it against me; he shouldn't be that good-looking. It's not fair. "Yeah. I, um—I'm going to… Yeah," I ramble, before going to pick up my keys.

Wrong move.

I land on my sore ankle, end up twisting it again and stumble. I wince in pain, wishing the world would swallow me up.

This is embarrassing.

"Fuck," I hear him mutter, before his strong arms wrap underneath my knees and behind my back and lift me off my feet.

"Hey! What are you doing?" I screech, my gaze on his tattooed neck. I'm tempted to lean in and press my lips against the vein pulsing there. It's calling to me like a dry land calls for water.

If I didn't think I was attracted to him before, I knew right then I definitely was. I've never had improper thoughts about anyone before. But his scent, the feel of his chest rising and falling against me, has my brain short-circuiting.

"You're hurt," he states, not looking at me. "Keys?"

"You can put me down. I'm fine."

"Keys?"

Huffing at being ignored, and uncomfortable about being in some hot guy's arms, I grumble my response. "On the floor."

I also feel tense; not because he's holding me, but because I like the way it feels to be in his arms. I don't know what to think of that.

He looks around, before bending—with me still in his arms. He snatches the keys off the floor and opens the door. He flicks the switch on like he's been here before, which surprises me. Even family still have a hard time locating shit in my place. And they really have been here before.

He moves with ease until he notices the empty flat. He looks around, confusion crinkling his forehead.

Roxy comes strutting over, wagging her tail excitedly and sniffing the new person.

"Roxy! Sit!" I order, wishing the ground would swallow me up when she starts sniffing around my butt—no doubt his… um, junk.

"The landlord said you've lived here a few years."

Well, if it wasn't already uncomfortable…

"I'm getting the place redecorated," I comment, almost quietly.

"I can see. Um, let's get you to my place—"

"What? No! Put me down. You can't just take me to your place. I don't know you," I screech, trying to wiggle out of his arms.

Roxy barks but he ignores her.

His grip tightens as he ignores my pleas and walks me out of my flat, past my smashed-up Chinese, which I had been excited to have since I woke up craving it this morning, and into his.

Unlike mine, his is full of furniture. What surprises me is he's building shelves from scratch—no Ikea bull where it says it's easier, but it's not. Instead he has a sturdy table with an electric saw and wood shavings all over the place.

Roxy runs ahead of us, making herself comfortable on a blanket near the covered TV set and settles down, resting her head on her paws.

Traitor.

"My name is Beau. I know you don't know me, but I promise I'm not going to hurt you. I'm going to take a look at your ankle, get you an icepack and some paracetamol, and run down to the Chinese and order whatever food I just destroyed of yours. Is that okay?"

My mouth opens to argue, but nothing comes out as he sits me down on a round table he clearly also made by hand.

And why didn't I argue? Because how can I when he's being incredibly sweet, even if a little demanding.

"Thank you," I whisper, staring at the top of his head as he slips my shoe off.

Hearing me, he lifts his head, his eyes piercing mine, and for a second—okay, maybe longer—I get lost in his gaze. Something shifts in his emerald stare and he clears his throat, breaking whatever just transpired between us.

The feather-soft touch on my ankle startles me. I can feel my cheeks heat as I look down, feeling at a loss for what to do.

And the silence… I've never been one to be quiet whilst in the company of others. It just feels stilled, awkward. My facial expressions also give me away, so it will only make the situation even more intense.

Another thing that's startling is the fact I can't seem to look away from him. He is immensely watchable—you know, being a walking, talking equivalent of a model you'd find in some raunchy romance novel.

"I'm Faith. My name, that is." I inwardly groan at my ramble, feeling my cheeks heat further.

His eyes meet mine, crinkling at the corners as his lips twitch in amusement. "Hey, Faith." He looks back down to my ankle, pressing into the tender flesh and making me wince. "It's bruised and a little swollen, but it's not broken. I'll get some ice for it. It will help take the swelling down."

"Thank you."

He walks over to the open kitchen, grabbing a frozen gel compress and a towel. When he walks away, towards the sofa at the other end of the room, I'm confused. He rips the plastic protective sheeting off before turning back to me.

He moves towards me with predatory steps, his eyes narrowed as he considers me. I open my mouth but again, nothing comes out as he lifts me up, then walks me over to the sofa where he sits me down.

"I'll be back in five with the Chinese."

"Wait!" I call out. "You don't have to do that. I dropped it, it's my fault. I can just go get another." I can't; I'm totally skint and don't want to waste another fifteen pounds on food.

"I'm hungry." He shrugs. "And I was the one who scared you."

With that, he grabs his wallet and walks out, leaving the door open so I can see into my flat. I'm tempted to go back, lock my door and pretend none of this happened, but the throbbing pain in my ankle prevents me.

And yes, the intriguing Beau is another reason.

I want to know more.

Oh, Faith, he'll probably get you a Chinese and throw you back in your own flat. Hell, he probably just feels guilty for scaring you.

But even as my inner voice mocks me, I don't believe he did it out of guilt. He helped me because he's a good person.

By the time he comes back, I'm a nervous wreck. I don't know what to do with myself. Do I sit back, make myself at home and come across as rude and overly confident? Or should I stay sitting with my back straight, uncomfortable, and looking an awkward mess.

My worries are answered when he pulls out some plates and forks, watching me intently.

"Sit back and relax. Eat your food, then I'll take you across the hall. You need to keep ice on your foot for a while. Leave it on for twenty, off for thirty, until you fall asleep." As soon as Roxy hears the word *food*, she's up, walking over to him and sniffing the bag. "Lay down," he orders easily, and Roxy, who never listens to anyone other than me, follows his command and lays down.

Not even my cousins, uncles or parents can get her to listen, and it's them that take turns to walk her on the days I work long hours.

"Thank you for helping me. And for the dinner." I smile shyly.

He looks like he wants to say something but shrugs instead, passing me a plate and fork before digging into the bag.

"I guessed what you liked by the smell. I'm sorry if it's wrong," he tells me sheepishly, handing me a container filled with Singapore fried rice.

"It's my favourite," I admit, and dig in.

I'm starving. I missed lunch today due to the walk-in emergencies. Susan even came in early to help, but it still kept me busy most of the day, which is why I was late coming home.

"Did you live around here before? Your Aunt never said anything when she informed me you were moving in," I say, starting conversation and slipping in the fact that I know he's our landlords' nephew.

He looks at me from the corner of his eye before finishing his bite of food. "I moved around a lot due to work. The last place I lived in properly was half an hour from here."

He doesn't give me more than that. I bite my lip, wondering what to say next, but he jumps in to save me before I embarrass myself.

"They put up new security before I came. Is it working out for you?"

I smile at that. Martin had been beside himself when he found out. He reminds me a lot of my great-granddad before he passed. He just had that aura about him that screamed grandfather.

"Yeah. Martin even came to overlook the construction, making sure they did it right. He was a bear to deal with."

A deep chuckle slips past his lips and I watch, transfixed on the laugh lines wrinkling his face.

My cheeks heat, as well as my chest, and I have to look away before I do something stupid like kiss him.

"He's stubborn as hell. Have they caught who did it?" he asks. I feel my eyebrows pinch and my stomach drop as Noah is so casually brought up, and he frowns. "Sorry, none of my business."

"Sorry, it's still sore to talk about. It's been hard living there knowing someone invaded my personal space, touched my stuff... Well, the stuff that survived."

"Is that why there's a ton of paint in your living room?"

"Yeah, I'm hoping it will help me see the flat differently, make it feel like a home again."

Something passes through his eyes and for a few painfully long seconds, he doesn't say anything. He seems to be taking something in or figuring out how to approach the subject.

Whatever was on his mind disappears because the look is soon gone and a smile forces its way on his beautiful lips.

"How about we finish this and then you ice your foot while I paint?"

"No! I'll be fine, honestly. You don't need to do that, it's my own stupid fault for being so jumpy. I should have remembered you were living here."

He shakes his head at me, his lips twitching in amusement. "You'd actually be doing me a favour. I've had a lot of energy to burn through since moving here. I've been working on putting stuff together here, but I'm done once I clean it all away."

"You really don't need to," I tell him quietly, feeling a weight on my chest at his kindness and generosity.

"I know." He smiles big, nearly blinding me. "But my uncle would have my head if I didn't help you, and I really don't mind. Plus, we're neighbours now; we can get to know one another better."

When he says it, a picture of us together runs through my mind. I know when he'd said *get to know one another*, he hadn't meant it like that, so my cheeks heat further. I'm thankful he can't read my thoughts. I'd probably combust.

"Okay. I can let you know about Maisy, the owner of the hairdresser's downstairs. Trust me, you'll need the downlow if you ever bump into her on a Monday."

He grins, helping me up off the sofa. "What about your plates?" I ask when he starts to bend, no doubt to carry me into my flat.

"I'll do it when I'm finished at yours. It's fine. It's not going anywhere, so stop worrying. Now come on, I need to know about his Maisy chick. Roxy, come."

Roxy barks, gets to her feet, and heads home, where she goes straight to her food dish and sits. I giggle at her expression, knowing it must have killed her to sit through us eating. She normally pinches food off my plate when I'm finished, but not tonight.

And like he belongs, Beau places me down on the makeshift sofa I have shoved under my window. It's basically a bunch of pillows my mum bought and blankets Nina's mum got me, piled so I've got something comfy to sit on.

It does the job. It's also been a bed since it was comfier than the air mattress Aiden bought me. I'd been so glad when my mattress had been delivered; my back couldn't take it anymore. Tomorrow, my bedframe will arrive and everything will start going back to normal.

After placing me down, he moves off to the kitchen area, looking through cupboards for Roxy's food.

It's a few hours later, after watching him paint my living area, that my eyelids become heavy and I fall asleep.

If I had stayed awake, I would have felt him cover me with a blanket. I would have seen him start my bedroom, painting with the deep shade of purple I'd bought before the robbery.

And I would have heard him whisper goodnight before he left.

THREE

I**T'S BEEN TWO DAYS SINCE I LAST** saw Beau, my new neighbour. A hot, sexy neighbour who'd painted not only my living room, but my bedroom.

It hadn't even occurred to me to ask him what he did for a living, but I doubt being a painter had you travelling across the country. And the only other thing I knew about him was that he liked to build things, and I don't see that causing the need to travel for work.

The first thing I did when I woke up the morning after I met Beau was look at my foot, which was surprisingly not as tender as it had been the night before.

The second was to admire the incredible job he did on my flat.

The third was to call Lily and tell her all about my new neighbour. As a bookworm, she lives for this stuff, and when she lays eyes on Beau, I wouldn't be surprised if she starts drooling over him. He is a force to be reckoned with.

Then I was startled by a knock on my front door. Instead of it being said hot, sexy neighbour, it was my sofa.

I spent the rest of the day catching up on housework, Beau constantly on my mind. I wanted to see him again, if only so I could thank him.

When I woke up the following morning, I made a batch of cookies and took them to his place. I told myself it was just to say thank you, but when he didn't answer, the disappointment I felt told me there was more to it.

I was starting to believe I'd made him up in my head. I never heard him drilling, moving around or coming to and from his flat.

Shaking away my thoughts of Beau, I concentrate on the task at hand. The red-brick building with tall ceilings seems intimidating as I look up from the bottom of the steps.

Collings called me this morning to come in and meet with his new officer at the police station. Apparently, this guy is good at profiling and stuff like that, but if he hasn't managed to catch Noah yet, he can't be as good as Collings has made out.

Guilt immediately hits me. They're only trying to help me and there's only so much they can do. I should be thanking them, not dismissing them.

I walk inside with a new perspective. I'm not going to cry or scream if they give me bad news. I'm going to take it on the chin and pull my big girl pants on.

Because I've noticed since the break-in that it's slowly begun to control my life. It's taken my home away from me because I let it. It's made me scared to sleep, wondering if he'll come back. I even jump when my phone beeps with an email because I keep thinking it's him.

It never is.

Any doubt I had that it couldn't have been Noah was immediately dismissed when his account suddenly disappeared. When it happened, my first suspect was Noah, but then I felt bad for accusing someone who could be innocent. Now, there is no doubt in my mind.

"Hi, I'm here to see——"

"Faith, hi. You can come on through," Collings interrupts, opening the side door for me to enter. I smile politely at the officer on the front desk and follow Collings.

When we walk into a pretty cosy room, I'm surprised. I kept picturing a metal table with screwed down metal chairs and a one-way mirror. Instead, there's a grey sofa against the wall, a small table with a vase of bright, colourful flowers and a round table and chairs. Nothing formal or intimidating, like I'd presumed.

He sees me looking around in surprise. "Not what you expected?"

Laughing, I shake my head. "No. The way my brothers and cousins go on about it, you'd think it was dank and dirty."

"Any chance your brother is Ashton Carter?"

My eyebrows rise. "No, he's my cousin," I tell him slowly. "Why?"

"He's a regular in here. Has been since he turned fifteen. The kid even talks the female officers into buying him food. Sometimes I think he pulls stuff just to get pampered."

My brain tries to conjure up what Ashton could have possibly done. At eighteen, he's always up to something, but the one Carter rule is to never get caught. Not that we commit crimes, only minor infractions. The guys just get into a lot of fights, a few pranks, and possibly nearly set an old church on fire with fireworks. But I've never actually picked Ashton up from here. That privilege went to my brothers and other cousins.

"That sounds about right. He loves his food, especially desserts. Can't see why he'd be brought in though. He's actually the tamest of my family."

He laughs at that, his eyes crinkling at the corners. "I know. I was just starting out when your uncle Max kept getting brought in. He made my job hell. Ashton always gets brought in for drunk and disorderly, but whenever he gets here, he's sober as a judge and laying on the charm."

My laughter spills free, because that really does sound like Aston, but it soon dies when the door opens and in walks Beau, decked out in police uniform, looking utterly sinful.

My mouth opens, then closes, before I finally manage to speak. "I baked cookies for you. You weren't in," I blurt out, feeling my cheeks heat.

His lips twitch as he eyes Collings, before turning back to me. "Hey, Faith."

"You two know each other?" Collings asks, eyebrows raised.

I don't need a mirror to know my cheeks are flaming red. "He's my neighbour."

"Oh, well, look at that."

"I only found out who you were today. If you'd like another officer working your case, let me know," Beau says.

I snap out of my daze, out of the shock of seeing him.

In freaking uniform.

Looking like every woman's wet dream.

And if a woman denies she's ever had one… she's freaking lying.

"Um, no, you can work me. I mean, work for me. I mean my case," I ramble, groaning out loud.

His deep, masculine chuckle sends a tingle shooting down to my sex. "All right, take a seat. We need go over everything one more time. It's probably going to be the same questions, but you might remember something you didn't before. Okay?"

I nod before finding my voice, "Yeah, that's fine."

"We managed to get printed copies of the emails that transpired between you and Noah Anderson, thanks to One Love communicating and working with us. So, I guess, we need to start off from that night." He holds up a small pile of papers before continuing. "Where did you get ready?"

I'm feeling on edge as I sit straighter in my seat. I can't seem to look away from him, from his lips, from the way he moves or the way his tattooed fingers grip his pen. I'm being incredibly gawky, and it's making the whole thing intense.

"I got ready at home, with my friend, Nina."

He looks down to one of the pieces of paper, reading something over. "Nina, she's your best friend?"

"Yes."

"Okay, so you left your flat. Was there anyone in the hallway or outside the main door?"

I think back but see nothing in my mind. "No. No one lived next door then, so it was empty. We met the taxi outside and I didn't see or notice anything out of the ordinary, but then I wasn't really looking for anything. It was late and most of the town was closed. It was also raining pretty heavily."

"And your friend went to the restaurant with you?"

My fingers entwine on my lap. I'm beginning to feel like I'm being interrogated, like I'm the one who did something wrong.

"She came with me in the taxi, but as soon as we arrived, we said our goodbyes. She walked over the road to the bar and I went inside."

"Straight away?"

My eyebrows draw together. "Yes. It was raining and my feet were soaked, so I ran in."

"And then what?"

"The male host asked for the name the table had been booked under, and I told him Anderson. It was the name Noah told me to——"

"He booked it?" Beau interrupts, startling me.

I nod, trying to remember if I'd already told them that. "Yes. It's hard to get a table there. My friend, Nina, was going to eat there too, in case he turned out to be a creep, but they don't book singles. By the time she got someone to agree to go with her, they were already fully booked."

My palms begin to sweat as I ramble on, having no idea where this is going.

Beau looks to Collings and gives him a nod.

"I'll be back in a moment. It's been a while, they probably won't find anything," Collings says before leaving.

"What's going on?" I ask nervously.

"Collings is just going to check if anyone had Rosa's call records checked and if there was any payment information left. Normally, with restaurants like that, you have to put down a deposit."

Ah, I see.

"I'm not sure. He just said to leave it to him."

He gives me gentle, warm smile, and I feel myself melt against the table, feeling like he just handed me a gift.

"Okay, so, you booked in and went to sit down?"

I think back, trying to remember moments I hadn't considered before. No one had gone into this much detail with me in my previous interviews. They had been more focussed on my journey home; what I saw, what I didn't see and what was taken. No one had stopped to really ask about Rosa's, other than to confirm I was there at the time of the burglary.

"No. The host told me to wait in the bar until my table was ready, so I did."

"Did you sit next to someone, near someone?"

"No. I sat on a small couch by the fire. No one sat on the one opposite or next to me. There were a few couples sat at tables nearby, but I paid no attention. I was texting Nina, worried because he hadn't arrived."

He nods, then looks back down to his paper. "What happened after? Did you get seated or did you wait there until you left?"

"Anderson was called, so I stepped up and let the waitress walk me to the table." I pause, remembering something that slipped my mind when the police questioned me. In my defence, I had just been robbed of everything, of every penny I had, and my precious necklace was taken.

"What?"

I shake my head. "It's probably nothing," I whisper, feeling foolish.

"Let me be the judge of that." He smiles, eyeing me gently, as if I may break. My hands are shaking. I remove them from where I'd been gripping the table and back to my lap, hiding them.

"When I was getting shown to my seat, a man knocked into me. I can't even remember what he looked like, only that he had really dark eyes. I dropped my bag and the contents went everywhere." I gasp, feeling stupid. "Oh, my God. He could have been the one to take my things. I didn't even check whether I'd picked everything up. I was too freaking embarrassed. And he made me nervous—in a bad way. He said something… He said… something about a date. It stunned me. Yeah, it was the easiest assumption but—" I'm breathing hard, my hands back on the table as tears spring to my eyes.

How could I have been so stupid?

All this, because I'm a hopeless romantic.

Always, since as far back as I can remember, I have wanted to get married. I have wanted my Prince Charming. My forever. I have wanted the big wedding, the big, puffy, princess, wedding dress. I have wanted it all. It's why I've never settled. I'd never said yes to a boy, hoping, over time, I would know he was the one, because I knew when I did find my soul mate, I wouldn't need hope. I would just know, deep in my soul.

It was stupid.

Naïve.

Reckless.

"I'm so freaking stupid."

"You're not stupid, Faith. You didn't know. Thousands, if not millions of women and men use dating sites, and a majority of the time, they are successful. People find their other half and marry them. They find love. It's not stupid."

I wipe at my tears, feeling frustrated with myself. Nothing he says can make me feel better. "I am. I let a stranger into my life. I didn't even meet him and he screwed me over. What kind of person does that make me?"

"It makes you a faithful, trustworthy one. You didn't know what he was going to do. Nobody could have predicted that, Faith.

"Now, I know this is hard for you, but is there anything you can remember about the man you bumped into?"

My eyes close as I picture myself back in the restaurant, walking between tables and hearing the endless chatter around me.

When I get to the part where I'm bumped into, my mind goes fuzzy. All I can see is his eyes. They're brown, almost black, with no emotion inside them. There's just nothing there, like he has no soul.

"All I can see is his eyes," I tell him, sagging with defeat. *Why can't I see his face?*

"That's fine. Hopefully, Rosa's will have something on camera."

My ears perk up. "Really? Oh, my God, does that mean you'll probably find him? Find my necklace?"

He takes my hand in his and my mouth falls open, a breath passing my lips. His skin is warm, calloused—probably from all the woodwork he does.

My eyes snap to his, and seemingly without thought, he rubs his thumb over the top of my hand as he stares back at me with a feverish intensity.

Collings walking in has us splitting apart, and Beau quickly turns his attention to the papers in front of him. "I've got Mathews on the case. Did I interrupt something?" he asks, looking at us both with a raised eyebrow.

"No, we're good. We've got more to go on now. As for your necklace, it will probably be a lost cause," he tells me, wincing at his words.

I can tell my face crumbles, because I can feel it, the hurt that must be showing in my eyes. It's all reflecting off his expression, filled with pity, as tears fall down my cheeks.

"No," I choke out on a breath. "I need it, it's mine."

His arms tenses, like he's forcing himself not to reach for me. There's a part of me that wishes he would, that he would take me in his arms, but that's just crazy. We hardly know each other.

"I'm sorry, Faith. We have been searching for it. All the pawn shops in a ten-mile radius have a description and picture to look out for. One of them will contact us if it turns up."

My head moves into a nod, but I'm not present. Deep down, I know the necklace is gone, but I can't accept it. After losing both my great-grandparents, I know how much it means to keep hold of the things that mean the most to you. That necklace was everything to me.

"Is that everything?" I whisper, not meeting his eyes.

"Yeah. Let me walk you out."

Again, I nod, but I don't pay attention. I walk mindlessly to the door, which he opens for me, and step out.

The second we're outside, the harsh weather hits me. It's raining, the wind whipping my hair around my face sharply.

"Where's your car?"

Fingers trembling, I point to the visitor's bay and start over, trying to duck my face into my chest to protect myself from the wind.

I open my car door and am just about to get in when he stops me and turns me to face him, the rain pouring down, soaking us both.

"We will work our hardest to find who did this, Faith. From the look on your face, I can see the necklace means a lot to you."

I wipe my wet hair from my face and nod. "More than the money he took, and the things he trashed. It's irreplaceable."

"I need to get back, but I'll come over later and grab those cookies."

I wince. "My brother ate them. But I'll make some more."

"Looking forward to it," he says, then does the damnedest thing. He winks. Actually freaking winks, and my heart thunders in my chest.

Holy shit, that was hot.

I nod and just stand there, gawking like a moron. He leans down…

My eyes close, wondering if he's going to kiss me. I even stretch up on my toes, so he doesn't strain his neck. Hell, I'm practically begging him to kiss me. It's something I've imagined more than once since I first met him.

Which is so out of character for me.

I'm never like that.

I thought my female libido was broken or something.

But with Beau, it's on fire.

And I almost collapse… in disappointment when his warm lips press against my forehead. He knocks my chin with his knuckles. "See you later." And then he's off, running back into the police station.

"Holy Moses," I curse, looking up to the sky, my eyes blinking rapidly against the rain.

The icy water doesn't cool my burning body, or the fiery need swirling in the pool of my core.

My thighs clench together, and a throbbing needs pulses between my legs.

And he only kissed me on the head.

The freaking *head*.

Like I'm a relative or a close friend. Like I'm a child.

Thoroughly drenched head-to-toe, I get in my car, not caring about getting my seats wet, and head back home.

There, I'm going to make my weight's worth in cookies and eat them.

After I take a long, cold shower.

FOUR

THE EVENING WEARS ON AND I'M almost asleep when there's a knock on my door. I look at the clock, seeing it's only seven.

It's probably Aiden, wanting me to bake him some over the top cake so he can pretend he made it and impress one of the many girls he's always trying to hook up with.

Apparently, a guy who can cook is a keeper.

It's just a shame Aiden can't be kept. My mum would probably worry less if he settled down.

After I'd got home earlier and had my shower, I'd baked double my weight in cookies and curled up on the sofa with a blanket and binge-watched the Hallmark channel.

Roxy had cuddled into me, her weight welcome as she'd kept me warm. Now, her head pops up from my thighs and she jumps' off the sofa, before rushing to the door, barking.

I'm in my pyjamas; a long-sleeved blue top with lace lining the edge near my breasts, and a white pair of shorts, scattered with printed blue stars, that barely cover my arse. The only reason I didn't put on my wool bottoms was because of my awesome socks. They're knitted in a light and dark shade of blue, and the insides are white. The tops flip over, showing off the white wool, and are finished with a blue bow. They're the only pair I have now, but no doubt family and friends will start adding to my collection, buying them for me every chance they get.

They're normally my reading socks.

Yes, it's lame, but that's what they're called.

I love being snuggled in them while I sit and read my Kindle.

It's my sister's fault. She started the trend. Her addiction to these socks is ridiculous, but totally necessary.

Another knock on the door and I get up. My family see me dressed like this when they pop by unannounced, so it doesn't bother me. I don't think to check the peephole, so I'm startled when I find Beau standing there, leant against the doorframe, looking freshly showered and dressed, holding a bag of takeout. I hadn't been expecting him until later.

"Do you like Indian?"

My nerves ease and my racing heart calms down at his easy smile.

"Depends. Where did you buy it?"

He scrunches his face up at that. "Masala Spice."

I relax. "Then come on in. What are you waiting for?"

"Um, why was that important?" he asks, stepping inside.

"Because, the Indian down the road has given everyone I know food poisoning. Trust me, it's disgusting."

"Ah." He grins and walks into the kitchen, where he drops the bag on the kitchen side. When he turns, it's like he sees me for the first time. His eyes rake over my bare legs, down to my socks, which come up to my knees. He grins, his eyes sparkling. "Nice socks."

I blush under his scrutiny, wishing I had something to cover up. The only thing close by is an old and tatty, knitted cardigan; but it's long and great for curling up with on the sofa. So, I quickly step back, not wanting to turn and flash my arse, and put it on.

He grins at me, before grabbing some plates out of the cupboard. I clear my throat. "What made you stop by?"

He shrugs, and I don't think he's going to answer me, but he does, "I'm hungry and you promised cookies. It's boring eating alone. I also ordered too much food."

"Okay." I didn't really need an explanation. I like his company. It's why I don't argue. Plus, it's a win-win for me. I get him and free food. What more could a girl ask for?

IT's LATE AND Beau is still here. I'd flicked off the Hallmark channel hours ago and put on One Tree Hill, starting from the beginning.

"You're telling me he crushed so hard on that P girl, yet he ends up with Brooke? Not that I'm arguing—she's hot—but I'm confused. Why's he dating her when he likes the other one?"

"Because he secretly loves her but fears rejection. Brooke is easy—no pun intended," I tell him when he grins, his eyebrow arched. "She doesn't scare him the way Peyton does."

He shrugs and flicks his gaze over to me. "Still don't get it. Love isn't meant to be easy. It's meant to be scary, fulfilling and... What?"

I giggle. "Nothing. You just seem to have a strong opinion on the subject."

"You teasing me?" he asks, a grin tugging at his lips.

God, will I ever stop swooning over his smile? *Nope, don't think I will.*

"Maybe a little. My favourite couple is Hayley and Nathan," I comment absently, looking back at the screen.

"And they get married in another season?" he asks, genuinely interested.

"Yeah." I smile big, turning in my seat. "It's so romantic. She's a virgin and has always promised herself she'd wait for marriage before sleeping with someone. And Nathan... Even though he's a little bit of a d-i-c-k. in some episodes, he never pressures her—well, there's a scene where I think he's slyly pushing. He kind of stops kissing her because he doesn't want to pressure her."

I roll my eyes at that. "But deep down, I think he actually believes he's helping, though to me, it just seemed he was putting more pressure on her." When Beau gives me a funny look, one I can't quite figure out, I stop. "What?"

"You really love this show, huh?"

My face aches from smiling so much. "Yeah. But it's more than that. I love the relationships. They're real. And Hayley and Nathan go through so much, but always manage to find their way back to each other. I also like they got married, tying themselves to one another forever before getting intimate."

"You want to get married?"

My heart drops and my smile falls. "I did. Always have. But after this stuff with Noah, I'm not sure I ever want to date again."

His smile falls now, his eyes gentle. "Not everyone is like Noah, Faith. Any man would be lucky to have you."

He reaches out for my hand, and I let him. I notice him shift closer, his eyes staring intently into mine.

He opens his mouth to say something, when a thundering knock on the door has us both jumping apart.

"What the fuck?"

My heart pounds and my gaze flashes to the door. "Who is it?"

He looks at me, raising an eyebrow. "I'll go see. Wait here."

Like hell.

The door isn't that far away, so I'll be able to see whoever it is from here, but if it's someone coming back for me, I'd rather be standing next to Beau. He looks like he could pick up a truck if he was angry enough.

"Can I help you?" he asks.

"Who the fuck are you?"

I groan and rush over to the door. "Dad! What are you doing here?"

"Who's this punk?" Uncle Max pipes in, barging in past Beau and stepping into the flat.

"Dad?" I call, looking around Beau to find my dad staring him down. "Dad!"

He looks over at me, his expression softening. "We came to see you. We have, um… some information." He eyes Beau again distastefully.

"Hey, sis, who's this punk?" Aiden asks as he steps in and walks straight over to the counter, where my baked goods are. "Cookies. Awesome."

"Hey, Faith. We wanted to come for moral support. Just know, we're pissed we weren't invited." Mark, my eldest brother, walks in and kisses me on the cheek, before following Aiden over to the cookies.

"Invited?" I ask as Malik and Dad walk in next.

I notice Dad's knuckles are red, dried blood caking his skin. "Oh, my gosh, what happened? Are you okay? Where's Mum?"

Max laughs and I turn and glare at him, as I hear Beau shut the door. He stands in front of it, his arms crossed. That's when I remember he's a cop and it's clear my dad has gotten into a scuffle.

"He," Dad points to Max, "had Liam find out who this Noah kid is, and we went to pay him a visit. Unfortunately, your stuff wasn't there, and neither was he. According to his buddy, he's left town. Don't worry, we'll find him."

My heart races as my gaze shoots to Beau, then Dad. "Um, Dad, this is Beau Johnson, the new officer working my case, the one I told you about." I widen my eyes, giving him *the look*, but he seems undisturbed.

"I mean… we gave him a good talking to and told him, once we find his little friend, we'll be going straight to the police," Max quickly adds.

Aiden outright laughs, jumping up on my counter. "This should be fun."

"You gonna say something?" Dad asks Beau, giving him a death glare.

God, why did we open the door?

"Dad!" I scold, before looking to Beau. "Ignore him."

But Beau doesn't look at me, he just stares at my father a second longer, both locked in this weird macho showdown, before nodding. "Depends, give me his address so I can go pay a visit and I won't report what I've heard and witnessed. Maybe I could find out more."

"Crooked cop?" Aiden asks, bouncing from his perch on my counter.

I roll my eyes at my brother. "No, so he can go *question* him."

"Shut up."

"No, you shut up," I snap.

"I said it first." He grins triumphantly.

"Jesus, are you two…?" Max asks, looking at Beau and I.

My cheeks heat with embarrassment at acting so childish in front of Beau. When I turn my gaze his way, I see he's smiling, his head ducked a little.

As if feeling my attention, he raises it and gives me a wink before turning to my dad again. "Address?"

Dad nods and turns to Malik. "Go on."

I watch Malik eye Beau before speaking, "What are you doing here? I don't think eating and watching chick flicks is a part of your job."

Beau doesn't miss a beat. "No, it's not, but she's not just a case, she's my neighbour. A neighbour who, I might add, was left to walk home in the dark, and then stepped into a blackout. She was so scared that she nearly fell down the stairs and ended up twisting her ankle. She was also left to paint her own flat." He raises his eyebrow at Malik, waiting for him to answer, and I fall back in shame.

I'd told everyone I'd tripped walking Roxy, which was believable since she mostly walks me. It also got them to give her extra walks for me while my ankle still ached.

I'd also lied and told them Nina and her mum had helped me paint, so I didn't have much to do.

All eyes turn to me, every pair of them narrowed in anger. "Come again?" Dad asks.

"Um…"

"I told you to hold off on the painting until I could come round to help," Mark snaps, straightening his spine from his position on the floor, where he's been petting Roxy.

"What the fuck? I even offered to do it for a chocolate cake," Aiden pipes in.

"Girl, you're in a world of shit. When did you start doing shit on your own? This is a family; we help each other out," Malik grunts.

"I, um…" I start, looking around sheepishly.

Max looks up from his phone, grinning. "Your aunts and cousins are gonna be pissed. You're hiding too much shit from us." His phone beeps and he grin spreads wider. "Oh, your mum is so pissed. She won't be taking in any more strays while you find them homes."

Dad grunts at that. He's never liked the fact Mum always helped me out when it came to animals. We only had so much space for strays at the vets, and unfortunately, most older animals find it harder to be homed. We usually make an ad in a paper or get friends to hassle parents. My sister, Lily, has two cats. One only has one eye and the other has three legs.

"She wouldn't," I gasp, wondering what I'm going to do with the three small rabbits that had been brought in last week. They've got two more weeks at the shelter, but after that, we either have to put them down or send them to a bigger shelter. It's not in my nature to put a healthy animal down. It's not why I became a vet.

"Oh, she would." Max laughs and puts his phone away.

"I'm sorry. I didn't want you guys to keep worrying or force me to move back home. And I certainly didn't want Mark stinking up my sofa. I'm twenty-five, not five. You guys worry over us girls more than is necessary."

"Because we love you," Dad growls, his expression filled with hurt and annoyance.

"I'm sorry," I tell him, tears filling my eyes at the disappointment in his.

"Look, I didn't mean to get her into shit. I just wanted you to know I'm not here to fuck her over." He holds his hands out, speaking slowly to calm the situation.

"Or fuck her," Max snaps. "Cause cop or not, I'll break your legs. We've already had a pregnancy scare."

Oh, my god.

He did not just say that.

I can't even look at Beau. I'm dying of shame and ready to call Hayden, to get him back for doing this to me. If there's one thing Max can't control in his life, it's his wild daughter. She also loves getting him back for all the embarrassing shit he pulls on us.

"Noted." He walks over to Malik, no doubt getting Noah's address, as Dad walks over to me and pulls me into his arms.

"Squirt, you need to stop doing this to me. I'm old. You need to be open with us. I thought you could tell us anything."

Hearing the hurt in his voice is painful. "I really am sorry, Dad. More than you'll ever know. I just didn't want you worrying even more over me. I promise to keep you informed… on important stuff," I tell him, eyeing Beau.

His gaze flicks there too, and his shoulder sag. "Is he—are you two…" He rubs the back of his neck, trying to look anywhere but at me.

I want to giggle at his expression, but I'm mortified over where he's going with the conversation. Heat spreads up my neck and I feel like my face is on fire.

"No, Dad, we, um… we—we're neighbours," I stutter out.

He sags in relief. "If he, you know, touches you," he begins, pointing to my body, "remember what I taught you."

I roll my eyes, giggling. "Dad, I'm twenty-five. I'm not a teenager anymore."

"It still counts. If he makes a move, punch or knee him in the balls. Just don't… you know, touch them," he says, blushing.

I groan and close my eyes, before looking at him. "Dad, please shut up, or I'm calling Mum and telling her you're the reason she was never chosen to volunteer for school events."

He snorts. "He was eyeing your mum's arse. She was wearing a wedding ring."

"He was a teacher asking if she'd volunteer for the wild camp. You scared him so badly he pissed himself."

"You said you'd take it to your grave," he growls.

I smile sweetly. "And I will. *If* you stop interfering in *that* department. It's awkward as hell."

"It's kept you a virgin for twenty-five years," he yells, then stops short, his eyes wide and horrified as he breathes deeply.

I drop my head, utterly ashamed when it echoes around my walls.

"Well, this got awkward real quick. Let's go before you blurt out more shit," Max says, slapping Malik on the shoulder.

"Good going, Dad," Mark snaps.

I do love my brother.

"Yeah, we really didn't need to know that shit, but it's good to know we don't have to kill anyone… yet," Aiden adds, narrowing his eyes on Beau.

I can't even look at him.

If there was any chance of him being interested in me, it just died with Dad's proclamation of my virginity.

And meeting only a quarter of my family.

"Sorry," Dad grumbles, sounding sincere.

"Please, just go. I'll talk to you tomorrow."

He nods, looking tense, like he doesn't want to go with things so awkward. He leans down and kisses me on my forehead.

"It was nice meeting ya," Max says, and I turn to find him talking to Beau.

"Yeah, at least *you* didn't scream at me." Beau chuckles at the memory. I blush, knowing he's referring to me and how we met.

They all look confused, but Uncle Max takes it in stride and shrugs. "I'm only a screamer with the wife." With a wink, he walks out, patting Beau on the shoulder before he passes.

Beau chuckles under his breath, shaking his head as they all pile out.

I grab my brother's jacket, pulling him back inside as he goes to leave. "Put them back. Now!"

"Put what back?" Aiden asks innocently.

I roll my eyes at him. "My cookies. Now, Aiden, otherwise I'll never bake you a cake again."

He rears back, hand to chest as he feigns being hurt. "You wouldn't?"

"Oh, I would. They're Beau's cookies."

Aiden turns, glaring daggers at Beau, before stomping over to the counter and putting my plate—hidden under his top—back. "I won't forget this," he snaps at Beau, who doesn't even blink.

He follows Max out. Malik walks past next, rubbing my hair like I'm five again. Next is Mark, who leans down for a kiss on the cheek and a quick hug.

When it's just me, my dad and Beau, I start to feel uncomfortable again. The air is tense.

"If you hurt her, I'll do more than break your legs."

"Dad, we're just friends," I yell, pushing him towards the door.

"Understood," Beau grunts, not even correcting my dad on our non-relationship.

Dad stops me from pushing him out even more and pulls me into a hug. "I'll find your necklace. But if I don't, you won't need it. You have me, baby girl, and always will. My love for you grows stronger every day. Necklace or not, nothing can change that."

My eyes burn with unshed tears. "I know. I love you too."

He holds me a bit longer before pulling back. "Let's not tell your mum about the teacher, or me blurting out you're a—you know," he tells me, his voice low. "Or about tonight at all. She doesn't need to know."

"I make no promises. Now go, before you put your foot in your mouth. Again."

He nods before giving me one last kiss and walking down the stairs. I shut my door, plastering myself against it, and close my eyes.

It's only when I remember I have company do I open them, smiling sheepishly at Beau. He's moved over to the counter and is leaning against it as he watches me in amusement.

"I'm sorry about my family. They can be a little… crazy and full on."

He shrugs. "It's fine. They seem like good people, and they love you."

"They are. The best." Then I remember why they showed up in the first place. "Are you going to report what you heard tonight?"

He grins, shaking his head. "Any respectable father would protect their daughter."

"That doesn't answer my question," I reply hesitantly.

He runs a hand down my hair, lingering near my shoulder, where he coils a piece around his finger. I shudder and step closer—a subconscious movement.

"I'm not on duty, Faith. Plus, I heard nothing. I'll just say a tip came in with this address."

He steps back but takes my hand and pulls me over to the couch.

I still can't believe how comfortable I am with him, how it doesn't feel like we met only a few days ago. Everything with him seems to flow easily.

"Now, come on, I want to see if there's going to be a catfight between Brooke and Peyton."

I laugh and fall down on the sofa next to him, not even tensing when he pulls me into his side.

FIVE

A WEEK AFTER SPENDING THE NIGHT watching One Tree Hill with Beau, something inside me feels different. I feel different. I feel alive. Not that I hadn't before, but now I see everything as if through fresh eyes, feel things more intensely. It's a good change.

Whenever I hear the door across the hall open or close, my heart races in anticipation. When he drops by to say hi or, like Tuesday, cook me dinner, I feel like he's knocking all my walls down. I never want him to leave.

The excitement that swirls inside me whenever I spend time with him, increases every moment I'm in his presence.

I'm seeing him again tonight, and this time, I'm the one cooking dinner.

Every time I see him, I get to know him a little bit more. And the more I get to know him, the more I find myself liking the man I'm crushing on.

I can't seem to help myself.

My walk to Lily's is suddenly stopped short when Roxy pulls on her lead, which is strange because she's usually pulling me forwards. "Roxy, what are you doing now?"

I'm still righting myself when I hear her growling. Shocked she'd do such a thing, I rush to tug at her leash. I'm startled when I see she's snarling at a man in a black hoody.

"I'm sorry. She's not usually like this."

I stroke her fur, trying to calm her down, but it's not helping. She keeps on snarling, growling at the man in front of me.

"Be glad she's on a leash. It would a shame if something were to happen to her," the man warns in a waspish voice. The hairs on the back of my neck stand on end.

My head snaps up at his cruel words, ready to give him a piece of my mind, but he's already walking away.

Roxy whimpers and my attention turns back to her. "It's okay, girl. It's okay. Come on, let's go see Lily. I bet she has some tasty treats for you."

Roxy barks and we carry on walking, turning onto the street that houses the library that Charlotte owns. She lives around the back, in a small house that connects with Lily's garden. Lily's cottage, a few other houses, and an old, closed-down church are also on the street.

No one liked living here before, but Lily took one look at my dad's new investment and wanted it.

My uncle Mason had put in a claim to buy the library building when it threatened to go bust. Charlotte loves working in the library. She gets to do both what makes her happy. When my dad and other uncles found out, they all invested too. All of them now own the building. Since then, Dad's also invested in other properties on the street. The street now looks liveable, even if it is still empty on the far end. But it's quiet, something Lily treasures.

We walk up to her cottage and I let myself in, inwardly chiding her for never locking her door. The only other people on the street are elderly. She doesn't think they'd be a nuisance. But if the past four months have taught me anything, it's that nothing is certain.

"Lily?" I call, dodging Willa, Lily's one-eyed cat. Willa doesn't let her disability stop her from doing anything, including attacking Roxy when she sees her. Roxy ignores her and steps into the house, no doubt sniffing for Peggy, Lily's three-legged cat.

"We're in here," Hayden calls.

"Stop shouting," Maddox groans.

I roll my eyes. I should have known he'd be here. Hungover.

I walk in, grinning at a suffering Maddox who is curled up on the sofa, his head on Lily's lap. Hayden is sitting in the armchair, Mark slumped at her feet.

Since Lily only owns a three-seater and an armchair, and Maddox's large-framed body is currently taking up most of the sofa, I do the only thing a respectful cousin would do: I jump on his legs, squashing him.

"Faith, I feel sick," he groans.

"Shouldn't drink so much."

"There was a hot blonde," he explains.

Mark grunts in agreement.

"There always is," I mutter sarcastically.

"How you doing?" Hayden asks. "You know, after your dad blurted out you were still a virgin in front of the hot guy."

"Mark!" I yell, glaring at my big-mouth brother.

He holds his hands up in surrender. "Um, I didn't tell anyone."

My eyes narrow in doubt, but then my mind drifts to Aiden. Oh, I'm going to kill him when I see him. "It wasn't Aiden either. My dad told us." Hayden rolls her eyes. "We told him it wasn't funny, but he said the guy's face was priceless."

"What face?" I ask, horrified.

"Not sure, just said it was a picture moment. Wished he had his phone handy and everything. Said he'd put in his pocket before the juicy stuff got said."

"I'm going to kill him. Gah! Why does he always have to make an embarrassing situation worse?" I ask.

I already know the answer before they even say it.

"It's Dad."

"It's Max." Is chorused throughout the room.

I sigh and lean back against the sofa, ignoring Maddox when he shifts his legs from under me and puts them on my lap instead.

"Dad said the guy looks like a dick and we should watch out for you," Maddox puts in. "I'm thinking of paying him a visit. Have a talk about your virginity staying intact."

"Maddox," I screech. Roxy comes powering in, Peggy following at a much slower pace. "Don't you dare do that to me. I mean it. None of you are to go near him. If you do, I'm going to start spilling secrets to certain parents. I mean, you wouldn't want your mother finding out it was you who crashed Madison's near date's car into the lake, would you?"

He gasps and shoots up, as he narrows his eyes on me. "You wouldn't?" he shouts, before wincing and grabbing his head.

I giggle at his expression. He deserves it for threatening to speak to Beau. "I so would." I shrug, ducking my head. "He's just a friend anyway."

"Who likes to spend time with you? Cook you dinner? Tuck you into bed when you fall asleep on him?" Hayden asks, her gaze on her phone.

My eyes nearly pop out of their sockets when she announces it to the room. Lily knew, but she's my sister; I tell her pretty much everything. The boys, on the other hand, no. You can't tell them anything, especially stuff like this. They'd overreact and start doing shit that would get normal people arrested. People around our area are too scared to mess with a Carter, or try to get payback. One tried and never succeeded. He ended up with slashed tyres and shaved eyebrows.

"Hayden!"

She looks up at me, her expression confused for a second, before realisation dawns across her face and she has the audacity to look ashamed. "Sorry."

"He does what?" Mark growls.

I close my eyes for a second and groan. "Mark, please, shut up. I don't need you interfering."

"I thought he was just a friend?" he asks pointedly.

I glare at Hayden. "Just you wait."

"I said I'm sorry."

I shrug before addressing my brother. "We are. I promise. You know I can rarely stay awake after nine. I'm like an old lady. He's just being a friend."

"No, he isn't. I would have just left you where you fell asleep," Maddox adds, and I slap his thigh.

"That's because you're a jackass. And you've never been to a girl's house to watch a movie before."

"What's the point in wasting time watching movies when I get what I want in the beginning?"

Total freaking jackass.

"You really need to man up. One day some girl is going to come in and sweep the floor from underneath you," I warn him, narrowing my eyes on my brother when he grunts.

"Never gonna happen," he tells me, kicking my legs.

"It will, Madz. And when that day comes, don't expect me to have sympathy. The way I see it, you should be treating every woman how you treat us," Lily adds.

"But sleeping with you would be incest," Mark points out, looking sick.

She shakes her head at him. "That's not what I meant. We're your sisters, Mark. The girls you sleep with are someone's sister, someone's daughter. Would you like it if we were all treated like that?"

"No, 'cause I'd break their fucking legs," Maddox growls fiercely, always the most protective over Lily. They're closer than we are, and we're sisters.

"Exactly. Just think of how their family feels when they see how upset their daughters or sisters are."

"But they know what they're getting into."

"Really? Then why is Aiden always telling girls everything they want to hear, including getting Faith to bake them goods, when all he wants is a good time? He lies to them to get himself what he wants," Hayden says, turning her nose up at the boys.

I knew I loved her.

"I'm not getting into his sex life, girls. I get where you're coming from, but he makes them no promises. They all love him," Maddox argues.

"You're all dawgs."

"Lily, you love me. And, speaking of, where's my lunch? You promised me a BLT."

Lily rolls her eyes. "No, you promised me lunch because I made you breakfast this morning. And if you haven't seen the time, lunch passed hours ago."

I glance at my phone and see that Lily is right. I'd completely lost track and now I'm running late. The chicken for mine and Beau's dinner tonight needs to go in the oven.

"Guys, I hate to leave ya, but, well… I'm going. I've got stuff to do."

"More like a dinner to cook for your fancy boyfriend, and we're not invited." Mark pouts, his chin to his chest as he looks at me.

"I swear, you were too spoiled as a kid. Get Mum to make you dinner."

"Whatever. I'm going out tonight anyway."

"I bet you are, sulky pants. Tell you what, I'll cook dinner for you next week," I tell him.

His ears perk up. "Promise?"

"Yeah." I laugh, throw Maddox's legs off me and get up. "Roxy, come, girl."

I put her leash on before giving everyone a hug goodbye. Then we leave and make our way home to get dinner started.

I'M TIRED FROM the walk back from Lily's, but I remember to grab my post before I slug myself up the stairs.

I really wish I hadn't offered to make dinner and instead said I'd get him a takeout. It's too late to start the chicken now. It seems Roxy wanted to take the scenic route.

I walk into the flat and kick the door closed, not bothering to check if it's shut properly. I didn't sleep well last night. In fact, the past few days I've struggled to sleep. It's starting to catch up with me, especially with the long days at work.

Roxy barks when I flop down on the sofa face first. My hand slowly reaches out and I pat her head as I turn to look at her.

"I'll get you a fresh bowl of water in a sec, girl. Mummy just needs two minutes rest."

She barks and rests her head on the edge of the sofa, watching me with those big brown eyes of hers.

Sighing, because she isn't going to give up, I drag myself off the sofa and over to the kitchen, where I pour her some water.

"Here you go, girl."

The pile of post on the counter calls to me, so I walk over, grabbing the mysterious package first. I hadn't ordered anything, but then again, it could be a book Charlotte had recommended that I'd forgotten about. I'm always doing that.

Tearing it open, I pour the contents over the counter and find myself confused by what's inside. In there is a DVD and a note. I turn the DVD over, and a gasp leaves my throat when I recognise the writing.

It's mine.

Something I'd thought had been taken during my break in.

I grab the disc and the note before rushing over to the DVD player, wanting to make sure it's what I think it is before I overreact.

Maddox's fourteen-year-old face pops onto the screen, smiling big. Though still a child, he looks the size of an adult.

"He's going to bring a girl," Maddox says, rubbing his hands together.

"Don't you dare do anything to her," Madison warns him, her eyes narrowed on her twin brother. "He'll be so mad. And Daddy said you can't touch girls."

Maddox rolls his eyes as she walks off. Aiden comes into view next. My brother is only eleven in the video, but he looks around fifteen. Maddox drags him and a twelve-year-old Ashton away from the crowd, where they huddle in a circle.

Behind the camera, you can hear me say something to Lily as we move closer to listen, the picture bouncing with our steps.

I was nineteen when this video was taken, Lily was eighteen. I remember because we had moved out a few weeks before Mark's thirteenth birthday and were feeling a little homesick.

You don't hear what my cousins and brother plan, but when Aiden and Ashton move away, they have massive grins on their faces and are high-fiving each other.

"What did you do, Maddox?" Lily asks, walking over to Maddox when he's alone.

When he turns to her, he smiles, and his eyes soften. "Nothing he can't handle."

Suddenly, a high-pitched squeal echoes across the garden. I turn the camera in the direction of the sound and my laughter echoes through the speakers.

Aiden has pulled Mark's shorts down to his knees and he's going commando while Ashton has shoved a cake in his face.

My dad and Max come running out of the house, their faces priceless as they look torn between laughing and yelling.

Malik wins when he walks right up to Maddox and slaps him across his head. *"Kid, you turn sixteen in two years. Two years!"*

"And?" Maddox shrugs, unaffected.

A small grin tugs at Malik's lips. "And, he has two years to plan how to get you back."

Maddox pales and I start laughing behind the camera again.

Tearing my gaze from the screen and back to the note, I feel the blood rush from my face and I gag.

Call off those hooligans, otherwise I'm coming for you.

Tears fall onto the letter, the video still playing in the background. I can't move. I can't think. There's nothing but fear, eating away at me.

He sent me something he'd taken from me.

He's telling me he can come back at any time.

And I could be here next time, not at some restaurant waiting for someone who isn't going to show.

More tears fall and a sob breaks from my lips.

I'm not sure how long I sit there. The television has long turned off, and the sky outside has blackened.

"Faith?" A voice calls in the distance, but I'm too lost in my own nightmare to register it belonging to Beau.

I whimper as Roxy gets up with a whimper of her own, her feet padding across the floor.

"Faith?"

The lights switch on and I blink. The tears have longed since dried up, but I know without seeing myself that I look a mess.

I always do when I cry.

I get horrible red eyes, dark bags under them, and a snotty nose.

"Jesus. What's wrong? What happened?" he demands, coming to kneel in front of me.

My gaze meets his, the first thing I've concentrated on since the words on the letter were no longer visible due to my tears and blurred vision.

"I—" I croak out, my throat raw from crying. It hurts, feeling dry and scratchy.

"What's this?" he asks, and looks down at the note. He takes it out of my hand and growls when his eyes rake over the words. "When did you get this, baby?"

Baby.

The soft words reach me and I relax somewhat, but tears once again fill my eyes. I didn't think I had any more, having dried up… however long ago.

"When I got back." I manage to find my voice, but it still comes out hoarse. "It came with…."

"It came with what?" he asks, gripping his fingers around mine. They're warm, something I'm not at the moment. I bask in it, needing it.

"One of my homemade DVD's. I filmed a lot as a teenager. Just birthday parties, Christmas', New Year. He sent one with the note."

"Where's the envelope?"

I look around, having forgotten, then see it still sat on the kitchen counter. I point to where it is and he eyes it, nodding. When he starts looking around, searching for something, I get confused.

"What are you looking for?" I ask, looking with him, even though I have no idea what he's searching for.

"Where's your phone, baby?"

I feel my brows scrunch together and answer, "On the table."

He nods and picks it up, wasting no time in swiping across the screen before holding it to his ear. I open my mouth to ask what he's doing, but he holds his finger up, stopping me.

"No, it's Beau Johnson. Your daughter's friend. No. She received a note today from whoever robbed her, along with a DVD. Can you come over and sit with her, so I can take this into evidence? Yeah, no problem." He ends the call, looking back at me.

"Who did you call?"

I want to know if it was my mum or dad. That way I can prepare to handle my mum when she comes.

When I was five, I was involved in an explosion at the club my uncles owned. It was my uncle Mason's wedding and we were all there, but I'd got caught under some rubble and, for a moment, my mum had thought I was dead.

She's never been able to get over that night. It's why she's so darn protective and can't handle anything—even something insignificant—happening to us.

"Your dad." I relax onto the chair, my back protesting since I've been sitting straight for however long. "They should be here in fifteen minutes."

"They?"

"I think your mum was in the background asking what was wrong. I also heard someone else, but not sure who."

"God," I groan, covering my face.

"Hey, it will be okay. I'm going to find out who did this."

Uncovering my eyes, I look at him sitting next to me, a thought occurring to me. "Collings said you've been working this case a while. Why?"

He runs a hand over his face, seeming a little guarded. "I became a PI after I left my job at the police station. To them, I work this case because someone hired me, but it's not because of that. My neighbour, a single mum to four kids, used the same dating site you did. She met a Noah Henderson online, and they got talking. He was a widow with two girls, he'd said, and they instantly clicked. Whilst she went out on the date, her three youngest stayed at a neighbour's house. Her eldest stayed home to do homework."

I gasp, not liking where this is going. This Noah guy made sure I was at the restaurant before robbing me. He must have done the same with this woman. But he couldn't have anticipated the kid being at home.

"Did he do something to him?"

His guarded expression turns cold, angry. "Yeah. He beat him up. He had broken and bruised ribs, a fractured arm in three places and was badly beaten. He had to have surgery on his cheekbone."

Tears fall down my cheeks. "He's a monster."

My thoughts are with the boy and how scared he must have been. I'm also grateful right now that I didn't back out of my date and stay home, which is something I had wanted to do. Nina had talked me out of it.

"Yeah, baby. She was a close friend. I looked after her kids when she worked nights and couldn't find a sitter. It's why I took on her case without been asked. Her son never fully recovered. He was withdrawn, jumpy, and couldn't go back into their home. The neighbours did a fundraiser to help with moving costs, having known the family for a long time."

"I can see why he wouldn't go back. When I found the mess that had been made of my home, I was inconsolable. It wasn't until the police asked me if I had somewhere to go until they processed the place that I realised I'd have to come back.

"I stayed at Nina's, my best friend's place, the first night. They called the second night to tell me it was okay for me to come back, but I didn't want to, not at first. But I knew if I didn't, I would end up moving, and with no money, no furniture, it wasn't going to happen. I didn't want to move back to my parents; they would have asked questions.

"The week after the robbery, my great-grandparents died. They were second parents to us all, always there for each and every one of us. They were everything. We all grew up with each other you see. We might not have lived in the same house, but we were basically brought up in one another's shoes. Hell, my uncle Mason and aunt Denny live in my aunt Harlow's backyard. My grandparents lived next door and my mum and dad lived two doors down. It would have been too much on them if I had told them."

He rubs my back. I didn't even realise a few tears had fallen until he started rubbing my back, soothing me. "It's okay. Everything will be fine. You did great coming back here and not letting him run you out."

"I could have been here that night, just like that little boy."

He looks at me strangely. "Why would you have?"

"Because I hadn't really wanted to go. You heard my dad the other night," I remind him, blushing at the memory of Dad informing the world I was a virgin. "I'm twenty-five, Beau, and I've never been in a relationship. It's not because people haven't wanted to date me, but because I haven't wanted to date them. They weren't who I was looking for. It eventually got to the point I decided it wasn't going to happen for me. I wasn't going to meet my person, my special someone. I felt like I should just try to settle, so I did.

"Nina came up with the dating site, but I went along with it. Noah's profile made him seem like a decent guy, so I decided to give him a chance. That day though, I kept having doubts about the date. I berated myself for not waiting longer for the man I'd always dreamed of. If not for Nina encouraging me to go, I would have been here when he came. *If* he came."

He pulls me to him, rubbing his fingers through my hair affectionately to calm my fear. "I'm not going to let whoever this is get to you. We will find him. He's slipped up in sending you this message, which means your dad was onto something at Malone's place."

"Malone?" I ask, hearing the main door to our building open.

"Yeah, the guy your dad visited. He said he was just a friend of a friend who'd let Noah crash for the night. I'm thinking there's more to it and he's lying. He had to have contacted Noah to let him know we're looking for him."

"Faith?" Dad calls, rushing into my flat, Mum, Harlow and Malik close behind.

"I'm okay. I'm okay." I get up from the sofa when I see he's not going to stop. He pulls me into his arms and squishes my body to him. Mum comes around us and hugs me from behind.

"Sweetie, you need to stop scaring your mother like this," she whispers. I can hear the tears in her voice, causing a knot to form in my throat. I hate worrying her. She's been through enough in her life without to have to deal with this.

And my brothers.

She needs a medal for dealing with them.

"Are you okay?" Dad asks, pulling back to search my face. He looks torn between wanting to shred someone to pieces and hold me even tighter.

"Let up, I can't breathe," I tease lightly. He loosens his hold, but doesn't let go. He puts his arm over my shoulder, pulling me to his side as he faces Beau. Mum fusses over me, but my eyes are trained on Beau as he talks quietly to Malik and Harlow.

"She's coming home with us," Dad declares, and I want to groan.

I knew this was coming.

It's not that I don't want to stay with them, it's just that... Yeah, I don't want to stay with them.

They're madly in love with each other and have no problems with PDA's. I'd had eighteen years of seeing it; I didn't need to see any more—or hear it.

"Dad, I want to stay here. I have Roxy to think about, it's easier to get to and from work, and I have a police officer living across the hall. Plus, and I mean no offence when I say this, but I never, and I mean never, want to walk in on you and Mum on the kitchen table ever again." I shudder dramatically. I hadn't really seen anything. Hadn't needed to. I'd heard them the minute I opened the door and decided not to proceed. But they don't need to know that. It had taught them to never do it out of the bedroom again.

I hope.

My mum smacks my arm lightly, probably knowing I'd lied about walking in on them, but my dad turns ten shades of red.

Malik chuckles along with Harlow. "You can come stay with us."

I glance to my uncle. "Yeah, that's a big no, too. You forget; I get along with my cousins and know for a fact you two are loud when you think no one is home."

Malik grunts, unaffected, but Aunt Harlow blushes and curses at Malik. I ignore them and turn back to my father.

"I can't leave. I'll never come back."

"Fine by me."

Jesus. "Dad, this is my home. I can't let him win and run me out," I tell him, using Beau's words.

"If it makes you feel better, I can stay over here," Beau offers, and I'm not opposed to that idea.

"Yeah, that doesn't make it better," Dad growls, narrowing his eyes on Beau.

"At all," Malik adds, arms crossed over his chest.

I roll my eyes at them both. "Can we give it a few days? See how things go on my own?"

Dad's eyes soften when they land on me. "A few days, but if we still haven't caught this guy, you're either coming to stay with me or with your sister."

And he's only offering Lily's because he knows Maddox stays there a lot. And Maddox, although more protective over Lily since they share something we don't, is still protective over us girls. In fact, he hates any girl being threatened. He's never told us why it triggers his anger, but I know Lily is aware and often talks to him about it.

"Okay. But please, just keep it between us?" Mum bites her lip and Dad looks anywhere but at me. "What?"

"We were out with Max and Lake when we got the call. They had to, um, do something."

And Max will tell every family member and close friend. I groan, silently cursing Beau. "I need to go, but I'll be back as soon as I can."

"We aren't going anywhere," Dad tells Beau. "And thank you—for calling us."

Beau glances at me, his expression softening from the determined and angry one he had been wearing, before looking back at my dad and shrugging. "She loves you. You love her. And from what she's told me about you guys, you're all close."

"Yeah," Dad replies gruffly, looking at Beau differently. It's a look I've never seen him give a male that isn't family. It's weird and something I'm totally going to question when we're alone.

SIX

Since getting the letter from Noah four days ago, I've not been left alone. The first day, my parents didn't leave until Beau came back from handing the letter in to Collings. The second, my brothers and cousins, Landon, Ciara, and Charlotte came over. The third, I worked late, but when I got back, Beau was waiting for me.

He'd made me go inside and run a bath while he cooked us dinner. We then sat down for the rest of the night and chatted, our gazes only going to the TV once or twice the whole night.

He's an only child and has two cousins he never sees, since they live in Scotland with his dad's brother and wife. He has another aunt and uncle nearby, but they couldn't have kids. They doted on their niece and nephews.

His parents live an hour away and are very much involved in his life. He'd even added to the conversation about meeting them when they next visit.

It was nice to get to know another side of him. A side that wasn't my neighbour or the officer working on finding the person who'd stolen my belongings. He was different. He could be charming, funny, gentle and demanding, and if his choice of movies is anything to go by, a total badass.

He took control of life, of everything in front of him, and he did it in a way that wasn't arrogant or big-headed. He just did it.

And I really like that about him.

Okay, more than like it.

"What has you thinking so hard?" Lily asks, flopping down on my sofa, next to me.

"Huh?" I ask, glancing her way.

She giggles and throws a pillow in my face. "You are so lost in your own head. I've been talking to you for ten minutes about a little girl in my class and you've completely ignored me."

I'm mortified. "You were?"

She nods. "So, what were you thinking about? Or should I say *who?*"

My cheeks heat when I tell her. "Beau."

Her smile grows. "Ah, the hot neighbour. Do I want to know what you were thinking about?"

I throw the pillow back at her, laughing. "Lily! And he's just… I don't know. I like him, okay."

"Well duh! You go gooey-eyed when he's mentioned, narrowed-eyed when the boys threaten him, and gush when the mums ask about him. Does he like you the same way?"

That's a loaded question.

I just don't know.

"Lily, I wouldn't even know how to find out. He does all this stuff for me; cooks me dinners and hangs out with me. The other night, he ran me a bath and told me to relax. He's amazing. However, it could be just who he is. He could be a nice person in general; a generous, caring, seriously hot person."

"He's lived here a few weeks now. Has he brought any girls home?"

My heart twists at the suggestion. Most of the time I fall asleep before he even leaves to go home. On the times that I'm awake, we say goodnight and I end up in bed watching my soaps.

"It's not like I stalk his front door or anything, but no. If he isn't here, he's at work. What do you think?"

"I'm not really sure, since I don't have any more experience than you, but from what I've seen with our cousins, men don't do something that nice for just anybody. Not with the stuff he's doing for you. Look at our family; Maddox doesn't treat girls like crap, but he doesn't sit with them most nights or run them baths either. And Ashton; he's never cooked himself a meal, let alone someone else. And they're good men. The best."

I think it over. She's right. Our cousins, dads and uncles are the best men we know, the best we've ever known. They stick together through thick and thin. They've only ever treated our mums with the utmost respect. They love them unconditionally.

They've groomed the boys in our family to be the best they can be, made sure they always treated women with respect and care. They may act like total dawgs, but none of them would intentionally hurt a girl, physically or emotionally.

"What if I make a fool out of myself by saying something to him?"

"You'll never know unless you do something. This has been the first male to *ever* capture your attention for more than five minutes. He must be special."

At that I smile. "He really is. Actually, he should be here soon. He always pops in after work."

She pales a little. Lily hates being around strangers. It's why she got a job teaching five-year olds; they're not threatening or intimidating. Personally, I'd be more scared of the five-year olds.

She picks at her fingernails, and I know she's struggling with something. I'm unsure whether she's going to say whatever is on her mind, but she surprises me, saying, "I heard Mum and Dad talking about the note and DVD."

"Yeah?" I ask quietly.

I hate worrying my parents. We all do. Even my brothers, who often run them through the wringer. We love them. And anything hurting them, no matter how big or small, hurts us.

She picks imaginary lint off her leggings before her gaze meets mine. "Are you scared?"

I haven't admitted how I truly feel to anyone, knowing it will only make them worry more. However, this is Lily, my sister, my best friend. She's the one person I tell everything to. Maybe it's because of how we became sisters or because of our close upbringing, but she's the only one out of the family I can easily confide in, despite how close we all are.

"It's terrifying knowing he's still out there. Beau said he usually moves on, so knowing he's still here, possibly because of me, is scary as hell. I'm struggling to stay asleep most nights. Little noises keep waking me up. I don't even know if it's him that scares me or the thought of him and what he did," I admit, feeling my chest tighten.

It's been hard to come to terms with.

"Faith, why didn't you say anything? Are you sure staying here is safe?" She worries at her lip, cupping her mug of tea closer to her, like she's warding off the cold.

"Because I knew you'd all worry and I didn't want that. I didn't want Mum and Dad to talk me into moving back home. You know it was hard saying goodbye to them the first time. And I have Beau across the way now. It's not like I'm alone here with no neighbours."

Lily slowly nods her head. "And I suppose they have put extra security in. I'm just worried for you. You never think something like this could happen to you or someone you love."

"Agreed. I didn't think anything like this would happen to me. It was a topic you'd read about in the papers or on the internet. It was never real." I sigh. "It's been a lot to deal with, especially since he hasn't been caught. The picture he had on his profile is clearly fake, so we're not sure what he looks like. The only thing we do know is that he has done it before and his real name is most likely Noah."

She nods, stroking Roxy's fur. "Just be safe. If it gets too much for you, come stay with me, or swallow your pride and go back to Mum and Dad. It won't be forever, but for now. They'll understand that, and Mum won't be a wreck like she was before. We were the first to move out and she found it hard."

Yeah, she did.

I've never seen her cry like she did on the days we both left home. I'd been seconds away from saying 'fuck it' and moving back in. Fortunately, Dad intervened by whispering something in Mum's ear that made her blush. It was gross.

Mark and Aiden both live at home still, but most of the time they sleep at friends' houses or crash at one of ours, to give Mum and Dad space. Mark has been looking for a place for a while though. We're all hoping Mum takes it better than she did with us girls.

"I will. Anyway, are we all set for the weekend?"

Every once in a while, we all plan to go away somewhere together. Sometimes it's for two weeks in the sun, others it's just a weekend away somewhere remote.

"Ah, about that, Kayla and Myles said Jacob can't come this year since he got drunk the last time he was with us. Josh isn't coming, but Imogen is. Ashton, Aiden, and Trent have also said they can't make it. Because of their new jobs, they haven't managed to get the time off."

"But we always go together." There's a knock on my door, and my complaint is cut short. I eye Lily with a grin. "Be right back."

I'm not even embarrassed to admit I skip to the door like a teenager, or that my heart beats wildly inside my chest.

It's Beau.

"Hey," I greet, smiling wide.

He grins at me. "Hey."

"Come in, there's someone I want you to meet." I take his hand and drag him inside.

He looks at me warily. "It's not another uncle or male cousin, is it?"

I laugh, knowing Landon really put him through the wringer when they met. You'd never think he was my uncle Max's son. They're nothing alike. In fact, if anything, I'd say he was more like my uncle Malik; broody, serious, and burly.

"No, it's my sister, Lily," I assure him, closing the door behind him. "Lily, this is Beau. Beau, this is my sister, Lily."

He pastes on his charming smile, giving her a chin lift. "Nice to meet you."

"They're right, you're hot," she blurts out, her cheeks turning pink. She groans as I laugh. "I just said that out loud, didn't I?"

Both Beau and I laugh at her remark, and her expression. Lily may be quiet, shy, and a little bit of a recluse, but she has no problems blurting stuff out.

She thinks it, she says it. Without even meaning to.

It's hilarious.

"Yeah, you did."

"Sorry," she says, wringing her hands together.

He smirks. "It's fine. It's good for my ego to hear it once in a while, especially from a pretty woman." I giggle at the reddening of her cheeks as she eyes him. "And it's my lucky day. I was going to take your sister out for dinner, since it's my turn to cook, but I'm not in the mood. Would you like to join us?"

Lily's flustered for a second, looking a little panicked. I smile, giving her a nod that it's okay. Now that she knows I like him, she'll probably feel uncomfortable, like the third wheel.

"Um, I can't. I promised my cousin Maddox I'd make him dinner tonight."

"Oh, that's a shame. I was looking forward to getting to know you. Faith speaks very fondly of you."

Lily smiles at that, knowing how much I love her. "If you'd like, we're going camping Friday till Monday. A few members of our family can't make it and we're at an odd number. Some of the activities require pairs."

"Camping?" he asks, looking at me doubtfully.

In the time we've got to know one another, he knows I'm not an outdoorsy person. I hate rain—it's miserable and wet—and since we live in England, ninety-five percent of the weather we have is rain. I'd rather sit and listen to it from inside my warm flat, preferably curled under a blanket.

"Don't get me started. It was Maddox's turn to choose where we went. Hayden, my other cousin, took us on an All-Star Retreat the last time we went away. She'd thought it was a club crawl weekend."

"What was it?" he asks, grinning.

Lily giggles. "An OAP venture retreat. They had knitting circles, bingo nights, singles nights, dance nights, back to the forties, and some other stuff."

"No!" He throws his head back, laughing. "And all your cousins I met did this?" he asks, looking at me now.

"Yeah. They didn't have a choice. It was actually a pretty good weekend, but poor Maddox and Jacob, who were sixteen at the time, kept getting hit on. The others stayed clear, bless them. In the end, Jacob got so drunk from sneaking their drinks, he had a hangover for a week. And Maddox…" I end up laughing too hard to carry on.

Lily continues for me, "Ended up in one of their rooms. He walked a group of ladies back to their apartments, but was so drunk he ended up crashing. His face the next day was priceless. We even have pictures. The old lady took selfies to show her friends in the home she lives in. She had breakfast with us the next day and told us all about him passing out, and the photos. Once Maddox stormed off, we got her to send them to us."

Beau can't stop laughing either. As bad as the trip started off—and being nothing like we had expected—it turned out to be one of the best holidays we've had.

"Oh, God, I'm definitely coming. What time are you leaving on Friday?"

I look at Lily, since she's helped Maddox organise this one. "In the morning, around seven. We want to get there early. It's a three-hour drive."

"I'm supposed to work till four, but Collings owes me a favour. I'll see if he can get someone to swap my shift. If not, I'll meet you there after work."

I grin, giddy with excitement. "What about the weekend? Don't you have to work?"

He shakes his head. "Nah, I have every other weekend off, remember."

"I'm so glad you're coming. No one likes sharing a room with Faith, or in this case, tent. She snores," Lily teases.

"I do not snore," I snap.

And I don't. I may breathe a little heavy, but I don't snore. And no one likes sharing with me because I move around a lot in my sleep.

Beau grins. "You do."

Lily's eyes widen at his words, putting two and two together and getting five. "Not what you think, Lily."

Beau turns his grin to her, winking. "It is."

I smack his arm lightly and he grabs my hand. He pulls me closer to him and wraps his arm around my shoulder. "She can't resist me. Her head hits my body and she's out like a light."

Okay, that may be a little true.

"It's 'cause you bore me."

"You're the one who wanted me to watch One Tree Hill. I can't help that I'm now invested."

Giggling, I look up at him, watching his face relax and soften.

Lily clears her throat, her smile wide and knowing. "I've got to go, but I'll message Faith with everything you'll need. I'll let you go out for your dinner."

I walk out from under Beau's shoulder and hug her. "Speak to you later. Text me when you get in."

"Will do. Bye, Beau. It was really nice to meet you."

"You too, Lily."

I say another goodbye before walking her out and turning to Beau.

"So, dinner… Where are you taking me?"

He grins at my excitement. "KFC."

"You wouldn't," I gasp in mock horror. Although, I do love KFC.

"Nah, I've got us a table at Paradise."

"Yummy. Give me fifteen minutes and I'll be ready." I rush over to my bedroom before stopping suddenly. "Wait, are we going now?"

He chuckles. "Yeah, babe. Get ready. I'll be back over in ten. Just need to change out of these."

"Okay, good." I nod for good measure, causing him to laugh. He walks over and kisses my forehead before heading to the door.

I'll never get tired of him doing that.

I just wish it was on my lips.

I'm always left wondering whether his kisses are just a friendly gesture or something more. With Beau, you can never tell.

I watch his fine, perky arse as he leaves, shutting the door behind him. The click of the lock makes me jump. I turn and rush into my room, wondering why the hell I offered up fifteen minutes.

I'm never going to find an outfit in fifteen minutes.

Holy fuck!

With that, I begin my frantic rush, hoping like hell I'm ready and looking half descent before my fifteen minutes are up.

SEVEN

WHEN LILY TRIED TO GET US ALL TO carpool together in a mini bus, I'm glad Maddox talked her out of it. With the storage space needed for pillows and the other shit we've all lugged together, it wasn't hard to talk her out of it without hurting her feelings.

I'm pretty sure Charlotte brought the most. At nineteen, she still has that childlike character about her. She's gentle, caring and puts others above all else. She's a gem.

When she'd informed us she brought some bird seeds and some feeders to place around the camp, it wasn't the least bit surprising. Neither was the amount of first-aid, spare clothes, and food she'd brought with her.

She doesn't go anywhere unprepared.

"She's not really going to make me eat veggie food, is she?"

When Maddox talked Lily down from the mini bus, he forgot to inform me we'd have to drive three hours with Aiden and Ashton, who'd decided to tag along at the last minute. Apparently, they managed to get time away from their schedules.

It's sucks.

For me.

Definitely for Beau.

For the first hour they'd filled Beau in on what to expect from the weekend. With all the shit they'd tried to scare him with, it was Charlotte and her need to sway people to the other side and become a vegetarian that had scared him the most.

"No—" I start, but I'm interrupted by Aiden.

"Yeah, as long as she has enough for herself. She hates it when we eat her burgers."

"You willingly eat that crap? My aunt is a vegetarian and I once ate one of her burgers. I puked and felt sick for days."

I feel rather than see Ashton shudder. "I puked my first time too."

"I bet," Beau mutters, looking a little green.

I roll my eyes. "Stop whining like pussies. They aren't that bad."

"Says you. Who cuts her burger first to make sure one of us haven't switched it?" Aiden comments.

I feel Beau's gaze cut to me and I swear my cheeks burst into flames when he starts chuckling. "Okay, I admit I like my meat. However, I hate it when Charlotte goes without. It's not like there's another vegetarian in the family to give her another option. You two are the worst for switching burgers."

"She only went without once," Aiden adds.

"And Dad made *me* go the shop and get her more."

"We're nearly there." Beau's voice interrupts whatever Aiden was going to say as we pull onto a long, dirt lane.

"I can't believe Jacob isn't allowed to come with us," Ashton whines, looking out at the scenery.

"You spiked his drink with vodka knowing he had already been pinching the old lady's alcoholic drinks."

"Whatev's." He pauses, and I hear his seat belt unclick. "What the hell is Hayden doing?" Ashton suddenly asks.

I squint and lean forward in my seat. "Um, I think she's beating Landon. Though it could be Liam. You can never tell with those three."

Ashton laughs, bouncing in his seat. "She just punched him in the nose."

"Are all your family violent?" Beau asks, sounding worried.

I bite my lip as I turn my gaze away from the fight going on in the back of Maddison's car and focus on Beau, trying to keep a straight face. "Um, not all of us."

"It's Liam. Landon's in the front. Look! He's trying to stop her from killing Liam," Aiden says, laughing.

Both he and Ashton have their seatbelts undone and are now sitting forwards, their heads perched on the headrests between me and Beau. When he turns to Beau, grinning, I know what's coming.

"It's Landon you have to be wary of. His dad might be a total goof, but he's all my uncle Malik. He's serious most of the time, protective and broody as all hell. Piss him off and you need to run. He doesn't pull punches."

"And we should know," Ashton laughs.

Ashton has just turned eighteen. If there's any one of us who doesn't take life seriously, it's him. He's actually more like my uncle Max than he is his own dad, Mason.

It's uncanny how many of us get traits from other family members.

We pull up, parking next to Madison. We all turn when the screaming continues, and see Liam fighting to get out of the car. I step outside, into the fresh air, and see him fall to his knees, trying to shuffle away. I lean against the car, ready to intervene if it gets out of hand. The boys won't do anything; they'll think it's hilarious Liam is getting beat up. They know he'd never touch her back, not even to restrain her.

"Calm down," Landon growls at the pair as he steps out of the car at a much slower pace. He's not even fazed by Hayden jumping on her brother's back and attacking him. He's had to live with it his whole life.

Beau meets me on my side of the car, leaning back, close to me. We watch as Landon pulls Hayden off kicking and screaming.

"What happened?" I ask Madison when she steps up on the other side of me.

Her gaze doesn't leave the chaos, a resigned look across her face. "Turns out she had a date last night."

"Uh-oh." My gaze goes back to Hayden who has broken free and is once again attacking a now screeching Liam.

"It didn't get that far," Madison adds, and my gaze cuts to her. "She knew Uncle Mason was working late and thought Liam would spend the night out with his mates. She agreed to be picked up, thinking she had a shot at a real date."

"This doesn't sound good," I murmur, watching her lips twitch.

"Liam kidnapped him."

Holy crap. Again? "What did he do to this one?"

"This one?" Beau asks, shuffling closer to listen in. My eyes flicker to his and find his attention fully on us. I'm not sure whether he's worried for his safety, or ready to inform the police. I'm about to warn Madison he's a police officer, but she's already answering before I can even give her a look.

"We got the whole story in the car. Under duress, I might add. She may have had his balls in her fist."

Beau shudders next to me. "Ouch, poor guy."

Madison scoffs. "He zip-tied her date and threw him into the back of his car. Liam drove it to the quarry down on Hurcott and did the usual—you know, threaten him and all that. He told him she was a trans and he wouldn't have some lad taking advantage of her newly changed body, not when she still had all the male equipment."

Beau starts choking, his eyes bugging out as he stares at us. He probably thinks she's full of it, but sadly, she's not. It's actually not the worst thing they've done to someone one of us have dated…or tried to date.

My only guess on why they haven't touched Beau is because he's built like a brickhouse, has tattoos, and an expression that says *don't fuck with me.*

But it's still early days.

Anything could happen.

However, it's still the longest a male—other than family—has lasted around us.

"He did what?" Beau finally manages to get out. I'm struggling to work out if he's trying not to laugh or he's mad. It's hard to tell.

"Remember, Beau is a police officer," I tell her, my eyes widening.

Madison turns red, her eyes rounding. "Crap, I forgot you're a police officer. I'm only joking though. The lad was willing. They went out for a drive and after a few non-threatening words, he agreed not to date Hayden. He certainly didn't do what I said he did. I swear…but not on oath."

Giggling, I place my hand on her shoulder. "How did she find out Liam had something to do with it?"

She eyes Beau for a moment longer, biting her bottom lip. He gapes at us for a few more seconds before turning back to Hayden and Liam with new eyes.

Probably wondering if he can get home before they do anything to him.

But that's just a guess.

"There's a lot of forest here," he whispers.

I giggle and turn back to Madison, nudging her to carry on.

"Oh, yeah, right. She messaged him a few choice words on the way here. She was pissed, and you know Hayden; she doesn't like being walked over. He didn't answer right away, but after an hour he sent her a message saying to stay away from him, otherwise he'll get a restraining order. You know the rest. One look at her brother and she knew. They'd been arguing for an hour before she finally went for the balls. Her restraint lasted longer this time. As soon as he confessed, she started to attack him."

"She did good then. Uncle Malik has been trying to get her to work on her anger issues."

"Yeah, but her dad is Max; she was never going to be all there."

"I hate my brother," Hayden growls, walking over to us.

Her light brown hair is a mess. It was in a messy bun to begin with, but now it looks like a bird has nested in it.

"I'm going to help put the tents up," Beau tells me. He gives Hayden a wide birth, eyeing her warily. I can't help but laugh.

"Make sure you don't help any of the other men here," she snaps. His eyes come to me before he rushes off to set up.

"Why?" I ask her, smiling because I know she didn't say it to be mean.

Her eyes light up. "*Because*, if I'm correct, they'll be sleeping outside in the wild. None of them have put a tent up in their life. Our dads always did it."

"Um, I'm pretty sure my dad always put your dad's tents up," I remind her. Max made such a fuss, my dad did it to shut him up.

She laughs, taking her hair out to tidy it up. "Exactly. Why do you think Dad always made out he couldn't do it?"

"Because he couldn't?" Madison asks, looking at me for answers. I shrug. Uncle Max isn't the brightest bulb in the box, even if he is one of the smartest people I know.

"*No*. He could. He just knew someone else would do it for him if he put up a stink."

"Oh, my God, is that why he says he can't cook—so others cook for him?" I ask.

Her grin is wide. "No, he really can't cook for shit. My mum does all that."

"What about pets? Is he really allergic to animals?" I have to ask. I've been trying to get my auntie Lake and uncle Max to adopt for years. Lake always seems to want to say yes, but Max always shoots it down.

Her eyes are twinkling now and I'm ready to kill my uncle. "Nope. Apparently, my mum had a cat called Splinter when they first got together. He terrorised the men in the family, but mostly Dad. Any time he's mentioned, you'll hear my dad mutter cockblocker under his breath. After that, he wouldn't have another animal attacking him."

"That—I'm so going to get him back for this," I growl, thinking of ways to make him pay.

We all turn when we hear the lads arguing, ready to tear each other to shreds. The girls carry on putting their tents up, looking in the lads' direction with a smirk.

It's Beau that makes me giggle. He's ignoring them too, putting his tent up quickly and with ease, like he's done it a thousand times.

———————————

It's NIGHTFALL BY the time we finish setting up. We'd had to stop after a couple of hours when Lily dragged us away, telling us to leave everything so we could go and sign up for the activities.

After, we'd walked for three hours, checking out the area with a guide who pointed out every little thing. He'd let us know what tracks to stay away from and which ones were best to take.

We'd spent another hour helping Charlotte set up the bird feeders. The guide looked pretty taken with her and was pleased with her contribution.

It didn't take Aiden, Liam and Mark long to lose him.

And when I say lose him, I mean they scared the poor soul shitless. At first it was small things; commenting on what had happened to the last person who spoke to her. They used Landon as an example. And with Landon being big, scary, and tatted up, the sod bought everything they said. He stayed clear of Charlotte after that.

Then they started whispering taunts about how Landon was watching him.

He really wasn't coping well with their constant threats.

But it was Landon growling over Charlotte accidently tripping over a log that did him in. Since the guide was trying to stay away, he walked ahead, but when Charlotte started to catch up to him, he started to walk faster. It was how she'd tripped up.

Landon noticed what was going on and flipped. He told the guide to fuck off before he lost some teeth.

Now it's nightfall and Maddox and Liam have finally talked the girls into setting up their tents. They'd asked Beau to help another brother out, but Beau just laughed and told them he had orders and didn't want to get on the wrong side of Hayden.

Lily and Imogen, my uncle Ethan's daughter, help them.

Beau stands from the fire he just made, looking a little smug at my cousins. They'd been trying for thirty minutes to no avail, and that was with matches, gasoline, and a lighter.

It had only taken Beau a few minutes.

"I'd reign in the smugness," I warn him on a whisper when he sits down next to me.

"Why? I'm not worried about what they'll do."

He looks so damn sure, but he has no idea. "Yeah, you might not, but I have to share a tent with you."

His chuckle is deep when he gauges my reaction. "You're serious? Don't worry, baby, I'll protect you."

It's my turn to laugh. "Oh, I'm not worried about me. They'll try to avoid me, but I might get caught in the crossfire. I'm worried for you."

"They can't be that bad," he says, but doesn't sound convinced of his own words.

"Oh, they're worse."

"Hey, what's on the agenda for tomorrow? I'm not climbing any more trees," Mark complains, eyeing Charlotte.

She smiles sweetly at him. "We put them all up today, Mark, don't worry. Thank you for helping me."

He flushes with guilt over moaning about doing it, and gives her a timid smile. "It's okay."

Lily grabs her rucksack and pulls out a booklet. "Up first is a trek to——." Everyone groans, but she ignores us. "When we get to the top, we are zip lining." Cheers ring out around the camp, and a few girls groan. "Then we have white water rafting at three. It's a team building experience and overlooks the sights the valley has to offer. We've booked two boats, each fit seven, and we'll have fifteen minutes for the instructor to go through everything. Is that okay with everyone?"

"What did you book for Sunday?" Maddox asks, bouncing in his seat excitedly.

Landon and Charlotte hand out beers and I take one, my gloved hands wrapping around the bottle.

Lily smiles at Maddox. "We have a bunch of stuff; archery, rock climbing—only the beginners climb. Then we have the jungle challenge, which is basically an assault course, but most of it is in the trees."

"Fuck, I've wanted to do that forever." Aiden hoots, throwing back his beer.

"Tobogganing on the adult slope is last. We have a choice of having dinner before the jungle challenge or after. But if I'm honest, with those activities, I think I can handle waiting to eat. Then there's a party back at the main building where the restaurant and bar are. This weekend has been closed for under eighteens. Apparently, because next week is half term, they get packed with children, so they like to open it for adults only a week before."

"And Monday?" Beau asks what I'm thinking and I give him a smile. This is a lot to fit in in a few days.

"Not much. They only have canoeing on since they close at four. So, we'll be canoeing through the valley until we get to the drop off point. There, we will be met by some guides who will carry a change of our clothes, so we can hike back."

"More walking?" Liam groans.

"Afraid you can't keep up?" Hayden taunts, grinning.

He narrows his gaze on his sister. "No, I just don't want to put you guys to shame when you're all panting and gasping for air."

"Sorry to interrupt, but what about food?" Aiden asks Lily, causing her to frown.

I giggle under my breath, earning a glare from both my brothers.

"What do you mean?"

"Well, you've got all these activities planned but not once did I hear anything about food. How are we gonna eat if we're walking miles up a hill?"

"Um, it's after breakfast and before lunch."

His eyes bug out. "I'll starve to death."

"I'll be wasting away," Mark retorts. I snort, hiding in Beau's shoulder when his eyes come my way.

"I've brought snacks," she tells him gently, not wanting to poke the bear.

He scoffs, eyeing her bag with disgust. "If those bars are what you call snacks, then nope. They taste like cardboard."

"I've got snacks too," Charlotte informs him.

"Um, yeah… No," Aiden tells her.

Her face falls, and she looks at the both of them from under her lashes. "You don't want my food? I baked too."

They eye each other before their shoulders sag, and they glance back at Charlotte. "We can eat your baked goods."

Her smile brightens at their words. She bounces up from her seat and kisses them both on the cheek. "I'm going to get an early night before we have to walk for hours."

She waves at everyone before heading over to her tent, which is at the back, wedged between Hayden's and Imogen's. She's sharing with Landon, not wanting to be unprotected in the case of a bear attack. We did explain there are no bears here, only a few snakes, but she wouldn't listen. Plus, her and Lily together would talk themselves into being scared for no reason. They'd feed each other's fears by jumping at every little sound.

But we love them.

Once she's out of sight, Aiden and Mark turn to me, like I'm going to give them permission. "Please let us go get rid of them before she makes us eat them. We can say a bear ate them."

I roll my eyes at their dramatics. Charlotte can't bake for shit. Plus, somehow, whatever she uses to bake with makes everything taste stale.

"You can't do that," I tell them, giving them a warning look. It would hurt her feelings, and not one of us would do that to her. We've all had to protect her a time or two from bullies, or from boys who'd tried it on with her as a bet.

It started at the end of primary school. She hasn't let it jade her or make her any less caring towards others. But it doesn't mean it hasn't affected her. It's why we're all so protective of her and Lily.

Both are too kind for their own good.

"Okay." Aiden sulks, grabbing another beer out the cooler.

"Throw us one?" Beau calls, and Aiden, without thinking, throws it. Beau catches it, not bothering to wait for the fizz to calm down before opening it. It drips over the sides but he sucks it back, before taking a long swig.

My eyes shift to Lily, who is frozen, her eyes on the beer in Beau's hand.

"Lily, it's okay," Maddox tells her gently.

She doesn't move, her gaze still on Beau. My hand reaches out blindly, pulling his arm down so he's not drinking it any longer.

"What?" he asks, then pauses when he notices it's quiet. He looks around in confusion. "Um, what's going on?"

Lily quickly stands, Maddox following her, and we all listen helplessly to the sound of her sob as he carries her away. "Nothing."

"Um, that wasn't nothing, babe. What did I do?"

"What makes you think you did something?" I ask him, forcing a smile. Everyone resumes chatting, even though I know they all want to check on her.

Why Lily can cope with some of us drinking but not others is still a shock. I remember when she first came to live with us and Dad pulled out a beer. She'd had a fit, which turned into a severe panic attack that led her to faint. It wasn't until the third time, when she'd had to be sedated, that we clicked on that beer was her trigger.

It took years for her to get over our dad and uncles' drinking. She's never fully divulged why she has that reaction. She said she didn't like the smell, the taste, or what people did when they drank it.

It had worried us all.

Still does, if I'm honest.

It's only Maddox that knows her full story, and obviously my parents. But her childhood wasn't like mine or the others. It was rough.

"Because all your cousins are pretending to be sly at glaring at me."

I groan, glancing at him. "It's my fault. I should have warned you, and Aiden shouldn't have given you a beer without asking her first."

"Asking her?" he asks, looking really confused now.

"Lily didn't have the same upbringing we did. Biologically, she's my dad's sister, but he didn't know about her until she was four. Her mum, *their mum*, was a crazy bitch. But Dad got custody of her and later adopted her. She's only ever spoken to my parents and Maddox about what happened to her, but she has confided in everyone that she can't be around alcohol with people she doesn't know. It took her years, and I mean years, to let our parents drink, and even longer for us. It's why she never goes out."

"Fuck! Is she okay? Did I just traumatise her?" he asks, running a hand over his chin.

My gaze follows his fingers as they run over his stubble, noticing his plump lips glistening with droplets of beer.

"No. She'll be fine. It took her by surprise is all. If we had asked her first, she would have said yes, and just not looked at you. Aiden throwing it at you like a basketball kind of pulled all her attention to it."

"That's fucked up. I feel like shit now."

"Don't. She'll apologise tomorrow. She probably ran off because of her reaction. She hates the panic attacks. She'll feel embarrassed."

"She hasn't got anything to be embarrassed about," he says fiercely, understanding shining in his eyes.

At that, my heart melts and I stare at him deeply, like I'm seeing him in a new light. I didn't think he could sit higher on his pedestal.

"Tell her that in the morning, if she brings it up. Let her know it's okay if she's not comfortable with it. It will make her feel better if she's not and wants you stop."

He nods. "I can do that."

"I'm sorry this is crazy for you. Bet your wishing you never came."

He grabs my chin between his fingers. "I'm glad I came along. I'm enjoying myself, but more than that, I love spending time with you."

My mouth gapes open, a breath gasping free as I stare at him, lost in his emerald green gaze. The light from the fire reflects in his eyes, enough for me see them darken. The air around us is charged, the sparks crackling between us.

"I love spending time with you too," I tell him, my voice airy and breathless. All I can feel is the magnetic air pulling me towards him. I'm sure he can hear my heart pounding against my chest.

His head bends a little and I hold my breath, waiting, wanting, needing. Before I can analyse anything though, Mark is interrupting with a bite in his tone, "We should follow the others. We have an early morning again and I'm wiped."

My gaze reluctantly leaves Beau's and narrows in on my brother. "So, *go* to bed."

"We should all go," he says, punctuating each word.

I grit my teeth, hating him right now for interrupting what I had hoped was going to be a kiss. At least, I think it was going to be.

"Yeah, come on, Faith, I need to tuck you in… real snug," Beau announces, standing up and helping me to my feet. He gloats at my brothers who are now standing side by side, their arms crossed over their chests.

"You can sleep outside her tent," Aiden growls.

"No, thank you. I don't like bugs," Beau says as we walk towards them.

They step in front of us, both glaring at Beau. "She can stay with us then."

Oh, my God.

"Seriously you two? Go to bed and leave us alone. Neither of us are sleeping outside or with you."

"Yeah, you're really not my type," Beau taunts. I smack his back, wishing he'd stop putting his foot in it.

Mark grunts, but Aiden looks at Beau as if offended. "I'm everyone's type."

Beau snorts, his arm going around my waist and pulling me to him. "Goodnight, boys."

"We're not boys," Mark growls, turning to follow us.

We keep walking, heading towards our tent, but Aiden calls out, stopping us. "Don't forget, we're in the tent next to you, fucker. Touch her, we'll know, and you'll be fed to the bears."

"You said there weren't any bears," Charlotte shouts, sounding scared.

They both groan, looking in the direction of her tent.

"There isn't. Go to sleep," Landon tells her, his voice filled with amusement.

"Night, you pair." I turn to Beau as we reach our tent. "I'm going to check on Lily, then I'll be right back, okay?"

"Yeah, okay. Tell her I'm sorry."

"I will."

He unzips the tent and bends down to get in before I turn in the direction of Lily and Maddox's tent.

My heart is racing a mile a minute. When I'd said I wanted to check on Lily, it was a half lie. I really want to calm my raging hormones, because I'd honestly believed we'd been about to kiss. And I'd realised just how much I wanted it.

My crush for Beau is becoming uncontrollable.

I just hope I'm not reading the signals he's sending wrong. I don't want to make a fool out of myself.

With that, I call out Lily's name before stepping into her tent, praying Beau will be asleep by the time I get back.

EIGHT

BEAU WASN'T ASLEEP WHEN I GOT BACK. We didn't talk about what took place by the fire either—fortunately. Instead, we went and got dressed in the bathrooms allocated to our camp site and walked back to the tent. We shared some small talk before falling asleep, which I don't remember doing. I'd been so lost in his deep voice, trying to stay quiet so the others couldn't hear us, that the last thing I remembered was Beau talking about his parents.

I wake up feeling hot—too hot. Even though the weather is chilly outside—if the wind is anything to go by—I'm burning up like a furnace.

Why? Because my body is sprawled all over Beau's chest.

My right leg is hooked over his large thighs, my arm draped over his broad, tattoo-covered chest. I didn't get a good look last night since I didn't want to be caught gawking, but seeing his impressive chest covered in tribal markings was seriously hot.

How the fudge did I end up here, in his arms? We'd had a body width between us on the air mattress Beau brought with him and were in separate sleeping bags. Now, not so much.

It also feels like a blanket is over us.

Dread fills my stomach when I fully open both of my eyes. The tent has collapsed. I shoot up, pushing the roof of the tent away from me.

Beau stirs, a small grin on his lips. If I wasn't so panicked, I'd be checking him out a lot more. At a brief glance, he looks sexy as hell all tousled from sleep.

"Hey." His morning voice is husky.

He must see the panic in my expression before the destruction of the tent. His eyes widen and he shoots up, his mouth opening to say something. "What's—What the fuck?"

"Did it break?"

Laughter outside the tent brings me out of my panic, and I narrow my eyes towards the door.

"Your cousins!" Beau states, sounding annoyed.

"Yeah, it was bound to happen." I sigh, moving aside so we can shuffle through the mess to get to the entrance.

He finds the zip and unzips it. But before he can start on my cousins, he turns to me. "Revenge on your cousins, is it allowed?"

I grin at the look in his eyes. A Carter is accustomed to that look. It says payback is going to be a bitch. "Make 'em suffer."

He grins and winks at me before leaving the tent. I'm a breathless mess with that one look. God, it should be a crime to be that good-looking. He holds the flap up and I move forward, keeping the sleeping bag wrapped around me and one hand holding the tent flap up so I can look out. I'm going to wait until Beau kills my brothers and cousins before moving.

"Oi, dickheads. You made her have a panic attack," Beau growls. I know he's exaggerating, but they don't, and it brings a smile to my face.

He's only met them a few times and already he fits in, giving as good as he gets.

"What? Is she okay? We didn't mean to scare her like that. We couldn't get you to drink last night," Aiden confesses, sounding worried. He tries to look past Beau, to me, but Beau moves, blocking his view.

"We're sorry!" Ashton shouts, his head bouncing from side to side, trying to make eye contact with me.

I stifle a giggle as I bury further into my sleeping bag.

It's quiet for a few seconds, but then Beau speaks, low and dangerous, sending butterflies swirling in my stomach. "And why would I need to drink?"

Oh, crap!

Ashton seems wary when he mumbles. "Um…"

Aiden, not so much. He probably thinks being my brother will save him, so he doesn't have a problem boasting about what their plan was.

"We were going to drag you out on your blow-up bed and into the lake when you passed out from too much drink. We saw it in a movie and have wanted to do it ever since."

His laughter isn't followed by Beau's, and if his posture is anything to go by, he isn't happy about their plan.

"One: if you ever think of putting someone passed out drunk in a lake, make sure you're right next to them. They could fucking drown. Two: don't ever scare your sister and cousin again. You'll regret it."

Beau moves to the side and I watch as both Aiden and Ashton nod their heads compliantly. I'm completely shocked.

Laughter around the camp makes me jump, and I notice, for the first time, others are standing around and watching.

Ashton and Aiden turn around, tails tucked between their legs, and head back for their tent, but Beau clears his throat. "Um, where the fuck do you think you're going?"

They turn around, both clearly confused as they stare at each other, then look at Beau, their foreheads creased. "To go get ready?"

Beau shakes his head slowly. "Nope, you're gonna fucking put our tent back together while *we* get ready." They go to argue, but one look at Beau, with whatever expression he's giving them, has them nodding, gulping.

Beau turns around to face me, his expression amused. He's standing completely shirtless, tattoos covering his chest, arms and neck. His rock-hard body is drawn tight from the chill in the air, but even if it were warm, it's clear he'd still have the eight pack he's sporting. I've never seen anything sexier.

Absently, I check my mouth for drool, never taking my eyes off his chest. He's magnificent, beautifully sculpted.

"Eyes are here, babe."

At the sound of his voice, I jump, blushing at being caught. He laughs at my discomfort. "Shut up. Let's grab our stuff and get ready. I want to get breakfast before our trek."

"Breakfast," Aiden mutters, his lips pouty as he and Ashton get to work on the tent.

Out of the fourteen of us, it's mostly the boys moaning about the walk. Poor Imogen only brought pumps, so her feet have been hurting more than ours. The girl doesn't own a pair of trainers, so I'm surprised she owns a pair of pumps. If she had come in high-heeled boots or shoes, it wouldn't have been at all surprising. The girl is woman through and through.

We aren't far from the top, where we're meeting another guide to strap us to the zip line.

"For a group of young, athletic-looking guys, they sure bitch," Beau mutters next to me. I giggle, bumping my shoulder with his.

Speaking of age… "How old are you anyway?"

He looks at me funny, before grinning. "Shit, with everything we've shared, I've never actually told you how old I am, have I?"

"Nope."

Please don't let him be younger. He looks older than me, but with our generation, you can never be too sure. Jacob, our youngest family member, has been able to get into clubs since he was fourteen. Not that his parents know. They'd kick his arse.

"I'm twenty-nine."

"Ah, you're like the grandpa of the group," I tease. He feigns hurt, then a creepy smile reaches his lips. "What's that look for?"

A grin spreads across his face as he takes a step towards me. I take one back, not able to fight the smile spreading across my own face as excitement bubbles inside me.

"Don't be scared," he tells me as I take another step back. In a blink, he's in front of me, bent at the waist and hauling me over his shoulder.

I squeal loudly, but its soon followed by laughter. "Put me down."

"Oh, no. I'm going to find the grossest thing here in the woods and dunk you in it for calling me grandpa."

Laughter rings out around us, but he doesn't slow his pace. "No, no, no. Put me down. I'm sorry I called you old." I laugh harder, smacking his hard-muscled back.

"I don't believe you." He slaps my arse and I yell, smacking his back harder.

Lifting my head, my eyes meet Lily and Maddox's. "Tell him to put me down."

Lily laughs, shaking her head at me as Maddox's lips twitch in amusement. "I don't know. No dude wants to be called old."

"I was joking," I yell.

"She didn't sound like she was joking, right?" Beau asks, swinging me around. My head spins, along with the ground beneath his feet.

"Nope," Maddox, popping the 'P'.

Smug bastard.

"Traitor."

Beau spins back around and I lift my head to glare at my cousin. "You're so not my favourite anymore."

He waves me off, grinning. "We all know Ashton is your favourite."

"I'm your favourite?" Ashton asks, grinning like a mad man.

"If you get me down you will be."

He seems to think about it for a minute, but Beau turns, clearly giving Ashton a look, because when he spins me back around, still walking with me, Ashton gives me a sympathetic smile and shrugs.

"You'll still cook for me, right?"

"No. I'm going to make Charlotte bake you treats."

Charlotte skips up beside Ashton, all smiles. "I don't mind. I love cooking."

She just isn't any good at it.

Ashton pales, looking towards Beau again. I see him calculating. He's trying to see if he can get to me before Beau takes him out. It would be laughable if the blood wasn't rushing to my head and if my stomach didn't hurt from bouncing on his large shoulder every time he takes a step.

I groan. "Beau, please, I'm getting lightheaded."

He stops shortly and drags me down his body until my feet touch the ground. I stay flush against him, my body tightening as I meet his gaze. My hands clasp his large biceps, my fingers gripping them as they tense beneath my touch.

His green eyes sparkle as he stares down at me. "Sorry. We'll have to wait to get you back."

My lips twitch. "Yeah? What if I get you first?"

That makes him laugh. He tucks me against his chest, his arm draping over my shoulder. "Let's get this done. I want to see you fly."

It doesn't take us long to reach the top. I'd been fine all morning, not even a glimmer of fear, but the minute we get set up with our equipment, I'm a ball of freaking nerves. My hands are shaking and my breathing escalates. The closer in line we get, the more I begin to panic.

The boys are bouncing on their feet, ready to go, which doesn't surprise me. They live for this shit.

"You okay? You look a little green."

My gaze meets Beau's and I grimace. "Do I look that bad?"

His eyes scan my face, a look passing through them. "No, you look beautiful."

I melt against his side, my head resting on his shoulder. I watch as they strap Charlotte in, her mouth moving frantically at Landon. He just grins at her, saying something to the guy who is double-checking her straps. When the time comes, she shakes her head, not wanting to go, but Landon laughs and gives her a gentle push. Her scream echoes around us and my fear spikes.

"Holy crap." I take a step back, away from Beau and to the back of the queue. Still not taking my eyes away from where they're strapping Landon in, I take another, but stop when I suddenly bump into someone.

"Sorry," I squeak. My squeak turns into a squeal when Beau wraps me in his arms and pushes through the rest of our group. He stands behind Landon, who is getting ready to be strapped in.

"No, no, no, no," I chant.

"Hey!" Aiden gripes.

"She won't do it if she watches all of you going down. She needs to go next."

"Nope. I'll walk back and meet you at the rafting edge."

Beau holds me tighter, chuckling next to my ear. "You'll be fine."

Landon moves off, his arms reaching out, and howls. The boys behind howl back.

"Nope, can't do it. I'll run back if I have to."

Beau laughs, walking behind me now and moving me forward. I feel him nod—his chin knocking into my head—to the bloke to my left, and all of a sudden, hands are strapping me into a harness while another pair attaches me to the zip line. The one on my right checks my harness again, while the other rechecks the clip on the zip tie.

We wait a few more seconds, and then the one on my left asks me to take a step forward. I take one back.

"I can't do this. I really can't," I say, beginning to feel full-on panicked.

Beau moves out from behind me and steps next to me. He grabs my chin between his fingers and turns my face towards him. "You've got this."

"I'm scared," I admit.

"That's the fun of it. It's the fear inside you that feeds the adrenaline. Use it, enjoy it."

"I don't know if I can," I whisper, lost in his gaze.

His eyes meet mine for a second, before glancing down to my lips. My breath catches as he walks me closer to the edge, his eyes still on my lips, and I find myself swaying towards him.

Then it happens. Too fast. His lips press against mine. His tongue runs along the seam of my lips before entering my mouth. My eyes shut as the initial shock passes, and then I melt against him and kiss him back. He tastes like peppermint. A groan rumbles in the back of my throat.

He kisses me once more before his gaze meets mine, his eyes dilated and filled with lust.

"You've got this," he whispers.

Got what?

Then I'm flying.

Literally.

And screaming.

The kiss becomes forgotten as I panic.

The trees fly by below me. The wind roars in my ears. But the view… It's breath-taking, magnificent. My screaming dies in the face of its beauty. I've never seen anything like it. Trees as far as the eye can see surround me, birds chirping in the air, and the smell… it's all too much. The sun shimmers off the lake, make it almost glitter before me.

I lift my arms out and close my eyes, tipping my head to the sky as I take it all in.

It's not long before I begin to slow. In the distance, Madison, Landon, Lily and Maddox await with Charlotte. They're screaming and waving at me as they smile. I smile and wave back.

When they frown, I'm confused, until Maddox starts waving his hands, frantically pointing behind them. That's when I see the pile of straw and remember what our instructor told us.

My landing isn't as graceful as they said it would be. In fact, it hurts a little. I groan, rolling off the straw and onto the ground where another guide meets me, unclipping me from the harness and zip line.

I run over to the others. I'm buzzing with adrenaline, still feeling like I'm flying.

"Oh, my God, that was incredible. Did you see me?" I squeal, when I meet up with them.

"Wasn't it brilliant? That view was amazing," Madison gushes.

Landon laughs, walking up beside her. "Maddy, you were screaming the whole way down."

"And I'm pretty sure your eyes were closed," Maddox tells her, smiling.

She glares at them both. "I so wasn't. I saw everything. Well, not everything, but I did open my eyes for some of it."

I laugh at her honest answer, ready to reply, but movement from above catches my eye and I see Beau flying down, grinning.

My finger runs smoothly over my lips, still feeling swollen from our kiss. It was so unexpected, and I have no idea what it means. As I watch the men unclip him, thoughts run through my mind a mile a minute, wondering what the hell I should do. Do I ask him about it? Ignore it? Or do I run up and kiss him like I want to?

I'd rather do the latter, but nerves and fear get the better of me. Instead, I send him a small smile as he walks over.

"What did you think?" he asks, still grinning, and pulls me into his arms.

"Dude, personal space," Landon growls.

Beau looks over my shoulder at Landon and sees he's being serious, but he doesn't step back. "Jealous?"

"I'm not as easily intimidated as Ash and Aiden."

"Come on." Charlotte pulls on his arm. "Let's get a picture of the others as they come down."

Aiden screaming like a banshee distracts Landon long enough for her to pull him away, and I turn back to Beau, my voice breathless and hoarse. "It was incredible. The most amazing experience I've ever had."

"Yeah, it was," he tells me softly, but with the look in his eyes, I wonder if he's speaking about something else.

I smile, finding the courage to ask him about the kiss. But then my stupid brother interrupts us, bouncing into us like a caveman.

"Yo, don't kiss my sister again, like, ever. I don't care if you're mean and can probably put me in jail. I'll kick your arse."

He bounds off, luckily not talking loud enough for the others to listen. "Are they always like this?"

My face burns with embarrassment. My family will never be normal. "I'm sorry. They're just really protective. Overprotective if you ask me and every female in my family. I promise you, though, they're harmless."

"If you say so," he laughs. "What do you think they'd do if I kissed you again?"

"You want to kiss me again?" I blurt out, my eyes widening.

Hope.

That is what I feel. Hope blossoming in my chest. It doesn't feel real. He really wanted to kiss me. It wasn't to distract me long enough to push me over the edge. Literally.

"I want to do more than kiss you," he growls, pulling me against him.

I go willingly, my hands falling on his broad shoulders, and smile. I open my mouth to ask what he means when another body bounds into us, pulling us apart.

"Seriously, I want a body width between the two of you. No sharing a tent anymore either," Mark growls.

I stomp my foot, glaring at my brother. "Mark!"

He looks down at me, not even apologising. "Nope. Not gonna happen. You've got to stay single until you're forty, maybe older."

Beau scoffs, but all I am is embarrassed. "Mark! I'm older than you. Piss off."

"Just saying, don't kiss her again." Mark gives Beau a warning look, before bouncing off towards the others.

"I'm so—"

I'm cut off when his lips slam against mine, his hands framing my face so he can tilt my head for a better angle. I open my mouth, letting him slide his tongue inside. My lower belly coils, tightening, and I grip him harder, my body flush against his.

This is perfect.

He slows down, perfecting the kiss, being gentle. He moves his lips against mine like he has all the time in the world. His fingers run through my ponytail, tethering me as he grips the ends, pressing me tighter against him.

His bulge presses against my stomach, and though I want to tense against him, not having any experience in that department, I don't. I actually find myself feeling hot, craving more of his touch.

Too soon, he pulls away, his forehead pressing against mine as we both catch our breath.

"Damn, you can kiss," he whispers.

"You're dead," Aiden whispers, right next to us.

And I mean, right next to us. We part to find his face as close as he can get without joining in. He's scowling at Beau, who shrugs back.

"Was worth it."

My heart melts. He's willing to take my family on for a kiss. My smile falls when I turn back to Aiden. "You do anything and I'll never make you baked goods again."

"Like he'll let you cook for me," he scoffs, walking away.

Hayden whistles. "You two are hot." She runs off and jumps on Aiden's back.

I laugh at her brash words. I'm ready to kiss him again, but then Liam walks over, looking smug. "Bro, you're totally never leaving this place alive."

"You do realise I'm a cop, right?"

Liam looks confused. "What's that got to do with the price of chips?"

Beau looks to me before bursting into laughter. "You guys are gonna have to get used to it. I plan on kissing her a lot more."

"Your funeral," Liam sings.

We watch him catch up with the others. The boys stand with their arms crossed over their chest, their gazes downright scary. The girls, on the other hand, are grinning at us like fools.

I groan and take Beau's hand, but then quickly pull away, feeling like a stage-five clinger. When he pulls my hand back and smiles at me, I relax.

"Let's get this water rafting done. Maybe we can drown a few of them before bedtime."

He laughs and together, holding hands, we walk over to the others.

NINE

I WAKE UP EARLY, STILL FEELING PISSED off over yesterday's water rafting palaver.

Aiden had 'accidently' pushed Beau into the water. Then he'd nearly, accidentally, been knocked out with a paddle, when we'd gone over a bar of sand.

I'd gotten up to scream at the same time Ashton had to gloat. He'd ended up knocking me over too. The water had been freezing. I've never felt pain like I had in that the first second of falling in. It had felt like a thousand knives were stabbing into me. It didn't help that it started raining ten minutes into the rafting—something that hadn't been forecasted. But it happened, and it poured, chilling the air around us.

It was miserable.

By the time they'd pulled us both to safety in the raft, I just wanted to go home. Home to my bed, where I had heating and thick blankets.

Thankfully, Charlotte let us have two of the three spare blankets she'd brought along with her once we got back to our campsite.

We'd showered and dressed, and made the boys bring our food to the tent. At that point, I'd been ready to kill someone. I couldn't get warm for shit.

Fortunately, I'd had Beau with me. After their little stunt, they'd been in no position to tell me what do, so their plan to swap places and have me stay with one of them, failed.

Beau had wrapped me up in arms, making me feel like I was on cloud nine. After an hour of being cuddled against him, I soon warmed up.

It was the middle of the night when I'd felt him move from the tent, most likely to take a piss. As soon as we'd eaten dinner, we'd stayed in the tent, too cold to step outside and join the others.

When he'd returned, I had reverted to being a shivering mess. He'd been what felt like three hours outside, so he was chilled to the bone.

Now, I'm toasty warm under the comfort of Beau's body. It feels good to be here, in his arms. So much so I'm wondering if we can cancel today's activities and stay here.

I take him in while he's asleep. He looks younger, relaxed. Don't get me wrong, he's a mellow person, but he's also on guard for the unknown all the time.

Seeing him now, looking vulnerable, pushes me to want him more, to get to know him more. I want to know every little thing there is to know about him. There's just something about seeing him, *really* seeing him, that draws me to him.

My gaze moves down to his strong jaw, following it, and along to his lips. I don't know what compels me to do what I do next. I just know I can't fight the urge to feel his lips against mine any longer. My breath catches as I lean forward and press my lips against his. They're soft and full. Kissing him has never felt so right.

He stirs, his eyes fluttering open before they land on me. His expression softens, looking at me with a lazy smile. I can't help but return it, feeling wave of happiness flow through my body.

"Morning, beautiful. Did you—"

"What the fuck!" Aiden yells, fear evident in his voice.

I'm still staring down at Beau, so I see the knowing grin spread across his face. He shoots up, taking me with him.

He opens the tent as another squeal rumbles outside.

"It's hissing at us," Ashton squeals, almost sounding like Charlotte.

"Stop fucking moving," Aiden yells at Ashton.

My eyes widen when I look over at their tent. It's unpegged and both their heads are holding the roof up. It's only a two-man tent, so they're stretching the material.

"It's staring at me." Ashton screams again.

Landon walks out of his tent looking pissed off. He storms over to the boys, probably to knock some sense into them. Beau chuckles under his breath at their screeching.

"What did you do?" I whisper.

"It's coming for me," Ashton wails, sounding close to tears.

"It's gonna fucking eat us. Someone, anyone, help!"

Beau's laugh rings through the tent. "You'll see." He winks at me, smirking.

My gaze moves back over to the boys' tent, watching as Landon unzips it. He doesn't get a chance to look inside because Aston and Aiden both fall out and knock Landon over.

"What the fuck?" Landon growls.

The two culprits fall onto their arses and shuffle backwards, looking at the tent with wide, fear-filled eyes. There's no guessing what's in there, and with those two, it could be anything from a cat to a money spider. They are just that dramatic.

When Landon's eyes also widen, I try to look into the tent. He moves back at a fast pace, looking scared, and I begin to worry. I glance back over to the tent opening for another look and start laughing.

A grass snake slithers out, clearly in distress and feeling threatened. Its body is inflated and it's hissing between its teeth as it heads back towards the forest.

I'm stunned as I glance at Beau. "How?"

Beau chuckles. "My dad's friend breeds snakes. He showed me a thing or two, including where to find them."

"You are so crafty." I begin to giggle, gaining everyone's attention. I hadn't realised everyone had come out to see what the commotion was about. I was too enthralled by the entertainment Aiden and Ashton were putting on.

"You?" Ashton growls, getting up from the ground. He points at Beau, breathing heavily.

"Me?" Beau asks, pointing his own finger at his chest innocently.

"You did this?" Aiden asks, almost in awe. Well, he would be if he wasn't so scared.

Everyone looks at Beau with stunned expressions. At first, I'm worried about their reaction and if it will cause a rift between Beau and my family. But then Maddox, followed by the rest of them, start laughing uproariously, so I relax and join in.

"I told you payback's a bitch."

"You could have killed us!" Ashton squeals, throwing his arms up.

Beau scoffs. "It was a grass snake, not a cobra."

"That wasn't just some *grass snake*. It had fucking fangs and was hissing at us. It came at me."

"It touched me whilst I was sleeping," Aiden adds, looking pissed now.

"Where?" I blurt out.

He turns bright red, the veins in his neck pulsing. "It doesn't matter," he shouts louder.

I giggle, earning a glare. "It was harmless. I promise." My assurance falls on deaf ears.

"What would you know?"

My giggle turns into full laughter. "I'm a vet, remember."

He snarls, before grabbing his bag out of the tent. "I'm going to get ready. See you lot at breakfast."

"And I want an apology ready by the time we get back," Ashton barks. He glowers at Beau one last time before storming off after Aiden.

We're all silent for a few seconds before laughter fills our campsite.

"I cannot believe you did that," I say, turning to Beau.

He shrugs, playing it off. "It's actually fun to let my hair down. I didn't realise how uptight I was until this weekend with your family."

Uh-oh.

"Please don't let them rub off on you."

"Why?" He gives me his charming, boyish grin.

So not going to help right now.

"Because I already have a bunch of hooligans in my family. I don't need my… my…." I pause, wondering what Beau actually is to me.

Still grinning, he takes my shoulders and shakes me. "Don't worry, they aren't rubbing off on me. They just brought the old me out to play."

"Seriously, that *really* doesn't help."

He laughs at my expression. "Come on, let's go get ready. I want to kick your cousins' arses at archery."

"You've done it before?" I ask, shocked.

He winks at me. "No. But it will be fun to make them squirm thinking I have."

TURNS OUT, ARCHERY wasn't for everyone—okay, it wasn't for any of us. We all figured that out five minutes in to trying to aim and shoot.

Personally, I think I sucked because I couldn't keep my eyes off Beau's arse, or his bulging biceps. It was distracting. The instructor found it hard to take his eyes off him too, so I wasn't the only one affected.

Katniss Everdeen had made it look effortless in *The Hunger Games*.

As for rock climbing… Well, for us girls, it was a blast. For the boys, however, it was a competition, one that ended with us breaking up four fights.

The next activity is something none of us expected. Lily booked the wrong course. Instead of the jungle challenge, we are now doing the jungle mud course, which is going to get freaking messy.

We're all put into teams of two, and thankfully, I got paired with Beau.

"At each flag point, collect your team's colour and proceed to the next obstacle. The winners are whoever finishes the course first and manages to get all their flags."

"We got his," Imogen hoots, high-fiving Hayden.

Yeah, those two are the ones to worry about. Landon and Charlotte too, and maybe Maddox and Lily. The others have no hope against me and Beau. We're both active in our lives.

Mark scoffs, turning towards her. "You wish. See you at the finish line."

"Yeah, you'll see us waving to you from our winner's throne," Hayden sasses.

"Um, there isn't actually a throne." The instructor bites her lip.

"Right. More like waving at us to slow down," Liam laughs, goading his sister.

"All right, get into position."

I pull my coveralls over my clothes. When the instructor had offered them to us, I'd jumped at the chance. There is no way I'm going to ruin my Juicy Couture tracksuit. Not a chance in hell.

I pull my goggles over my eyes and high-five Beau, before stepping into place at the start of our first course.

Which happens to be a net of rope with thick, wet mud underneath.

"Ready, steady…" The horn blasts and we move.

I'm under the net first, laughing and squealing at the feel of the mud already seeping through my clothes.

So much for protecting my Juicy Couture.

Beau is behind me, shouting at me to hurry, to move as fast as I can. But I'm sinking into the mud, which is making it hard to move anywhere.

The instructor never gave us rules like the other guides did, so I turn on my back, grabbing the rope above me, and use it to pull me across the mud. I slide easily and look down at Beau, a few feet behind me. He's grinning, already covered in mud, and does the same.

We're first out, but a quick glance shows Maddox and Landon's teams aren't far behind us. The next is a wooden log, already covered in mud, with a rope above to help guide you along. We make it over with only a few slips before coming to a wall.

"I'll go first. Once I'm at the top, I'll help you up."

"Is this a sexist thing?" I ask, narrowing my eyes.

He laughs. "No, this is a me wanting us to win thing."

I don't get chance to argue because he's already leaping up the wall and grabbing the rope. I watch his firm arse until it's out of sight. He reaches down, and after a few steps backwards, I run and then leap to catch his hands. He easily lifts me to the stage, and I gasp, falling on top of him.

"Well…" he grins, grabbing my arse.

I giggle into his throat. Then Landon jumps up next to us, startling us. He reaches down to grab Charlotte, so I roll off Beau and down the other side.

I want to groan and rethink this whole mud challenge. I'm wet, and my muscles are already burning. But one look behind me, at a gloating Aiden, makes me forget the aches and move forward. If I lose to him, I'll never hear the last of it.

The first flag is just on the other side of the next course, which happens to be a lot of elastic rope and a puddle of mud. First, we run across the bridge, and then dive into the thick mud.

"Fuck, we need to go under, otherwise we could get caught in the elastic."

I push back the hair that has fallen over my goggles and nod, now realising why we needed the goggles and were instructed never to take them off.

As we head under the first part, trying not to put our heads all the way beneath the mud, something catches my leg and tries to pull me back. I kick out, hitting something hard, and keep moving forward. I don't bother turning back to find out if was one of the boys. Instead, I follow Beau, as he makes it easier for me to move through the mud. A quick glance to my side reveals Landon assisting Charlotte, laughing at her expression. Her face, her hair… Everything is covered in mud.

I start to giggle as we get out of the net.

I'm actually having fun. Even if I am getting filthy in the process.

We grab the flag as we reach the post. Once it's sealed safety in our pouch, we run onwards, following the arrows to the next course. It moves around, deeper into the forest. Footsteps running behind us let me know the others are close.

But once we exit a copse of trees, I gasp. I'm out of breath and startled by what is in front of us.

A water mudslide, so steep I'm concerned about how we're going to make it up there. Why couldn't it be a slide we went down? Now that, I'd flipping enjoy. Instead, we've got a single rope, for each group, to help us up.

"Shit." Beau laughs. "Come on, let's go."

I gaze at the top and find another flag sitting on a post by a tree. Another two to go before the end. That's if we make it up this hill.

I grab the rope and climb, using both my feet and hands. It's hard, and a few times I slip a little. More than once, Beau pushes my arse to keep me going.

I'm near the top when I hear Beau yell out. I look behind me to find him sliding down, Aiden next to him.

Damn my brother.

We were so close.

I keep moving until I reach the top, my arms burning from pulling my weight. I'm thankful I didn't slip and have to do it all again.

My body is like jelly as I slump towards the flag post. Once I've grabbed our colour, I look down the hill, keeping away from the edge, so I don't slip.

Beau is climbing up our rope again, Aiden to his left and Maddox to his right. The girls are further up, nearly at the top, thanks to the men below them.

Hayden falls down next to me, breathing hard. She grins, her eyes dancing with delight. "This shit is awesome." She pauses, squinting behind me. "Hey, what the hell is Beau doing?"

Laughter bubbles from my lips when Beau kicks out at Aiden, making him fall back down.

"Hey, you fucker," Aiden screams, sliding down on his side.

Beau moves to do the same to Maddox, but Maddox catches on and shoves Beau in the shoulder. He falls and slides down the slope, laughing. I should be pissed. We could lose. But it's so funny to watch as they all fight to get up here first.

Maddox, having looked away from his primary goal, misses Lily slipping, and they both slide down in a heap.

"Shit!" he yells.

"Oh, my God," I laugh, my hand covering my mouth.

"Come on, Imogen, we've got this," Hayden shouts.

Liam, hearing his sister, grins. He swings the rope he's on and dives on Immy. Both of them slide down. Hayden and Immy both start cursing, but Liam just laughs, moving back to his rope. Immy, pissed at Liam, pushes him over. He falls on the floor, grunting.

"I'm so going to drown him."

"We're never going to make it to the finish line if they keep this up." I'm still giggling when Charlotte reaches us. She's still covered in mud, but the splatters on her face have dried up.

"I'm going to kill Lily when we get back." She tries her best to move the fallen hair out of her face, but fails.

"At this rate, we won't have any family members left," I tell her, laughing hard.

My eyes fall to the slide again. Beau and Mark are now tying. The muscles in their arms bulging. I'm glad Beau only wore a T-shirt now, because seeing him like this is seriously hot. He looks like he's in his element.

The others are scrambling in the mud to get back to the rope, falling down the mudslide leading up to it. It seems to be getting wetter and wetter every time one of them falls. It's turned into a stream of muddy water rather than actual mud.

I start laughing when Aiden tries to punch Maddox in the face for pushing him off his rope, but instead of hitting him, he hits Ashton. Ashton curses, pushing him a few feet down to where the water and mud are gathering. Clearly, they've forgotten they're on the same team.

"Ashton," Aiden screams, spluttering muddy water from his mouth.

I shuffle backwards on my knees when Beau is close. I'm holding my breath, hoping Mark doesn't play any tricks on him. The only ones we have to worry about right now is Landon and Imogen, as they are both half way up the hill.

Beau grins when he reaches the top, tagging my arm. As soon as I'm on my feet, we're running. I'm laughing, not having had so much fun in my life.

This has to be the best getaway we've ever done.

A bunch of tyres come into view and we quickly manoeuvre our way through, laughing at Hayden shouting at us to wait.

Yeah, like that will happen.

"You snooze, you lose," I yell, running to keep up with Beau.

A long line of different logs at different heights are in front of us. In white spray paint is written whether we have to go over or under.

The first one is low. We slide under, easily slipping through, before crawling to the next one, both of us rolling over it.

I'm laughing so hard I feel weak, and when we go under another one, I feel hands on my ankles once again.

"Oh, no you don't, bitch," Hayden laughs, trying to drag me back.

Weak with exertion, I let her, and when we come eye level, I push her away and start crawling over her, laughing.

Imogen is cursing Landon as he starts dragging her backwards too. I'm still a laughing mess as I flop over the next log.

Beau is ahead of me, trying his best to jump for the next one, which is pretty high. He does it, rolling over and landing on the other side.

I'm fucked.

There is no way I'll reach the log to get over it. Beau must read my apprehension in my expression, because he grins. He walks under the log and links his hands together, to give me a leg up. I giggle, placing my foot in his hands. I'm just getting my leg over when Landon throws himself over easily. I glare when he ducks under to help Charlotte out.

"Let's go," Beau laughs, grabbing my hand. Together we run through some more tyres on the ground, again reaching another flag.

Beau grabs this one and shoves it into his pocket. We keep running, following the arrows around another bend.

A wide-roped ladder is against a wall and we sprint towards it, knowing this must be the last obstacle. I look around for the flag, not seeing one, but still carry on up.

Landon and Hayden are right behind us, both jumping as far up the net as they can go. Beau reaches the top first, leaning down to reach for me. A wicked grin on his face as he pulls me up.

I see why once I reach the top. We're on a massive hill that is soaked with mud and water. Plastic sheeting is underneath, so this part of the course has been built by them. Dirty water runs from small taps on the side.

My laughter is loud as I sit on the edge next to Beau. "Let's do this." I grab his hand, and together, we shoot down the slide, screaming and laughing.

"Fuck yeah," Hayden yells.

We reach the bottom too soon and jump to our feet, before running to the finish line a few meters ahead of us, the flag blowing brightly in the wind.

We grab it together, jumping up and down. I leap into his arms and wrap my legs around his waist. I must take him by surprise because he falls back a step, grunting.

Completely in the moment, I lean back to look at him. "We won!" Then I kiss him, full on the lips, deep and wet. My fingers run through his hair to the back of his neck, where I grip him to pull him closer.

I'm snatched out of his arms and I squeal in shock. "What did I tell you about kissing my sister?" Aiden growls. Mark stands next to him, scowling at us.

Beau grins. "She kissed *me*."

That really isn't helping.

Aiden drops me to my feet and I whirl on him. "Never pull me away like that again."

His face reddens—with anger or embarrassment remains to be seen. "I'm telling Dad you kissed him."

"You wouldn't?" I gasp, stepping back.

What a traitor.

"Oh, I totally freaking would. You wait until we get home."

"I hate you," I scream, before turning and going to storming off. I stop short and pivot back to him, poking him in the chest. "And we won! *Us*. Loser!" I hold my fingers in an L shape against my forehead and stick my tongue out.

He sputters before storming off to lick his wounds. He doesn't even try to hide that he's a sore loser.

Beau walks over to me and wraps his arm around my waist from behind. "You told him, baby."

Turning around in his arms, I grin up at him. "We totally kicked all their arses. I've had so much fun, but I'll be glad to get out of these clothes and shower the mud out of my hair."

He laughs, his eyes twinkling as he runs his fingers through my mud-covered hair. "I dunno; I think you kind of look sexy."

I roll my eyes despite the flutter in my stomach. I love it when he says things like that.

"And I'm hungry. Feed me." I grin, still jumping with excitement from winning. "And losers, you're paying," I shout.

They all groan, shaking their heads at my antics.

Next is tobogganing, and I can't wait to show them up.

TEN

Come Monday afternoon, I'm glad to be home. My hangover from last night is still pounding away behind my eyes. But it was so worth it.

The adult tobogganing slopes had a fully-stocked bar on the side and, if you can believe it, disco lights. With the weather cooling down, they even had heat lights by the patio. We had fun running up and down with sledges, and drinking in between. The little stunts the boys tried to do were hilarious.

The whole weekend was brilliant, but for me, Sunday was one of the best days of my life. It was incredible. We all had so much fun, and we have the photos to prove it. Ciara, Josh, Trent and Jacob and Hope are going to be furious when they find out what we all got up to.

Now, it's back to reality, though I am over the moon to be home.

Beau dropped me off at home before leaving to take the evening shift at work. He won't be finishing until two in the morning. I sort of feel bad he swapped all his shifts with shitty late ones, so he could come along with us.

I mean it when I say I *sort of* feel bad, because I'd loved having him with us. His sacrifice is appreciated.

However, I wish I knew where we stood. How do I bring up the fact we've acted like a couple all weekend? It's a hard topic to talk about—certainly not something I've ever had to do before. I have no idea what to do when it comes to men, especially Beau.

It's not like I can ask my cousins or sister for help; none of them have had a boyfriend either. They've dated, but with the men in our family, progressing past that getting-to-know-each-other stage is hard. Trying to get the guys to understand we're grown adults is like trying to get blood out of a stone.

With all the secrecy in her life, Hayden is the only one who gets away with hiding stuff so easily, and she still lives with my uncle Max and aunt Lake. None of us know what she does when she's not with us, or why she sneaks out at ungodly hours. She thinks none of us know, but we're not stupid. Only her brothers and parents don't see it. How? I have no idea.

The need to speak to Beau is going to keep playing on my mind. It's not something we can avoid forever. We need to talk about what happened between us. I want to know where we stand with each other. I mean, are we a couple? I'm hoping the answer is yes, but I don't want to come across clingy or needy. I've had enough friends get dumped because they've wanted too much too soon. Sad, but true. I don't want to ruin what we have, even if that means we'll only ever be friends.

My lips lift into a smile as I think of how easily we'd fit the role of being a couple. Kissing him had been like a dream, and I thought nothing could be better than spending time with him. It felt like we had been doing it for months, after having known each other for years. It's eerie how casual and aware we are of each other. I had been at ease the whole time with him, only feeling anxious when we'd been alone in the tent, and that was only because I hadn't wanted to make a fool out of myself by showing just how inexperienced I am.

I've never felt this way about a man before. I'm a dreamer, so when my expectations of the perfect man were never met, I moved on. I may have seemed small-minded to some people, but I never wanted to lead someone on.

I didn't want to give them false hope. It wasn't fair on them or me. With Beau, he's beyond any expectations I ever had. He's more than I ever wished for. It sounds sappy, but it's true.

My phone starts blaring from my bag by the door. I'm thinking about ignoring it, but Beau enters my mind. It could be him. With that thought, I practically bounce off the sofa and rush over to my bag.

The screen flashes with 'work' and for a second, I'm half-tempted to switch it to silent. I still have today off.

However, I wouldn't be who I was if I ignored it. Animals are a huge part of my life, and if one is in pain, I want to be there to help and comfort them.

"Hello?"

Nina answers, sounding tired. It's eight at night and we're normally closed. It feels later though, with autumn passing and the night's drawing in early.

"Hey, we need you to come in. We've just had a walk-in emergency. A dog has been run over and we're prepping him for surgery. We can't get hold of Susan. She's out on Hoo Farm, tending to the pregnant horse."

I'm grabbing my keys before she's even finished telling me. "How long has it been since he was run over?" I ask, running down the stairs.

"Not long. It happened around the corner. The car didn't even stop. A passer-by watched what happened and immediately brought him here. He has a broken leg, and although he's a chubby dog, he's underweight and malnourished. We think he's got internal bleeding."

That's good. Well, not good he got run over, but good he was brought in straight away. It's usually cats we have brought in after being hit by a vehicle, and ninety-six percent of the time, it's too late for them. They aren't brought to us in time. It's sickening how the world can overlook them, labelling them as feral animals. They aren't. They're someone's pets, a part of their family, their life. They become their everything.

If I had the power to change the law, I would. Sadly, I don't.

"I'm on my way. Keep him comfortable until I get there. Can you get reception to call my mum and let her know I won't be picking Roxy up until tomorrow?"

"Will do."

My legs move faster. I need to reach the building in time to scrub up and perform surgery. When it comes into view, I relax a little, my hangover all but gone.

The smell as I rush in is familiar. It's like a second home to me. Owning a veterinary surgery has been my dream and life goal for so long, I couldn't picture doing anything else.

The only other thing I'd like to do, which I'm saving up for, is own a shelter for stray animals. We don't have the funding or the resources at the centre. We just don't have the room. We're a small company, started up by me and Susan and a few investors my grandma Mary got for us. I'd met Susan at university, and although she's a lot older than me, we became friends. Our ideas for our future had been the same, and together, we made our dreams a reality.

I rush in and clean up, putting on my scrubs before meeting my colleagues in theatre, resting my mind so I can focus on one thing.

Saving his life.

AFTER CLEANING UP for the night, I head back into the kennels to check on Buster—a name I granted him when I'd seen the chubby English Bull Dog.

At first glance, I'd say he's homeless or a runaway. He's been living off scraps, not the hearty meals an English Bulldog is supposed to have. He isn't chipped, but it's still our duty as vets to try and find his owners—if he has any.

"Hey, buddy, you doing okay?" I coo, bending down to open his cage. I run my hand over him soothingly. He whines in the back of his throat, lifting his head into my hand. I giggle, stroking his head through the cone we've put on so he doesn't disturb his stiches. "You like that, huh? You're gonna be okay. I'll be back in the morning to check on you."

His head lifts, his eyes filled with sadness, like he can understand my words. I feel tears build when he whines again.

"I'm sorry, but I gotta go."

He whines again and tries to stand. This is always the hardest part of my job; walking away. I shut the cage when he struggles and make my way out, turning the big lights off as I go.

We have nightlights inside all the kennels, due to some of the animals being unsettled in a new environment. I'm hoping these additions will settle him when I'm finally gone.

Everyone's left for the night, so the place is deserted. I'm proud of my accomplishments, but I never would have been able to do it without my grandma Mary's help. She provided me the funds to kickstart my adventure, along with willing investors. Every day I miss her but having this place keeps her in my memory. It's like I still have a piece of her with me.

After setting the alarm, I lock up, feeling the chill since I forgot to pick up my coat in my rush to get here. Thankfully, I remembered my phone and keys. The last thing I need is to wake my mum and dad up at this time of night to tell them I've locked myself out. I'd never hear the end of it.

The streets are quiet, something I've always enjoyed at this time of night. At midnight, the place is no longer buzzing with people, loud chatter or horns honking. It's just peaceful. Still.

I'm passing Poundstretcher when someone wearing a dark hood steps out in front of me and reaches out to grab me. Out of instinct, I punch my attacker in the face, surprising them. My entire body chills and I scream as I run back towards the centre, hearing footsteps and cursing behind me. I'm nearly back at my building when I'm grabbed from behind, propelling me forward before gravity takes hold and I crash down, fast and hard.

I ignore the pain in my knees and hands as I hit the unforgiving concrete, especially when a hand fists a chunk of my hair and slams my face into the ground.

"Please, I don't have any money. Please!" I beg.

I'm forced up by my hair and turned to face him—at least, I think he's a he, going by his shape and strength. I grunt at the rough, jerky movements. I'm barely able to blink when pain, like nothing I've ever felt before, begins to throb in my cheek.

I kick out, not hitting anything, my hands doing the same. I'm a fighter; my dad and uncles made sure I was. That we all were.

Nothing could have prepared me for the real thing though. I've never been in a physical fight.

"Please, I don't have any money. Leave me alone." I struggle to get free, my top tearing as he grabs at it. I roll over, going against everything my family taught me, and try to crawl away. Once again, he smacks my head on the concrete. I'm stunned, my vision blurring and my mind fuzzy. I fight to stay conscious.

"You think this is about money?" The deepness of the masculine voice startles me, confirming my suspicions on my attacker being a male. If evil had a voice, it would sound like the man dragging me around, my shoulders scraping on the ground.

"What do you want?" I scream, still fighting. I manage to get my leg up enough to kick him in the gut, but he comes back with a sharper punch to my chest, knocking the wind out of me.

It hurts, but there's no way I'm going down without a fight.

Not a chance in hell.

I'm still screaming, my voice hoarse and heavy.

His fingers pinch my cheeks, no doubt leaving bruises. "I told you to call off your dogs. You're still searching for me. Whoever your geek of a fucking boyfriend is, call him off. Otherwise things are going to get ugly, and not only will I be back for you, but I'll be back for him too. Killing that dog will just be the beginning."

My mind is foggy, so his words don't register. "Who are you? I don't even know you," I scream, struggling to get free. My hand connects with his face, but he grabs it roughly and slams it down on the pavement. I cry out in pain, feeling something snap in my wrist. My back slams against the concrete and I choke on air, fighting to keep conscious.

"You know me as Noah Anderson. Now, are you going to call him off?"

My eyes bug out, and I fight harder, needing to get away. There's no knowing how far he'll take this, or what he'll do.

And he hurt Buster? A poor innocent animal. I scream out for the pain he's put him through, but it's useless.

I bend my neck to alleviate the pain of his left hand still clutching my hair forcefully.

"Please, leave me alone and I'll tell them to stop."

A flash of teeth under his hood reveals his sneer. I can't see his eyes, just his mouth and the colour of his skin.

I'm scared, terrified out of my mind, and acting on adrenaline. I need to get away from him. He's unpredictable.

"Why are you doing this to me?" I scream in his face, tears running down my cheeks. "I didn't do anything to you."

He laughs hauntingly. "You bitches are all the fucking same. You're easy. You advertise yourselves to me. Me! If you weren't so desperate, you'd realise you had a predator watching you."

My skin crawls at the venom in his voice. He really believes we asked for it. That we set ourselves up for him to take everything away from us.

"You're not going to get away with this."

"Listen up, whore, I already have. Now you need to pay and let me carry on doing what I do."

I'm taken aback by him calling me a whore and too busy trying to fight against his hands pinning me down to notice his head coming at me.

Everything disappears, including the pain.

I GROAN AWAKE, my face and body hurting badly. I roll to my side and hurl, my limbs weak and shaky.

Everything, from Noah jumping out at me to the last thing he whispered in my ear, plays over in my mind.

I'm beyond terrified. I've never experienced anything like this in my life.

But there's one thing Noah didn't count on. I'm not the type of girl to keep my mouth shut because she's scared. I can see why there are thousands of women out there that do. A part of me wants to lock myself away and tell everyone to drop it, but I'd never be able to live with myself if he did this to another woman. And he will. It's just a matter of time.

A noise from the end of the dark alley has me jerking to my feet, crying out in pain. All I can see is darkness and a few shadows.

If he's there, I don't want him to hurt me any more than he already has. My whole body, especially my face and wrist, are killing me. I'd rather die than go through that again.

With a battle cry, I turn and run. I run with everything left inside me, even when it pains me to do it. It's ten minutes to the police station. Ten minutes. I can make it.

I stumble and throw up a more times than I care to remember, but when I make it to the police station, I fall at the bottom of the steps, crying out again as tears fall.

I'm so close.

So very close.

The door opens and a few men and women walk out. With blurred vision, I manage to see them all pause before jumping into action.

It's his voice that has me dropping my head on the second step.

He's here.

"Faith? Fuck! Drew, get the car running, we need to get her to the hospital."

"Beau, we should wait for the ambulance. Mandy called one."

"Fuck the ambulance. She needs a hospital now!" he roars, making me wince.

"Baby, can I lift you?" he asks gently, watching my expression carefully.

I nod, but it causes me to wince in pain. Everything hurts. Hurts so goddamn badly. I have to bite my lip to stop myself from screaming out when his arms go under me. He notices me tense, and sorrow and regret fill his eyes for hurting me. He lifts me, trying to be as gentle as possible.

"I'm sorry, Faith. We'll get you to the hospital, okay?"

"Yeah. Call Mum and Dad," I croak out, before dropping my head on his shoulder and closing my eyes.

MY EYES DRIFT open and, the minute I see both my parents beside me, they water. My dad has my mum in his arms as she cries quietly into his shoulder.

"Mum?" I croak.

Their heads snap in my direction when they hear my voice. My mum nearly trips over her own feet to get to me.

A heart-breaking sob tears from my mum as she looks down at me with a broken expression. Dad pulls her to his front, looking just as broken as he stares down at me.

"My baby girl. My baby."

"It's okay, Mum. I'm okay."

She looks up at my dad before turning her disbelievingly stare my way. "Okay? You're not okay! Mav, did you hear our girl? She said she's okay!"

"I heard, darlin'. Faith, you scared us half to death. Do you remember what happened?"

I nod, tears slipping free. My face stings as they touch raw skin, but I don't care. I'm just glad my parents are here.

Mum takes my hand in hers, and for the first time I notice it's in a cast. "It's broken?" I ask in a hoarse whisper, dread filling my bones.

"Yeah," Mum tells me, trying to force a smile.

"Can I—can I still operate?"

Dad, seeing where I'm going, places his large hand on my knee. "The doctor said it should heal just fine. There wasn't any nerve damage. But to be sure, you'll need to come back and have another scan."

"I can't lose my animals," I whisper.

My job means the world to me. If I lose the ability to perform surgery, I'll have lost everything.

"You won't." Dad says it like he knows for a fact that is the case, but he can't know. Neither of them can.

Another thought occurs to me. "Beau, he—he brought me here?"

Mum smiles, wiping her tears away. "Yeah, the young man called us on the way to the hospital. We could hear the sirens before he even spoke and knew something had happened to you. He explained everything he could. They just don't know who did it. He's outside in the waiting area with the rest of the family. Only two can come in so it's been me and your father in here. We didn't want to leave until you woke up."

"It was Noah." I try to sit up, but Mum fusses, telling me to lie back down. "No, Mum, it was Noah. The man who robbed me. He said to call off the person looking for him or he would come back to finish the job and hurt them. I know it's Liam, Dad. You need to warn him." My voice rises with hysteria and a nurse rushes in.

I remember what he did to that poor dog. I can't have him hurting anyone else I love. Liam is like another uncle to me, since he grew up with them.

"You need to relax. Let's take a look at your vitals."

I ignore her, staring at my dad. "Please, Dad."

"Okay, squirt. But you need to let the nurse look you over. I'll go out and get Max to call him."

He bends over the bed to kiss my forehead before walking out. I'm left with Mum and the horrible nurse, who's poking me.

"Did he really stay out there all night?" I ask, whispering.

Mum smiles, her eyes shining. "Yeah, baby, he did. The others got back yesterday, preparing to pull something on him, but the minute they got here, saw his bloodshot eyes and how he was covered in blood, they decided to give him a chance."

"He had blood on him?" I ask, eyes wide.

Her smile falls. "Yeah, girl. Your head was bleeding pretty badly. They've had to shave a bit to put in some stitches."

My eyes water further. I shouldn't be so vain as to worry over some shaved hair after everything that happened. I should be thankful I'm still alive. But it's my hair. "Can you see it?" I croak out. My hair is long and thick, something I've always taken care of. If I have to cut it off, it will gut me.

The nurse interrupts. "You won't be able to see it. You also can't wash your hair until they get taken out. You need to keep them dry. How are you feeling? Would you like some pain meds?"

"My entire body aches, but it's my head and wrist that hurt the most."

She nods in understanding. "I'll go get you some pain meds."

She leaves us, and as the door shuts behind her, someone knocks on it. Beau pokes his head round, still wearing his uniform, but instead of the vest and all the crap he keeps on his belt, he's only wearing his shirt, slacks and boots.

"Beau," I whisper, feeling my pulse pick up at the sight of him.

His expression softens at the sound of my voice. He looks like he's been in a wreck. The blood on his shirt…it makes my stomach turn. "Hey, your dad said you were awake."

"Yeah."

"How did you get past my offspring?" Mum asks, trying to lighten the mood.

He grins. "Aiden and Mark were busy fighting about who got to come in first, so they didn't even see me and Lily. Lily said to come in first since she didn't plan on leaving any time soon. She's waiting for your dad to come back. They said since your awake, you can have three visitors."

"Sounds about right. I'm just going to let everyone know you're okay and ask the doctors when you can come home."

Ahh, my mum thinks she's being tactful. She's not. It's written all over her face that she wants to give us some time alone. And I love her for it. I need to thank Beau for saving me.

"Okay."

"Love you. I won't be long. Is there anything you need me to get while I'm gone?"

"Can you get me some water? And I love you too, Mum."

She kisses my forehead, the same way my dad did, before leaving. I glance back at Beau, forcing a smile through the pain.

It occurred to me on the way to the station that I hadn't been running towards the police, I had been running towards Beau. The thought not only scared me, but exhilarated me. When I was at my worst, at my most frightened, I'd wanted him. Not my parents, not my brothers or sister… Him.

In my life, family means everything, and Beau coming first… it's monumental.

"You did good coming to the police station." My head snaps to attention at the sound of his voice. It's filled with so much heaviness and grievance.

"I wasn't running to the police station," I admit, not understanding why I blurted that out. I'm putting myself out there for a guy I hardly know, but feel like I've known my whole life.

I'll never understand how billions of people walk around every day without knowing a thing about each other, but then you meet one person, just one time, and you can feel like you know everything about them.

It's how I feel with Beau.

"What do you mean?" His brows scrunch up in confusion, making his tired and spent features look adorable.

I smile weakly, due to the amount of pain I'm enduring, and explain, my voice still a whisper, "I was running to you."

His eyes flash as he leans forwards, taking my broken hand in his. He runs his thumb across my cast. "What do you mean?"

If we were in another situation, I'd giggle at his repetition.

"I was running to you, Beau. When I woke up, I didn't want to move. It was like, for a split second I gave up and just wanted to die."

His grip on my hand tightens, but I reach out with my good hand—hooked up to an IV—and place it over his.

"Don't say shit like that. I thought I lost you, Faith. When you fell on those stairs, broken and in torn clothes…" He shakes his head, running a hand over his rough-shaven jaw. "I can't lose you."

I shake my head at him. "That's the thing, it was only for a split second. And then I knew I had to get to you, that you'd help me. You've got to find him, Beau. He hurt a dog to lure me to my office."

Tears fill his eyes and he scrubs a hand down his face, looking more exhausted than he did when he first entered.

"I'm so fucking sorry this happened to you. When I started at the police academy, I knew I wanted to help people. I wanted to give victims a voice, a chance at hope, to know they had someone on their side. I failed you last night. We knew he was closing in and making demands. I should have been more vigilant."

"You couldn't have predicted what he'd do and when. Like you said, you have a job to do, you help people. I'd never let you, or anyone, stop their lives for him. He doesn't get that, not from you, not from me, and not from all the other women he has hurt along the way. He knew exactly what he was doing when he cornered me. He thought I'd run and hide with my tail between my legs. But he didn't count on me being a Carter. We don't run, and we don't fucking hide. We stand and fight."

His expression softens, his lips forced into a small smile. "You really are an enigma, Faith Carter. You were so fucking brave last night, even if you did give me a heart attack."

"From what I remember, you seemed pretty in control. You got me here. You called my family and stayed with them. Thank you so much. For all of it."

We stare into each other's eyes, lost in the moment. Beau blinks, a regretful look crossing his face.

"I'm sorry but I need to get back to the station. I've got to give a statement about last night. I just couldn't leave without knowing you were okay, really okay. I know you're not, I can see that, but I just needed to be able to hear your voice and see those pretty eyes of yours."

My cheeks heat at the compliment. "You didn't need to do that, but thank you. What will happen with Noah now? Have they found him?" I ask before he rushes off to work where I won't be able to see him.

One's thing is for sure, I'm not relying on his colleagues to be upfront with me about everything. Beau has been honest from the very beginning of this case.

His eyes harden at the mention of Noah. "We haven't found him. We guessed where you were attacked last night and traced your footsteps. They found the crime scene and have started asking other store owners for any CCTV they have. A woman named Susan has already brought yours in. Apparently, some kids, a few weeks back, turned your camera from facing your front doors to face the street where you were attacked."

Yeah, thousands of pounds worth of equipment and somehow, some teenage kids with too much knowledge moved the sensors towards the street and not the doors.

"Did they tell her what the CCTV was for?" I ask, slightly worried. Susan will be going out of her mind and will no doubt be calling Nina. And, well, Nina in a crisis is a nightmare. She doesn't handle things well if something bad happens to the ones she loves. She'll be a wreck, even after seeing I'm okay.

"No. We reported a victim was attacked in the early hours of this morning and needed the footage. We're hoping we can get a description of him, something to go on."

I wince at that. "He's white and has a gravelly voice. That's all I can tell you. He had a hood pulled over his head and eyes, so I didn't see his face. He also targets women on chat sites because he thinks we're desperate. He must see us as helpless little women needing a date." I smile at the memory of my fist meeting his face and my nails scratching his skin. He might not have made much of a deal last night about it, but that shit will hurt this morning.

"Why are you smiling?" Beau asks, looking at me like I'm batshit crazy.

Maybe I am.

But I did fight back, something I've always been taught to do.

"I fought back, Beau. I hit him, scratched him. Even before he hurt me. He jumped out of the alley by Poundstretcher. He startled me, so I punched him in the face. It was a kneejerk reaction."

He forces a smile, his voice hoarse. "Well done, baby. Well done. We will get him. I promise. I won't rest until we do."

"I know——"

"She's my fucking sister. I want to see her," Aiden booms from somewhere outside my door. It bursts open to Aiden and Mark fighting their way in, getting stuck in the door-jam when they try pushing through together. I giggle a little.

Lily follows behind them more quietly, looking utterly worn out and distraught. She's not slept, I can tell. And from the way her hands keep fiddling with her dress, she's clearly having one of her anxiety episodes. I'm guessing being at the hospital isn't helping. She's never liked them since she was in one for a while when she was saved by the police.

"Boys," I snap, but it comes out hoarse.

They stop, each having the other in headlock as they turn to me, their eyes wide and filled with dread.

My eyes flick to Lily, who is still standing in the hall with tears running down her face. She looks so tiny and lost, and it's breaking my heart.

"Lily, baby, come here."

She doesn't unfreeze, her eyes never leaving the injuries on my body. I'm glad they put me in a gown and under a sheet, because I'd hate for her to see what I can only guess will be a mass of bruises on my body. But being in here and not being able to go to her is torture. She needs me. She needs—

"Lily," Mark calls softly, stepping over to her. "Aiden, can you go get Maddox?"

"No, I'm not leaving either of them. Ever again."

Beau chuckles, but respect flashes across his features. "I'll grab him. I need to get back to the station before I get fired."

"Fired?" I ask, panicked.

"I'm joking. I'll be back later." He leans over my body and kisses my forehead. I savour the feel of his cool lips on my burning skin, feeling relief course through me.

"See you later."

His eyes rake over me once more before he reluctantly leaves.

My attention reverts back to Lily who has stepped into the room, even though my heart feels like it left with Beau. He's gone and already I have the need burning inside me to cuddle next to him, to hear his voice.

"Lily, girl," I call again, my eyes feeling heavy. But I need to know she's okay before I pass out, this time from exhaustion.

"Lily," Maddox calls gently, stepping inside the room. He ignores me on the bed, and I know it must take some strength. He wants to concentrate on

Lily, and if he sees me he'll lose his mind, like my brother Aiden is seconds away from doing. He still hasn't looked away and it's unnerving. His eyes and expression are hard, his breathing laboured, and his hands are clenched into fists at the side of his body.

Hello, meet The Incredible Hulk.

"Maddox?" Lily's soft whisper calls.

"Yeah, it's me, Lils."

"He hurt her badly. Really badly," she chokes out, tears running down her face.

Mark walks over and takes the seat Beau had been sitting on. "She was holding it together outside, but we knew this would happen. It was only a matter of time. She was ready to explode. We didn't think she'd follow us in without Mum with her."

There's guilt in his voice, and I reach out to take his hand. "She had to see me, Mark. There's no covering this up." I gesture to my body, making him grimace.

"I'm going to fucking kill him," Aiden suddenly shouts, storming out of the room, but not before we get a look at his face. Tears were running down his cheeks and the veins in his head were pulsing.

Mark looks torn on what to do. I make the decision for him. "Go after him. I'm not going anywhere." My attempt to joke is met with a narrowed gaze.

"I'll sort him out and be back. Don't go anywhere. I love you." I give him a dry look then stare down at my body. "Ah, yeah. Won't be long."

He leaves as Maddox eases Lily into the room, sitting her down on the bed. "See, she's... awake."

He grits his teeth when he sees me for the first time. I'm sure he was about to say I was fine, but stopped himself before he could, getting a good look at me.

"Lily, I'll be okay. I promise. I remembered all the moves our dad and uncles taught us. I got away," I lie. I don't want to tell her I passed out, having no idea if he had left or stayed somewhere in the shadows. It will only make her worry more.

"Really?" she breathes, sitting closer.

I smile. "Yeah, punched him right in the nose and everything."

"I'm sorry this has happened to you. I'm sorry I can't be stronger for you."

My heart breaks at the sound of her own resentment. "Lily, you are one of the strongest people I know. Never doubt your worth or strength. You are our everything. You hold us together."

"She's right, Lils. Look at how many times you've saved your brothers from Faith trying to kill them, or your brothers killing each other. You organise our little getaways, so we can all be together. You're strong, Lils. You don't see it yet, but you will."

Maddox runs a hand down her hair. He loves her like a sister, like he loves Madison. But most of all, she's his best friend.

"I hate seeing you like this," Lily tells me, her eyes full of sadness.

"Me too. I promise I feel fine, just tired."

"We'll let you get some rest. Mum and Dad are going to stay here until the doctors release you. I'm going to head to yours and grab you some stuff, then head to Mum and Dads to do the same."

"Your too good to me."

"We love you, now get some rest."

She kisses me much the same as everyone else, only lingering longer, before walking to the door, where she waits for Maddox. He leans down and kisses my cheek before moving towards my ear.

"I promise you, Faith, once we find the fucker who did this, he's going to wish he never fucked with a Carter."

My throat closes with emotion as he leans back, showing me through his eyes how much he means it. The conviction and determination are there, bold as day.

I just hope none of them get into trouble.

But as he leaves, closing the door quietly behind him, a sick feeling fills my stomach.

ELEVEN

STAYING AT MY MUM AND DADS HAD been fun… for the first few days. But I've been here for two weeks recovering and now I'm ready to go home for some peace and quiet.

Everyone, at one time or another, has come to keep me company or check up on me. Beau has even been around most days, just not when he's at work or working late. Seeing him, though, made my day. I was worried when I first agreed to recover at my parents that I wouldn't get to see him, but I needn't have.

I needed my parents though, not just the safety of their presence and for peace of mind, but because I needed Mum's help. As much as I knew Beau would take care of me, without even being asked, I needed my mum to help me shower, so I didn't get my cast or stitches wet.

"Are you sure you don't want to stay another week?"

"I'm ready to go home, Mum. I'll have Beau across the hall and Roxy with me all the time." Roxy, who was sent to a neighbour's after Mum got the call, hasn't left my side since I returned home. She'd gone for walks with the boys, but always whined to come back, positioning herself in protective mode.

"She has been a little soldier. I thought she was going to tackle Landon when he walked in."

I giggle. "It did seem like he was sneaking in. She just didn't realise it's how he always walks."

Mum laughs. "All right, but the minute you feel like you want to come back, ring me or your dad and we'll be there. When is Beau picking you up?"

"Any second."

As if hearing me, a horn blares from outside. "Must be him."

Mum carries my bags to the front door. We're greeted by Beau and I smile like a goof at seeing him. He couldn't stop by yesterday since he was at work. It feels like it's been a week though.

"Hey." I wave, feeling lame.

"Hey, you ready?" He charms me with a grin as I nod eagerly. We step outside, Mum following us.

We're at the end of the walkway when we hear a commotion to our left. I jump, startled, but sigh with relief when I see Aiden, Ashton, Mark, Trent and Jacob running towards us. Jacob pushes Aiden into the bush outside Harlow and Malik's, and his feet flying in the air knock Trent forwards.

"What on earth?" Mum gasps.

"This should be fun," Beau chuckles.

"Faith," Aiden yells, getting back to his feet.

Mark tackles Ashton to the floor a few feet in front of us. It's Jacob, followed by Aiden and Trent who stand in front of us, gasping for air.

"Faith," Mark breathes out, panting.

"I'll come stay with you," Jacob offers.

Yeah, because his parents would let him.

"Dude, she's my fucking sister. I'm staying with her," Mark snaps.

"You've got your own place. I'll stay with her; I'm her favourite," Aiden yells at Mark. Mark pushes him back, before stepping further in front of me.

"I'll help do the cleaning." *Yeah, that will never happen.* "And take Roxy for a walk." *Okay, that would be nice.* "And I'll even cook dinner twice a week." *The earth will end before I get an edible meal out of him.*

I open my mouth, but Ashton interrupts. "I'll just stay with you. You've spent your whole life with those two goons, you don't need to see them any more than you already do. I'll stay with you. It's no problem."

"I said I'd stay with her," Trent argues, shoving Jacob.

Oh, for heavens sakes.

"Guys," I call out, but they ignore me, or don't hear me, over their own arguing. They keep shoving each other, fighting over who will be staying with me.

I knew this was going to happen. Landon had already offered to move in with me for a bit, but I'd declined his offer. And he can actually cook.

"You want me to move in with you don't you, Faith?" Ashton asks, still shoving Mark around.

"Guys," I call again. Once again, they ignore me and fight amongst themselves on who will be staying with me.

Mum sighs next to me before taking a deep breath. "Boys! Move away from each other this instant. Faith has something she wants to say."

They all stand to attention at the sound of Mum's voice and I roll my eyes. I wish she'd tell them I didn't want any of them staying. They'd probably take it better and not answer back. Instead, she had to put me on the spot.

Thanks, Mum.

"Did you pick me?" Ashton asks, pouting.

Those eyes really don't work on me.

Okay, they don't work on me anymore.

"Guys, I think it's amazing you all want to stay with me." They beam with pride, their chests puffed out. *Jesus.*

"We can't all stay with you, you don't have the room. I'm your baby brother, Faith, it should be me."

"No, dickhead, as the oldest it should be me. I can protect her," Mark puts in. I groan, looking to the heavens for strength.

"You saying I can't look after my own sister because I'm younger? I'd fucking kill for her," Aiden yells, glaring at Mark. He looks ready to kill him. If I wasn't still pretty banged up, I'd clip them both around the ear.

"I didn't say that, Aiden. You're being sensitive again."

"Me being sensitive? It was me who said I'd move in with her first."

"Because you want to move out of Mum and Dad's," Mark yells, throwing his hands up.

"Faith, pick one. You can't have us both," Aiden demands, staring pointedly at me.

I take a breath, preparing myself for the ear-lashing I'm going to get when I give them my answer.

"I'll be staying with, Faith," Beau tells them, his voice steady as he eyes my brothers and cousins. My heart stops for a minute as I slowly turn to face him. He's serious. I'm not sure what to think or feel just yet. At the moment, I just want to get home. Although, the thought of spending time with him in close proximity does excite me.

"That isn't fair, you live next door," Ashton yells.

"Can I move into yours?" Aiden asks with no shame.

"No! Now let me get your sister home. She still needs to rest."

Their eyes come to me, their expressions ashamed.

God, I really do love them.

"I'm sorry, Faith," Mark tells me.

"Me too," Aiden adds, still pouting. "Are you sure I can't——"

"Nope," Beau tells him before he can finish.

"We'll let you go, but if you need us, call us," Jacob tells me before he walks off with Trent.

"I love you for offering, but I'll be fine."

"Yeah, she'll have me," Beau gloats, earning a glare from each brother.

"Come on, before they tackle you to the ground," I tell him, fighting back a laugh.

I turn back to Mum and pull her into a hug. "I love you, Mum. Thank you for being here for me."

"Always. There isn't anything in the world that could pull me away from my children. I love you. Please call me if you want to come home or need me to come over. I'll pop in tomorrow with some shopping. Your dad didn't have a chance to fill your cupboards."

Her sheepish look gives everything away. "You mean he thought by not filling them that I would stay here?"

She looks away before grinning. "Yeah, kinda. He got the idea from your uncle Max."

"That doesn't surprise me. Love you, Mum. See you tomorrow."

We give each other another hug before pulling away. Beau helps me into the car and even straps me in, before getting in himself. Mum is still standing at the end of the path, watching with a smile on her face. She winks at me as she waves goodbye.

I wave back, rolling my eyes at her. She's continues waving until we lose sight of her. As soon as we pull out of the street, I relax back into my seat.

The peace and quiet is welcome.

———————————

"I DON'T FUCKING believe this!" Beau yells, sitting on the edge of the sofa. "How the fuck can this happen to her after everything she's already been through?"

I fight the laughter threatening to bubble free. I'd answer his questions but I'm too entertained by his theatrics.

"I can't deal with this. Please tell me this is a mistake?"

"I'm sorry, Beau, I can't." It's hard to keep a straight face, but I manage.

"You're telling me she went back to Tree Hill to start a family and she can't have kids? First, she gets a foster kid, but the chick changes her mind at the last possible second, and now this? She doesn't deserve it. She should have offered that Haylee chick more money for Jamie."

At that, I burst out laughing, falling back on the sofa. "Oh, my God, Beau, it's a TV series."

He glares at me. "It is *not* just a TV show. It's Brooke Davis. And Jamie is pretty fucking cool."

"My brothers would so lay into you right now." I laugh.

"I'm comfortable enough in my own skin to admit this show is the shit. What are we gonna start after?" He looks so eager, I can't help but melt.

"Well, Hayden recommended *Game of Thrones*. She found it in her mum's boxsets at home. What do you think?" I ask, liking that he wants to keep up our series nights. We've had them ever since we met. One Tree Hill has been our thing from the beginning, it's just a shame it ends at season nine.

"Sounds like a plan," he agrees, his eyes back on the screen. I laugh when Quinn starts trying to sing, *Eye of the Tiger*.

I love this show.

"What do you want for dinner? I can cook or we can just order in."

I don't even need to think about it. "Chinese, please. I love my mum's cooking and all, but I miss my junk."

He laughs at that. "Chinese it is. Anything special?"

"Everything on the menu," I tease, half joking.

He gets up and walks over to the kitchen where he left his phone on charge. He makes quick work of ordering for us before sitting back down.

We've been back for nine hours and I've yet to bring up the conversation about us. It's been playing on my mind since we got back from our trip. I felt that if I brought it up whilst I was recovering, I wouldn't get an honest answer. I don't want him to feel sorry for me, or say things just to appease my feelings.

I'm also conflicted over him actually wanting to be with me. He's given me no indication that he doesn't want to be, so it's not that. It's because Noah is still a threat in my life. How do I pursue this thing between us when he hangs over our head like a stormy cloud?

Still, I can't not talk to him about it any longer. So, whilst Quinn talks Alex into opening for an act, I build up the courage.

"Beau, I, um… Can we—I mean… can I talk to you for a moment?"

He pulls his gaze away from the screen, giving me his full attention, something any other male I know wouldn't do if something was on the television.

It's just another positive attribute to his charming personality.

"Why do you look so nervous? Do *I* need to be nervous?"

"No… Yes—no. Oh, God." I groan, covering my face with my hands. "I'm not doing this right."

"Hey, look at me." He waits until I've lifted my head to continue. "You can talk to me about anything. Are you in pain? Do you need help going the bathroom or something?"

Just let me die.

My face must be scarlet, because it feels like it's on fire. "No. I'm good, thank you. It's actually about us."

My eyes drift down to my hands, too scared to see the expression on his face.

His finger presses under my chin, lifting my head until my gaze meets his. "What about us, baby?"

Baby. I like it when he calls me that.

"I'm not sure—okay, I'm a little… We kiss—well, you kiss me. I—I don't know." I want to throttle myself for how wrong this is coming out. I'm never this freaking shy, but I've discovered a lot of new things about myself when it comes to Beau.

"Are you trying to ask if we're in a relationship?" He asks so calmly, no clamming up and making a fool out of himself, unlike me. I want to throttle *him* now. His lips twitch into a smirk, and I have the urge to stomp my foot.

"Yes!"

He full-on smiles, showing all his straight, white teeth. *God, he's perfect.*

"For starters, I don't kiss my friends, or fantasise about them either. What did you think was happening here?"

He genuinely wants to know, I can see it in his eyes. He's not asking to tease me or put me on the spot. He wants to know where I'm at. I kind of like that.

And he fantasises about me? My belly tightens, wanting to ask him what kind of fantasies.

"You heard my dad. He wasn't lying when he blurted out about my lack of sexual experience. This is all new to me, so I'm going to need you to spell it out so I don't get my hopes up."

His eyes heat at that. "Yeah, still have no fucking clue how a girl like you stays innocent. You could have anyone you wanted."

I scoff. "We'll get back to that later. *Much later*. Answer."

His deep chuckle hits me all the way down to my toes. So does his smouldering gaze.

"I'm hoping we can take things steady, see where this goes between us. I really like you, Faith. I've never felt instant chemistry—beyond sexual—with someone before. Before you were assaulted, I was drawn to you. I thought it was because you were different—you're Faith. But after you were attacked, I knew for sure I was into you, like really into you."

My insides are going crazy at the knowledge he sees me as more than a quick dunk and roll. My belly flutters at the thought of him wanting to see where this goes. But I still feel like I'm back at the beginning, like he didn't answer my questions.

"You're going to have to explain, Beau," I whisper, unsure. "What is it you want from me? Are we in a relationship? Are we friends who kiss? Will you see other people? Expect *me* too? This really is all new to me."

His hands go around my waist and pull me onto his lap. "I'm sorry. I'm new to this too. I've only been in a few relationships, baby, and none of them were like this. We weren't friends like how we are together. It's one of the most important parts of a relationship and it was constantly missing in all of mine. To answer your questions, I don't expect anything from you. I'm not even sure what you meant by the question. Do I *expect* you to have sex with me? No! Do I expect you to clean and cook? No! I don't want anything *from* you. I just want to be with you."

I grow soft in his arms, dropping my head against his and closing my eyes. I've heard so many people ask their other halves that question, and not one of them answered like that. They always gave a list of demands; they wanted them to be there for them, to listen to them and love them. Beau, my handsome and rugged Beau, had just given the most perfect answer I've ever heard. It cuts deep into my heart, and I know it will stay with me forever.

"Beau," I whisper, feeling myself tear up.

He kisses my lips once before looking intently into my eyes. "Are we in a relationship? Yes, we most certainly are, but only if that is something *you* want. I'm not going to be dating anyone else—hasn't even crossed my mind since you screamed in my face the first time we met." I laugh, remembering our first encounter, which feels like years ago. "I also don't like the thought of you seeing someone else. But most of all, yes, we are friends who kiss, and in the future, we will be lovers who have sex."

A tingle spreads in my core at the mention of sex. All these years I'd presumed I was frigid, that something wrong with my lady bits, but from the moment I'd met Beau, it was like they awakened. But still…

"I don't know if I'm ready for that."

He smiles, his expression soft as he tucks my hair behind my ear. It's been a pain to wear it down all the time—it still hurts to put it up.

"We're good, Faith. Never feel rushed, ever. But I do have to ask, can we do other stuff that isn't sexual intercourse?"

He looks at me hopefully, and his professor voice makes me giggle. "We can try, but I've never done that either."

His eyes heat and his smile falls. "You've never had a—"

Blushing bright red, I place my hand over his mouth. "Nope. Nothing but kiss. Now shush, a good part is about to come on."

"But—"

"Nope! Just shush, you'll regret it if you miss this."

"Bossy," he mutters, before turning to the screen. He keeps me on his lap and I stay there, resting my back against the arm of the sofa and leaning my head on his shoulder.

Ten minutes later, I look away from the television to stare at Beau's face, a smile nearly splitting my cheeks apart. His eyes are misty from what just played on screen.

"Are you okay?" I ask, not able to hide the amusement from my voice.

He snaps his head to me, like he forgot I was even there. "She's having a baby."

I grin at the joy in his voice. "I know."

"She's pregnant," he cheers, squeezing me to death.

"You do realise this is just a show, right?"

I'm given a glare in answer. "This is not just a show. I can't believe she's pregnant. Imagine being Chase, though, getting a phone call to say *he* was pregnant. Wonder what his doctor thought at those results, or what he thought about Alex being pregnant." He laughs as he continues to think on it.

"As I said, you do realise this is a show? I doubt they thought anything."

"Nah, I bet the doctor was ready to admit him and perform science experiments. And that he wanted to pass the fuck out when he thought Alex was pregnant. But fuck, never has a show made me truly happy for its characters.

I have to agree. "They are good actors and real-life story plots. Plus, Brooke crying? Always sets off the waterworks."

He nods, still smiling for the fictional couple on screen. It's another side to Beau that I've come to love. He has so many sides to him, it's hard to keep up. He's caring, kind, thoughtful, protective, badass, outspoken, brave, funny, charming, sexy, and sensitive to those around him.

And now this man is mine.

Even Brooke Davis couldn't be happier than I am right now.

Because I think I just found my future, my life. My prince.

TWELVE

EVEN THOUGH IT'S BEEN TWO AND A HALF weeks since my attack, I've still not been cleared to go back to work, and won't be until my cast comes off and the doctors are happy it's healed properly. It still hasn't stopped me coming in and looking things over. Buster is still in the kennels and today is the last day he's allowed here.

"And you've put up posters, posted on social network sites?" I ask Nina again as I run my fingers over his head. He's getting better every day, healing quicker than I am.

"Yes. We've had over twenty-five thousand shares, and still nothing. I'm sorry, Faith. I know you hate this part of your job."

I do. If we send Buster to our local dog home, he will be put down if he isn't rehomed in time. Animals' lives become a ticking time bomb the minute they are referred there. We only refer puppies, since they are rehomed right away, but older dogs, like Buster, are harder.

I feel a connection to Buster. He was run over because of me; I feel like it's my duty to take care of him. And he's a really cute freaking dog.

Nina brought him round to see me when she'd been on one of her daily dog walks. I had been staying at my parents'. Buster had comforted me, just like Roxy, and something would pass through me every time he stared into my eyes. Guilt and love on my part? Yes. But I felt the kinship between us.

He didn't make me feel helpless. I saw strength in him, and I fed off it.

"I'm going to take him home with me."

Nina doesn't look surprised, only doubtful. "Faith, you have a huge heart when it comes to animals, but you need to think about this. You live in a small two-bedroomed flat. You don't have the space for two big dogs. And you work a lot."

She's right, I do work a lot, but I won't let him be passed through the system like he means nothing. He means something to me.

"I've been saving to buy a house closer to my family. It means I'll have to get a car to come to work, but it also means I'll have a garden for them to run around in. I'm going to hire another surgeon to help with the caseload we seem to be accumulating here too. It's something I've been wanting to do for a while, but something always came up and I made excuses, waiting until the next time."

Her smile is radiant. "That's amazing. You've always wanted a house closer to your parents. You Carter's will own that neighbourhood soon."

I laugh and sit back in my desk chair. "Don't be dramatic. We only own, like, five houses on that street."

"Yeah, *that* street. What about the one where Lake's parents live? Don't you own three on that one?"

"What can I say, my dad is awesome at real estate. I'm gonna grab some things and head home with Buster."

Buster's ears perk up and he makes a noise at the back of his throat, which makes me giggle.

"I'll come with you. I'm finished for the day."

I nod, knowing she would have called one of my brothers if she wasn't. None of them will leave me alone for five minutes. The only peace and quiet I get nowadays is in the bathroom, where none of them can follow. Unless your name is Aiden and you just barge in, embarrassing us both.

"Okay."

"Just give me five. Do you want to grab something to eat?"

"Yeah, I'm a bit hungry. We can just order in though, right? I feel like being lazy."

She shrugs. "All right."

THE TWO DOGS seem to be getting on fine. Roxy is resting her head on Buster's large belly, snoring lightly. Both are tuckered out after their walks around the park.

It's getting late. I'm expecting one of my cousins or brothers to turn up, but so far, nothing. My phone rings and I look down at the screen, seeing Hayden's name.

"Hey, sweets, what's up?"

"Just thought I'd ring you to let you know the plans for next week have changed. We're going out for a meal first and then going clubbing. Immy is still demanding we go out in fancy dress."

Crap, I forgot it was the triplets' nineteenth birthday.

"It's October, it's freezing, especially if she wants us to wear skimpy outfits."

She laughs down the line. "Too right. I've shut her down for now, but she'll keep trying. There's no way I'm going to a restaurant dressed like that. Pissed up and out on the town, I don't give a shit."

It's my turn to laugh. Hayden drunk is hilarious. She gets us doing random shit. Even if the night starts out normal, it always ends up with one of us falling for something she's conjured up.

"Okay. I don't mind either way, just keep me informed."

"Will do. How is that man of yours?"

She's been hassling me for a few days about what is going between me and Beau. I've not told my family anything, because the minute I tell them we're in a relationship, they'll start asking me if we've done it. And that is something I do not want to share with them.

Just… no.

It's bad enough he stays almost every night to keep an eye on me. They think something has happened between us, but it hasn't. We've done nothing but kiss, and it's all I'm ready for at the moment.

"He's good."

A knock on the door startles me. I look over to Nina, who is flicking through the movies on Netflix.

"Can you grab that? It's the pizza."

She nods, getting up to answer the door.

"Is that him?" Hayden booms down the phone excitedly.

"Um, no, it's Nina. I'm going to have to go, our food is here."

"Okay, I'll call in tomorrow. I wanted to get your opinion on the dresses I've picked for my birthday."

"Sounds awesome. See you then."

We end the call and I turn to see Nina holding a shoe box and not the pizza I had hoped would be here. I'm starving. I sigh in disappointment.

"What's that?" I ask, noting she's looking a little pale.

"Um, I—"

The door opens behind her and Beau steps in. "Hey, beautiful, I'm home," Beau sings. "Did you cook dinner?"

"Um, Beau…"

He notices Nina and loses his smile. "Is everything okay?"

"I don't know. Nina opened the door thinking it was the pizza bloke, but she came in with that." I point to the box in her hands. "I was on the phone." Once I've finish explaining, I walk up to her. Her hands are shaking and she's still looking down at the box. "Nina, girl, what is it?"

"It's a… it's a—"

Beau takes the box from her hands. "It's okay, I got it." He walks over to the counter. I tend to Nina, rubbing her arms, which are covered in goose bumps. I bite my lip, worried about what she saw.

"Fuck!" Beau curses, running a hand through his hair.

"What is it?"

He looks over his shoulder at me, his eyes hard. "It's nothing. I'll deal with this."

Yeah, that isn't going to happen.

Stepping around Nina, I walk over to the counter with determination. "Beau, I can handle this. Trust me. I want to know—no, I need to know. It's spooked Nina."

He sighs, looking conflicted, before flicking the box open. I peep inside and cringe at the sight. A dead rat lays on its side, blood pouring from a wound in his neck.

I flip the lid closed again and close my eyes, counting to ten.

"Are you okay? I knew I shouldn't have let you look."

Beau pulls me into his arms and I go, resting my head on his shoulder. "No, I'm fine. I'm just fucking mad he killed an animal to prove something. Who does he think he is? Couldn't he have just sent me a fucking picture of a rat instead of using a real, defenceless one?"

"It was a real rat," Nina whispers.

Turning in her direction, I wince. She freaking hates rats. Out of all the animals we deal with, she still hasn't gotten over her fear of the disease-spreading rodents. They're her worst nightmare. She constantly refuses to work on any that come in.

"Are you okay?" I ask as a knock on the door echoes throughout the room. "Mmm, pizza."

Nina gags and Beau looks at me like I'm crazy. He walks over to the door and I step towards Nina.

"It was a real rat. I nearly touched it," she whispers. "I need to wash my hands—bleach them. Yeah, I need to bleach them."

I watch her stumble to the bathroom, biting my lip to hold in my giggle. I shouldn't find it funny that Noah sent me a message, calling me a rat. What did he expect, me to sit at home and pray he doesn't hurt me or someone else again? Not a chance. There was no remorse in the man who attacked me, no chance of him changing.

I'd like to think I'm capable of forgiveness, but a monster like him, someone who will never repent for his crimes, doesn't deserve my forgiveness, or anyone else's.

"She okay?" Beau asks, dropping the pizza onto my coffee table—completely avoiding the counter. Thank god, I don't want my food near the rat.

"She will be. She hates rats."

"Who likes them?" he asks. His eyebrows scrunched up, seeming to really think about it.

"I like them. I like all animals, which is why I'm pissed. He's not going to leave me alone, is he?"

Beau's eyes harden. "No, he won't. We're gonna find him though, Faith. It's only a matter of time. I can't promise you it will be tomorrow, or next week, or even next month, but I will find him."

My heart softens at his declaration. "I know you will, Beau. You can't let it rule your life though. I'm not ready to walk outside on my own yet, but I'm not scared of him. I understand he's dangerous, but he's a coward. He's not going to ruin my life. I won't let him. Which is why I'm going to sit down, put my feet up, and eat my yummy pizza."

He looks dumbfounded when I flop back on the sofa and grab a slice of pizza out of the box.

"You're eating, after that?" Nina screeches.

I glance up from my mouth-watering pizza and shrug. I chew the piece I'd already greedily bitten off and swallow. "Yeah, I am. It's a dead rat. I deal with dead animals every day, so why he thought it would scare me is beyond me. He did more to you than he did to me. Though, I do feel bad for the rat."

I'm not heartless, don't get me wrong. I'm just not going to let some lowlife bring me down. I do feel guilt for the animal who was killed violently. It's sadistic. Cruel. He wasn't even a street rat. He was a pet rat, which makes it even worse.

Oh, my God, why didn't I think of that before.

"Beau!" I manage to shout around half a mouthful of food, before getting up. He startles, jumping back as he eyes me. I wave my hand at him, holding him off when he takes a step towards me. "It was a pet rat."

He still looks confused, and when I glance to Nina for help as I chew as quickly as I can, she looks at me with disgust. "It's a rat, Faith. They're all dirty rodents." She shudders dramatically.

I glare at my best friend. "You really need to get over your fear, Nina." I shake my head at her before turning back to Beau. "He was a pet rat. Now I'm just guessing here, but I don't think Noah had a rat on hand, unless he robbed one from his last victim."

"I'm still not following," Beau tells me, standing with his arms crossed.

I roll my eyes. *Men.* "It means he bought it from a pet store. The only pet stores within a six-mile radius are Malley's Pets and Lincoln Pet Store."

Realisation dawns across his expression. "I'll be back. I'm going to go back to the police station."

He heads to the door before running back and bringing his lips to mine in a heated kiss. I kiss him back, gripping the bottom of his shirt in my hands.

When he pulls away, I'm breathless. "Go."

"Take the rat with you," Nina adds on a shout, giving the box a wide birth as she moves to sit on the sofa.

"No!" he says, eyeing the rat with disgust.

"Um, yeah. Won't you need it for evidence? Plus, you need to check there isn't anything under the rat, or lying in the blood."

He looks back at the box, his shoulders sagging. I bite the inside of my cheeks to keep from laughing at his horrified expression.

"Shit. Okay. I'll be back later. If anything comes up, I'll let you know."

"All right. Want us to save you some pizza?"

He looks a little green as he holds the shoe box and looks at the pizza. "I'll pass. I'm not really all that hungry, come to think of it."

He walks out the door and I burst out laughing, falling back on the sofa. "Did you see his face?"

Nina chuckles, clicking on a Nicholas Sparks movie. My favourite. "Such a baby. I thought he was meant to be a big, badass police officer?" My head lazily turns to Nina, and I give her an 'are you kidding me' expression. "What?"

She grabs a piece of pizza as I answer. "You went deathly pale, screamed, and then scolded me for eating over the same rat."

"I'm a girl with a fear of rats."

"I still don't understand that. You like spiders, and in my book, they're fucking freaky."

"Oh, my God, they're tiny."

"Exactly! Tiny: they can get anywhere."

She rolls her eyes at me. "They're just harmless spiders. Rats? They bite, they infect, they are ugly and smell bad. And why do they need long tails? They're just freaky."

I giggle at her extensive knowledge. "You've really thought about rats, huh?"

She shudders. "My cousin Brody had one and scared me shitless with it. I've never recovered."

"I can tell." I smile in amusement as she glares at me.

"Shut up, eat your pizza and watch the damn movie."

"Did you get the tissues?" I ask her as I grab another slice. Some things you should always have at the ready; a pillow to hold on to, a tissue to wipe away tears and snot, and popcorn to chew when the emotion becomes too much.

"Shit. Be back."

THIRTEEN

THE SECOND MOVIE FINISHES AND I'M proud to say only two boxes of tissues were needed. I blow my snotty nose and turn to my best friend. "I've watched this movie, like, a million times, and each time I cry like the world is ending."

"Me too. I feel so invested that my own heart is breaking. They finally find their way back to each other, Faith, and it's taken away."

"But he gives his heart to her son. Losing her child would have been worse."

She nods, still choked-up over the movie. "Let's talk about something happy before I have to walk home in the dreadful rain."

I look out the window behind us. The rain is pouring and has been for the past two hours. "It is pretty bad. Are you coming out for the triplets' birthday?"

"Yeah, I am. I can't wait to have a night out. Just make sure they are on their best behaviour this year. Last year it took me a long time to recover."

"You drank my uncles' disgusting drink, didn't you?"

"Yeah, whoever invented that had the devil in them. God, I want to gag just thinking about it."

I laugh when she shudders. The drink is pretty vile. I've only ever had a sip. I'm one of those people who will wait until someone else has taste-tested. In my case, I watched Aiden drink it. When he was severely ill, to the point he nearly had to go to hospital, I decided to never touch the stuff again. It was enough.

"I'm going to try and get a new dress Friday," I tell her.

"Oh, did the bank sort your money out. I forgot to ask."

"Yeah. It came through over the weekend. After Collings spoke with them, they kind of rushed it through. I'm just glad I had insurance."

Her smile is sad when she looks at me. "Yeah. I keep wanting to ask how you're really doing. I want you to be honest with me, not tell me what you think I want to hear. I know you tell your family you're fine, but I know you, Faith. This has to be freaking you out. You couldn't even watch that film with Jenifer Lopez in."

I shudder. "That neighbour may have been hot, but he was a creep."

She points at me. "See, that there. If a movie can affect you, then this has to be permanently scarring you."

My mouth opens, ready to tell her I'm okay, but the look on her face has me revisiting my decision.

"It's hard to describe to be honest. It doesn't feel real enough."

She scoffs, giving me a pointed look. "Not real enough? The guy beat you up."

I glare at her. "I know. I didn't mean for it to sound so callous. It's like I'm seeing and hearing what is happening, but a part of me isn't feeling it. I know it's happening to me, but sometimes, it feels like it's not. The whole situation is bizarre."

"I kind of understand. When my dad beat my mum before he left, it didn't feel like it was happening. I watched from the doorway, trying to figure out what I was seeing. It was like I was in a bubble where everything around me seemed foggy."

I soften in my seat. Nina's mum is the best, but her dad… well, he's a monster. He was abusive, at first emotionally, but it soon turned physical when her mum tried to leave him. She never talks about him, not like this anyway.

"You get it."

"I'm glad you went to the police," she whispers, her eyes watering.

I take her hands in mine and pull them onto my lap as I cross my legs and face her. "He really did mess with the wrong girl. I'm not saying others who didn't go to the police are weak, but look where it gets them. Nowhere. Nothing good can come from them not going. It just gives him more control. They'll be scared every day of their lives that he will come back. They will have to live with everything he did after. It's a vicious circle. But it's hard to not defend them when I know how easily you want to forget it all happened."

"I can see what you're saying. He relies on the fear he feeds them. He doesn't expect them to fight back, which is what you're doing."

"Too right I am. It's easier to let his threats get to me, but I won't. I know what that rat tonight meant. He wanted to rattle me, but I can't sit back and let him terrorize me."

"What has Beau said?"

A goofy smile falls on my lips at the mention of Beau. "He's been protective ever since I was attacked. He's determined to find him."

She grins at my expression. "I bet. How are things with him? He's still staying here, right?"

"Yeah, but only in the spare room. He's been the perfect gentlemen."

"You seem disappointed," she teases.

I kind of am.

"I am. He drives me mad. There's just something about him that I can't get enough of."

She begins to giggle, pulling me in for a hug. "My girl is taking the next step to womanhood." She pulls back, a wide smile on her face. "You are falling in love with him."

I give her a doubtful expression. "I'm not. I swear, I'm not. I can't be."

Am I?

She laughs. "Oh, I don't know, the expression on your dopy face tells me otherwise."

I push her shoulder lightly. "Shut up and stop teasing me."

"So, you haven't—you know?"

I blush. "No."

"But he knows?"

I smile at that. "Yeah. And he doesn't mind in the slightest."

"I bet," she grins, winking at me.

"What?"

She rolls her eyes, most likely at my naivety. "Faith, most men would kill to be with you, especially if they found out you're a virgin. You're like a mystical creature."

I scoff. "You make me sound like I'm the only one."

"Well, there aren't many of you out there, sweets. I lost mine when I was fifteen, my cousin was thirteen, and even my mum was sixteen when she lost hers."

"People are losing it younger and younger," I agree.

"Yeah, girls who have no knowledge of what it really means or how serious it actually is. Look at me. I did it because everyone else was doing it and thought it would mean I'd be cool. But all I got was two minutes of awkward foreplay, five minutes of excruciating pain, and a week of discomfort between my legs."

"Don't remind me of Alan. Me and Maddox wanted to kill him for what he did."

"We can't really blame him. I bought everything he told me. But it's like I said, we have no knowledge at that age. You waiting until you were mature enough was the right thing to do."

Alan was a jerk and went around school telling everyone she was easy. Every girl in school had a crush on him, he was just that good-looking. Even I can admit he was a gorgeous lad and I didn't like him. For two weeks he pursued Nina, making everyone know he was into her. He went out of his way to see her, to buy her stuff and make her feel good.

Somehow, he manipulated her into having sex with him one night when we were all out at the park, drinking. He took advantage of her being drunk.

After, he said he wasn't looking for a girlfriend and then told everyone what happened, bragging.

Her experience didn't put me off sex though. I always knew I'd wait for the right one, and Mum always drummed it into my head that I shouldn't just let anyone get that far with me. They needed to respect and appreciate me.

"He knows and he hasn't pushed me to do anything. Honestly, he hasn't even brought it up again."

"But you want to?"

"I do, but at the moment, I'm not ready. I need to be a hundred-percent certain."

"I get that." She looks at her phone and winces. "I'm sorry, but I need to get back. It's half nine and I've still got to stop and get shopping."

"Thanks for keeping me company. I've missed this."

We may work together, but lately we've rarely had time to just chat about girl stuff. I've missed her.

"Yeah. We have next Wednesday afternoon off if you want to do lunch?"

I smile at that. "Yeah, we can go to Nando's."

"Deal. I'll see you tomorrow."

"Night, hon."

I walk her to the door and give her a hug goodbye. When I turn back to my living room, Roxy and Buster are sitting side by side, their heads tilted and watching me.

I laugh, walking over to the cupboard that hoards their food.

"Okay, you pair, food, then bed."

———————————

A KEY BEING put into the lock steals my attention from the ten o'clock news.

"Hey." I smile when his eyes lift to meet mine. When he frowns and rushes over to me, I lean further back into the sofa. "Um, is everything okay? Did something happen?"

"You tell me, you've been crying, Faith."

My body melts at his affection. He tucks my hair behind my ear, searching my face for what could be wrong.

"I'm fine, I—"

"I knew I shouldn't have left you." He gets to his feet and paces. "When I left you seemed fine, otherwise I wouldn't have gone. Dammit. I suck at keeping you safe."

My head falls back on the sofa as a laugh tumbles free. "You think I'm upset about the rat?"

He stops shortly, looking down at me in confusion. It's adorable. "Aren't you?"

"No."

"Then why the hell are your eyes red and blotchy from crying?"

He runs a hand through his hair, frustrated. Most likely to do with the fact he can't figure me out. One minute I'm happily eating pizza, then he finds me on the sofa, tucked under my blanket, with red-rimmed eyes.

I stand up, taking his hands in mine to get him to look at me, and smile when he does.

"Because I watched two Nicholas Sparks movies."

His eyes scrunch up. "The dude who only makes sad movies?"

I roll my eyes. "He actually wrote sad books that were made into movies. And yes, him."

"And they made you look like someone run over your dog?"

I take offence at that. "Hey, I'd be a lot worse if someone run over one of my babies."

He smiles, his hands grabbing my hips. "I know, I'm teasing. You're really doing okay?"

I run my hands up his chest and around his neck, stroking my thumbs on his stubble. "Yes, I really am doing okay. He's hurt me enough, Beau. I'm not just scared and upset now, I'm angry."

He holds my cheeks in his hands. "I know you are, baby. We're looking into the rat. Collings went to the pet store that confirmed they sold a rat two days ago."

"That's good right?"

He winces. "Yes and no. If he paid cash then we can't trace him. We will, however, finally have CCTV footage. The one we got from your business isn't clear. It's too dark and his hood is up. It's like he knew the cameras would get him."

"God, I hope this ends soon."

"Me too."

He really does mean that.

I gaze into his eyes for another beat before leaning up on my toes to press my lips against his. He kisses me back just as passionately, pulling me against him.

A shiver runs up my spine when his hands grip my arse and lift me. I wrap my legs around him, feeling flutters in my stomach when he sits down on the sofa with me straddling him.

We've kissed a lot since he started staying with me, but it's never felt this hot. I can't get enough of him. He's setting my body on fire.

It feels good. He feels good.

I run my fingers through his hair, grinding down on his lap. I don't know what possesses me to do it, but I do, and when a tingle spreads between my legs, I do it again, harder.

He's hard beneath me, and instead of being embarrassed or shy, I feel hot inside, like my blood is boiling.

I pull away, breathing hard as I keep rotating my hips, trying to find the right friction again.

"Beau," I whisper.

His hands on my hips steady my frantic movements, slowing them down to a torturous pace. He looks up at me, his eyes heated.

"Is this okay?" His breathing is just as heavy as mine, and I find it erotic that I'm turning him on as much as he is me.

"Yeah."

"Can I touch you?"

Understanding what he means, I nod my head, but pause my movements for a second. "I'm not ready to go all the way."

His smile is devilish. "Oh, baby, I'm about to show you that foreplay can be just as hot as sex."

Wetness seeps between my legs at his dirty words.

He doesn't wait for me to make a move. Indeed, his hands fall onto my shoulders, gently caressing me. I throw my head back at his touch, and when he flattens his hand against my chest, slowly moving down my body, I can't help but moan. It escapes on its own free will. The anticipation of what is going to happen is both exhilarating and frightening. I don't know what to expect, but with what he's doing to my body now, I know it can only be good.

When he reaches my waist, I drop my head to his shoulder, breathing heavily. I just about lose my mind when he grips my shirt and pulls it up and over my head. I let him, feeling a little self-conscious about being half naked in front him. I'm only wearing shorts and a bra. I'm about to cover up when I get a look at his expression. All sense of thought and insecurities leave me. That look will forever burn into me.

It feels good when he leans forwards, kissing and licking up the side of my sensitive neck. I give him better access, loving the feel of his tongue against me.

So much is happening it's hard to concentrate. His hands are moving up my ribs to below my breasts, and his tongue is tracing a path down to them too. It's hard to know which one feels better.

When his hands go behind my back and release my bra, I gasp at the sensation, feeling free.

I'm wetter, more turned on than before. However, my movements stop, as I struggle to concentrate on them. All I can focus on is what he is doing. Nothing has ever felt so sensual as his hands roaming over me.

Bra removed, his hands move back to my ribs before cupping my breasts. I moan, my auburn hair falling to my waist as I stare up at the ceiling. His thumbs rub over my sensitive nipples.

"Oh, God."

He chuckles against my chest, before gazing up at me, that sexy grin still in place. "Want to know what feels better?"

I don't get a chance to answer. All of a sudden, a sound I've never made before escapes me as his lips wrap around my nipple, his tongue flicking me in the most delicious way.

"Beau," I moan, sagging in his lap despite my body feeling coiled tight.

He sucks on my hardened nipple, sending me speechless. While his mouth is busy, his hands move down my ribs to my hips, which he slowly moves again.

The harder friction sends tingles to my core, and I begin to move on my own. Once it's clear I'm not going to stop moving, his fingers run along the seam of my shorts.

"Please," I beg.

His breath is harsh against my nipples as he pulls away, before taking my mouth with his. I kiss him back as his fingers slide into my knickers.

They run through my wetness like silk and I moan at the euphoria of sensations. He rubs my clit with his thumb in slow circles and my stomach tightens, something building inside me, something explosive. Wave after wave of pleasure assaults me to the point I can't think.

I'm startled when he flips me across the sofa and onto my back, and I yelp. He moves above me, and his hand repositions in my knickers as his mouth lands on mine in a hard, demanding kiss. My hips grind upwards to meet his touch. His finger circles my entrance, and for a split second I tense. I've never been touched down there before. But when he pulls back and gazes at me, I melt into the sofa.

"Are you okay?"

My cheeks feel like they're on fire and are no doubt pink. "God, yes."

His kisses me again and, slowly, pushes a finger inside me. *Oh, god, that feels so good.* I move against him, and he pushes in further. Other than there being a little discomfort, it feels incredible.

His thumb going back to my clit as his finger pushes in and out of me, drives me wild. I pull away from our kiss, needing more oxygen as I breathe deep. I'm gasping, fighting against whatever is building inside me.

God, is it getting hotter in here?

Tingles shoot up my spine and my movements become faster, more frantic. It's like I'm not in control anymore, like every instinct I've ever had has gone out of the window and all I see, crave, or feel is him.

Only him.

"Beau," I cry louder, biting down on his shoulder when his movements speed up.

"Let go, beautiful."

I don't understand, but my body seems to know exactly what he's saying. White light flashes before my eyes and I throw my head back, a cry of pleasure escaping me. It doesn't end. My body feels tight, yet relaxed, and the tingles shooting between my legs spread to my core.

Nothing, and I mean *nothing*, has ever felt so good.

Once the pleasure subsides, I sag against the sofa, my whole body spent. He slips his finger free and I twitch, still feeling sensitive down there.

He kisses the side of my neck, holding my naked chest against him as he turns us so I'm half lying on him. "You doing okay?"

I wait a few moments before pulling back, a lazy smile on my face. I'm completely drained—in the best kind of way. "That. Was. Amazing."

He laughs and kisses me hard. My lips feel bruised but I don't care. I'd do anything to feel that with him again.

"What about, you—you know?" I stutter, embarrassment overwhelming me.

He holds me tighter against him, kissing my head. "This was for you tonight, baby. Just you. We can explore another night."

I pull back again, fighting the need for sleep. "You promise?"

He looks deeply into my eyes, a soft smile reaching his lips. "I promise. Now, film or bed?"

"You can watch the football, I'm going to crash here. I don't think I could move if the house was on fire."

He chuckles and grabs my blanket, which had dropped to the floor, before pulling it over us. "Okay, but just so you know, I'd carry you out if the house was on fire."

"After you got the dogs out," I murmur quietly, my head resting on his chest. My eyes close, but my lips pull into a small smile when he chuckles.

"After the dogs."

"My hero," I whisper, a yawn escaping me before I fall into a deep slumber.

FOURTEEN

FOR THE FIRST TIME SINCE BEAU STARTED staying with me, I get to wake up next to him—or more precisely, on top of him.

I'd always thought positions like this in movies were forced. I mean, I've leant on my brothers' shoulders in the car and that shit gave me neck ache for a week.

But enjoying Beau's warmth beneath me, my head lay on his chest… I'm proved wrong. There's no other way I'd rather sleep now.

I've dreamt of this moment for so long. This feeling inside me is something I've craved, needed. All my life it's been this way, and I always knew it would be a blessing.

Now I have it and it's nothing like I ever dreamed of, ever craved or needed. It's so much more. It's not just a blessing, it's a gift. It's frightening and exhilarating, but most of all, completely wanted.

The feelings I have for him have only amplified with our time together. Every day is a new experience, but what stays the same is how I feel when I see him or hear him speak. Nothing else on this earth could ever make me feel that way.

And it scares me.

Seeing Beau asleep, I take my time running my gaze over him. I've always found is tattoos appealing. His body is a work of art on its own, but add those in and it's beyond hot.

I don't think I've seen tattoos look sexier on someone. Ever.

My fingers run down his bare chest, his skin soft like silk to touch. He's perfect. In every way.

I'm still unsure how he manages to stay in such good shape. His chest his hard, muscular. However, I've never seen him lift a weight, or known him to go to the gym.

My belly flutters when I run my finger between the lines of his abdomen muscles. It brings a smile to my face when he tenses and moans softly in his sleep. He's affected by my touch, just as I am his.

His eyes flutter open and a sexy smile greets me. "Morning, beautiful. You sleep okay?"

My cheeks burn. "I slept like the dead." Thanks to him and the incredible orgasm he gave me last night.

He notices my mild embarrassment and pulls me down on his chest, smiling cheekily. "Kiss me."

Obliging, I lean down and do just that. His lips feel soft against mine and I revel in the kiss. His hands go to my hips, gripping me tightly, like he did the night before. Wetness forms between my legs when I feel just how aroused he is.

My raging hormones are on fire, his touch burning me. It makes me want to do something I've never done before.

Touch him.

I pull back from the kiss, my eyelids heavy and my breath raspy. "Beau, can I... Can you—I mean, will you show me how to pleasure you?"

He looks stunned at my question, and at first, I begin to think he's going to reject me, but a blooming smile fills his face. His hard cock twitches against my thigh, and I gasp out loud. He chuckles, pulling me back down for another kiss.

When he's done, his eyes are burning into mine. The heat behind them have me trying to close my thighs together to get rid of the ache.

"Yeah, baby, I'll show you."

I feel my face light up with excitement, and he chuckles. I pull the blanket down, ready to take him in my hand. I may be a virgin and clueless, but I still hear things from other girls.

Before I can reach where I'm yearning to touch him, a knock on the front door interrupts us.

Breathing heavily, Beau sits up on his elbows. "Ignore it. It's probably one of your brothers or cousins. They'll go away. Eventually."

Whoever is at the door starts knocking again and I bite my lip. "Maybe we shouldn't. My brothers have keys, you know."

He groans, falling back on the bed. Before we can move off the bed, a voice I don't recognise calls through the door.

"Beau, are you in there? It's your mother and father."

My eyes widen in panic and I flip around to face Beau. He looks just as surprised as I do—more so when he falls out the bed.

"I think I heard him. He's coming, honey."

The male voice is deep and rugged, and I picture a mountain man in my head. He sounds just like one. I guess watching too many movies will make you imagine the strangest things.

Beau pulls on a pair of jogging bottoms before trying to straighten out his messy, unkept hair. I'd laugh if I wasn't so freaked out.

He's always so calm and collected that sometimes I get jealous over how perfect he is. Seeing him a complete wreck is kind of amusing.

I get out of bed, looking around the room for something to pull on, when I realise, for the first time since waking up, Beau put his T-shirt on me before bringing me to bed.

He rushes out the door first, me at a much slower pace.

Why are they here? Did he tell them he was staying here? God, so many questions are running through my mind when he opens the door and greets his mum and dad in a nervous voice.

"Mum, Dad, what are you guys doing here?"

His mum steps in, wasting no time in pulling her son in for a hug. Even though they are close, I know from conversations with Beau that they haven't seen each other in a while. You can see she's missed him.

She looks younger than the forty-six years Beau said she is. If I hadn't known her age to begin with, I'd have said she was beginning her forties— and that's pushing it. She's beautiful. She has pale skin, rosy pink cheeks and startling green eyes. The only thing that shows her age are the laughter lines at the side of her eyes.

I'm smiling when his dad pulls his wife back just so he can step in to hug his son. When his wife glares at him and rolls her eyes, I giggle, which turns her attention to me.

"Oh, my."

She gapes in shock as she takes me in, her fingers pressing into her cheeks. It's the tears in her eyes that have me worried though. I shift on my feet, feeling self-conscious, wondering why I'm receiving such a reaction.

Part of me worries it's because I'm not what they expected, that I'm not good enough for their son, but then my injuries come to mind, and I bite my lip. I don't know how to explain them without sounding like a walking disaster and someone putting their son in danger.

I know they can't see my bruises—most of them have healed, and the ones on my body are covered. The only thing to stir such a reaction is my cast.

"Mum, I'd like you to meet—"

"Faith! Oh, you are a beauty, just like my sister told me you were. She loves visiting with you when she does her six-month house inspection. Son, you didn't tell me she was this pretty."

I'm amused by the blush creeping up Beau's neck, but I can't study him for long because his mum pulls me against her, hugging me.

"Hi, Mrs. Johnson."

"None of that, call me Julie. We're practically family now. My son has told me so much about you," she gushes, beaming with pride as she takes my hands in hers. "Barry, just look at her."

"She's a beauty," his dad remarks, smiling at his wife. "Nice to meet you. I'm Barry."

"Hi, I'm Faith." I inwardly smack my own forehead for sounding so stupid. I just feel so out of my depth right now.

"Mum, think you could let her go?" Beau asks, grinning as he pulls me away slowly, like he's worried his mum will attack me. He tucks me into his side and I'm more than happy to be there.

His mum's eyes fill with even more tears, now threatening to spill over, and I begin to worry when she starts sobbing. I give Beau a panicked look, pleading with my eyes for him to do something. But he just rolls his own eyes at me, like he expected this kind of reaction.

"Come on, Jules, stop with the waterworks."

She slaps her husband's chest and glares up at him. "No. My baby boy is finally settling down. I've been waiting years for this, Barry. Years. And look at her." She points my way dramatically and I tuck myself further into Beau's side. "She's an absolute angel. Our grandbabies are going to beautiful, Barry. Beautiful!"

"Mum!" Beau groans, hiding his face in the top of my head.

I giggle under my breath and he squeezes me in warning. But what can I say, I'm a Carter; we live for the dramatic flair.

"Well, you will," she sniffles, her wide smile turning my way.

"They really will. Your son is so *beautiful*."

She giggles in Barry's chest, looking up at him. "She is an absolute gem." She turns back to us, her eyes looking around the flat, before landing on Roxy and Buster. "Oh, my, you have dogs. Barry, we should take these two for a walk and get some breakfast, let these two get on with making us some grandbabies."

"Mum!" Beau shouts, covering his face now. "We aren't making babies, so calm down, will ya. We've got stuff for breakfast and we can take the dogs for a walk later. First though, why didn't you call and let me know you were visiting?"

His dad grins before chuckling. It's his mum that answers, "Well, when Wendy phoned me after Harry had phoned her and told me you hadn't been coming to the flat for a while, I got worried."

"What?" Beau asks, looking at his dad now.

"Harry said he had some security put in after this flat got broken into. The feed runs to their house. He checks in to make sure nothing else happens. He said you had been staying over here for a while."

Beau sighs, looking at his dad a minute longer before turning his attention to his mum. "I have to fill you in on what happened, but first, Faith and I are going to get ready and meet you out here for breakfast. And I want to know if Faith is okay with me giving you the information."

Before my eyes I watch his dad straighten, looking like a man that could snap you in half and not the cuddly bear he seemed to be. He notes the seriousness in his son's voice no doubt and is ready for whatever he has to say.

And that is what Beau gets from his dad, because he looks too much like his mother. He has the same ash-blonde hair, and green eyes, although Julie's are sharper than her son's. His dad's hair must have been once brown but is now more silver, and his are blue. Beau gets his height and size from his dad, but after seeing his dad's reaction, they seem more alike than I first thought.

"Okay, we'll let you two get ready. Me and your mum will cook us up a nice healthy breakfast."

"You're supposed to be watching your cholesterol."

He rolls his eyes at his wife and pulls her over to the kitchen.

Beau pulls me away and towards my bedroom. I'm still feeling kind of dazed, so I don't question why he's coming with me. The spare clothes he left here—so he didn't have to keep heading across the hall each morning—are in the guest bedroom.

I hadn't expected a visit from his parents when I woke up this morning. I had wanted to explore things further with Beau, having thoroughly enjoyed last night. That said, I am intrigued to find out more about Beau. I want to know what he was like as a kid growing up. It's only fair, since my family have made it their mission to fill him in on every embarrassing detail of my life.

"Are you okay with them being here?"

A wide smile lights up my face. "Of course, I am. They seem awesome."

He rolls his eyes at me. "They're a little nutty. Well, my mum is. My dad just goes along for the ride. He said it's what drew him to her and wouldn't change her for the world."

I laugh at that. "Well, she can't be worse than my family."

His eyes light up in amusement. "Oh, she would probably give them a run for their money."

"Come on, let's get dressed so I can hear some embarrassing stories about you growing up."

His face drops and pales considerably. "Nope! No way."

Ha! "Oh, yes way. I'm totally going to ask your mum to send me baby pictures if she doesn't have any handy."

"You wouldn't want me to go snooping for your baby pictures, would you?"

I give him a wicked smile when I turn to look at him over my shoulder. "I was a cute baby. Look away."

He groans, running his fingers through his hair. "I'm so going to regret introducing you."

Just as the words leave his mouth, there's a knock on the front door, before we hear it open. We look at each other before turning towards my closed door.

Only a few members of my family have keys.

"Oh, aren't you handsome. I'm Beau's mother, Julie, and this is my husband, Barry."

"Cool!" Aiden booms, and I stare at Beau in horror. "Beau's parents, I'm Aiden, Faith's better brother."

"Any embarrassing stories?" Ashton adds, and more male chuckles fill the room.

Beau moves like lightening, tripping over his feet to get to the door. I start laughing as he races outside, running into the room next to mine. They all laugh after his door bangs, making me giggle. Seems today is going to be an interesting day.

"SO, YOU'RE TELLING me you are only staying here because there's a madman out for her, over something *he* did wrong?"

We've just finished telling his parents all about Noah. We'd had no choice since Aiden started telling them they were only allowing Beau here because he's protecting me. It had led to more questions, and embarrassing ones at that.

"That's not the only reason, Mum."

If I were to guess, I'd say Beau was blushing, but before I get the chance to confirm it, her eyes swing my way.

"So, you *are* a couple?"

I nod, smiling at the woman who, minutes ago, thought her dream of future grandchildren was over. She looks happy and I didn't want to be the one to point out we haven't known each other long and grandkids weren't going to happen any time soon.

It was then I realised I pictured a future with Beau, one where we did have kids and got married. It's premature to think of something like that—I've known girls who've been dumped because of it.

I guess when something feels right, there's nothing you can do but hold on to hope. And as far as things go, I'm hoping Beau feels the same and sees us going somewhere other than the bedroom.

"We've not been dating long."

Around a mouthful of food, Aiden interrupts, "She wouldn't be at all if we had our way, but Beau kind of bullied us."

Beau grunts under his breath, but stops short when his mum turns to him, her eyes frosty. "Beau Johnson, I taught you better than to bully people, especially people younger than you. They are still children." Beau doesn't seem fazed at his mum's rant, but when I turn to Aiden, his smug expressions falls at being called a child. Even if he does act like one. When her gaze turns his way, he sits up straighter, ready for the arse-rimming he's about to endure. "And you, what is wrong with my son?"

Aiden looks at everyone around my living room for answers, but none of my cousins who arrived with him back him up. He swallows his eggs as he prepares to answer. "Nothing, Julie. It's not Beau we have a problem with, it's the fact our baby sister/cousin is dating. We've worked hard to keep the boys away. It seems your son is immune to our threats."

Much to Beau's dismay, his mum actually melts at Aiden's confession. "Oh, dear, that is the sweetest thing I have ever heard in my life." She looks up at her husband who is sitting on the arm of my armchair. "Isn't that just sweet, Barry." Her gaze turns back to Aiden, all soft and mushy. I want to giggle but I'm worried if I do, Beau will find some way to pay me back. "You keep being protective of your sister, Aiden. If we had a daughter, we'd expect nothing less from Beau. But I do have to tell you, my boy is a good boy. He'll do right by your sister."

Aiden doesn't look convinced, but nods anyway.

"Sorry to interrupt," I start, my attention turning to my brother. "But why are you here this early? I didn't realise you ever even saw this time of day."

My cousins laugh, knowing how much my brother loves his sleeps. It was hard to get him to school when he was younger because he never wanted to get up. It wouldn't matter if he went to bed early, or in the early hours of the morning, he still hated getting up before midday.

He narrows his eyes at my dig, but then his face lights up with a smile. "I came to tell you I've found a house to move in to."

"A house?" I ask doubtfully, wondering what idiot rented a house out to him. I know for sure my dad wouldn't. Since we were teenagers, my dad always said that unless Aiden got his shit together, he wouldn't let him live in his shed, let alone one of his homes.

"Um, yeah."

"Wait for it." Mark grins as he gets up to take his plate to the kitchen.

"What am I missing?" I ask, looking at each of my cousins. Ashton is on the verge of laughing and Maddox looks ready to die—whether from a hangover or because what I'm about to be told is too funny, I don't know. It's only Landon who doesn't seem interested, busily typing away on his phone, frowning every now and then.

"Shut up, you lot. You're just jealous you won't have it so good."

"I still don't see how you think you'll have it good," Mark calls out from the kitchen, helping himself to another plate of food Julie and her husband cooked up.

"The suspense is killing me." Julie giggles, nearly bouncing in her seat.

With a sigh, Aiden faces me. "I'm moving in with an old lady on Sparks Lane. She's needed help around the house since she moved back from Cyprus two months ago."

Okay, so wasn't expecting that.

"Um, how old is this lady? And how did you qualify to help her out?"

Please don't say you slept with her. Please.

"Before you go thinking I slept with her, I didn't. She's sixty-two, for Christ sakes."

"I don't know, a woman a few doors down to us is in her sixties and she's married to a guy in his forties."

We all make a grossed-out face.

Aiden shakes his head. "Look, I didn't sleep with her. The ad only said they had a guest house to rent. When I got there, she took one look at my strapping body and made me a deal. She said if I helped fix up her house, she would knock rent off. The first few months will be basically free. The person who was supposed to be housekeeping, wasn't actually doing it. They were getting paid each month but never actually did any work."

"Oh, my, what a terrible thing," Julie gasps.

"You didn't tell us that," my other brother and cousins bark.

One thing we can't stand is people being mugged over, especially older people.

"Because I knew you would take the piss out of me. I wasn't going to say yes, not wanting to add more work to my schedule now that I'm starting work for Mason at the restaurant and starting culinary school next September. Then she told me about what happened and I couldn't refuse. The guest house is pretty cool. She had it extended above her garage."

The silence in the room is deafening. Even Landon looks up from his phone to gape up at Aiden in shock.

"You've got a job?"

He blushes. "Yeah, my other one wasn't something I could keep doing."

"And you're going to school?" I ask, still trying to wrap my head around this being real.

When he nods again, adding a shrug this time, I dive on him. He falls back, landing on the floor with a grunt. Roxie and Buster bark, rushing over to us and licking our faces. I laugh, shoving them off, but look down at my brother in awe.

"I'm so proud of you, Aiden. I never thought I'd see the day."

His cheeks have turned red now, but he carries on playing it off as I get up and move back to my seat, but not before giving him a peck on the cheek.

"It's not a big deal, for god's sake. It's just a job and school."

Mark shakes his head, his hand still frozen half way to his mouth from when Aiden told us what he's up to. He begins to choke before sorting himself out.

"Aiden, what the fuck? Why didn't you tell us?"

"Language, you're still young enough to go over the knee you know."

Mark audibly swallows. "Sorry, Mrs Johnson." He turns back to Aiden, still looking dazed. "This is a big deal. We didn't think you'd ever go to school and you're finally doing something you're good at."

"I don't know about that."

This time I roll my eyes. "Aiden, your cooking is amazing."

Aiden took a leaf out of my uncle Max's book and pretended he couldn't cook. Hearing he can will be a surprise to the others, that's for sure. But he knew if they knew, he'd be the one cooking at all the family meals.

"Yeah, but I can't bake for shi—sugar. And don't tell Mum or Dad, I want to tell them tonight. I just wanted you to know that I had found a place. But the reason I came over so early is because when she cleaned her shed out, she found a litter of kittens and their mum. She's taken them inside but she can't keep them. She thinks they're old enough to be rehomed. I told her I'd ask you."

I'm still reeling over him going to school, but I break out of my haze to answer him. "If you give me the address I can go over to take a look at them.

They'll need vaccinations and a full health check. She shouldn't have moved them. If they're stray they could be a little vicious when handled."

His eyes widen in alarm. "Should I go over and put them back? She said that once she got the kittens inside, the mum followed. The mum hid them in her boiler cupboard."

"Ah, sounds about right. They like it dark and warm, so that's perfect. If she hasn't tried to escape with them, then they should be fine. She'll also need to be checked for a chip. I'll go over tomorrow morning. Just let her know I'll be visiting."

He nods, taking his phone out. When I turn back to everyone, Julie is staring at me.

"You really are a wonder, Faith. You have a heart of gold and a beautiful family."

"Thank you." I blush at her praise and begin to fiddle with my fingers.

"We'd like to take you out later for dinner. Our treat. All of your family, dear. Beau said you're all really close. We're only here for the night, as Barry has to get back to work. We just wanted to make sure everything is okay."

Barry nods in agreement and Beau's hand tightens around mine. "Mum," he starts, seeming unsure—probably worried over the size of my family and the cost of feeding them.

And it doesn't pass my notice that it's the second time she's indicated she and Beau have spoken about me at great length. It actually feels pretty amazing to know that.

"It sounds like a plan, but for now, it should just be us four. My family is too big and could eat restaurants out of business."

"I take offence to that," Maddox growls.

I sigh. "Maddox, you're the reason we can never go back to the steak house. All you can eat salad bar doesn't mean eat the whole thing."

He rolls his eyes at me, grunting. "It said all you can eat. It was all I could eat and then some."

"Oh, dear." Julie giggles, taking us in.

"Sorry. As you can see, they can be a little difficult, but Beau and I would love to join you for dinner. Next time we have our family get together, I'll make sure to let you know so you can book it off work. With the weather cooling down, we have to find space for it as none of our houses are big enough to hold us all."

Her smile grows. "We'd love to, wouldn't we, Barry?"

"Sure would. Always up for some grub."

"We're going to pop over and see your aunt Wendy and uncle Harry. Is there anything you need while we're out?"

"No, thank you, Mum, we're covered."

She bites her lip, looking doubtful. "I'll just get a few things I think you'll need. Oh, and maybe some nice yummy treats for the dogs.

"Mum—" he starts, but she cuts him off.

"It's not every day I get to see my son finally settling down. Let me enjoy it. Now, we'll be back in a few hours. If you need to pop out, just send me a text message on my mobile."

He chuckles. "I will, Mum. I'll see you guys later."

We say goodbye to his parents and, not long after, to everyone else who'd raided my morning with Beau.

But as soon as the door shuts, I jump in his arms, demanding he take me to the bedroom to finish what we started this morning.

He grins against my lips and obeys my order with pleasure.

One thing is for certain: Beau Johnson is my person.

Life with him will never be boring.

FIFTEEN

LAST NIGHT'S MEAL WAS SO MUCH FUN, as well as eye-opening. I'd got to
see into Beau's past like I'd lived it alongside him. His parents were so
animated as they explained all the mischief he'd got into as a child.

It also got us onto the topic of Beau's friends. In the months I've known
him, I've yet to see a friend of any sort visit him. Apparently, the two best
friends he'd grown up with signed on for the army. He's only seen them a
handful of times over the past few years.

His other friends all drifted apart when he started working as a PI. He was
too focused on finding Noah, and still taking jobs to keep him afloat, to find the
time to keep in touch.

It made my heart hurt knowing he'd been alone for so long, but his parents
assured me they pestered him every chance they got, making sure he didn't
become a homebody.

The night was a blast, and although we planned it to be the four of us, my
parents invited themselves when Aiden told them what Barry and Julie were
planning. It was great, and a lot calmer than I thought it would be. My dad

even made an effort to ask questions, getting to know Beau that little bit more.

Beau and I had just finished waving goodbye to his parents and are standing outside my car. I'm off to go see Maggie, Aiden's new landlord.

"Are you sure about going out again tonight? We've still got my cousins' birthday meal tomorrow at my uncle's restaurant, and we're going out clubbing the night after."

Beau pulls me against him by my waist, smiling softly at me. "Yes, I'm sure. I want to treat you to a nice meal and the movies. It's what normal couples do. It only occurred to me last night when Mum mentioned it that we've only really gone out for something to eat a few times, and none of those were really a date as we were still friends."

My heart melts. "Okay. And are you sure you want to meet up with us after you've finished your shift on Saturday?"

Although Lake and Max had arranged a massive family meal tomorrow for the triplets' actual birthday, the triplets arranged their own party for Saturday, without the grownups. Beau had been invited to both, and although he had tomorrow off, he was working until midnight Saturday. But he'd promised he would meet us after. It just seems a lot for someone who will have been working a twelve-hour shift.

"Wouldn't miss it. I can't wait to dance with my girl."

I blush, picturing how dirty we can get while dancing. If I get turned on by just being near him, I'm worried what my reaction will be to grinding all over him.

"Well, in that case…"

He chuckles, taking my face into the palm of his hands, before bringing his head forwards and kissing me. It's soft at first, but then I reach behind his head for leverage as I flatten my body against his. He growls into my throat, his grip on my cheeks tightening as he presses his lips harder.

His hands run down my back and grip the cheeks of my arse in a soft squeeze, this time causing me to moan.

My body erupts with fire and, for a moment, I consider bailing on Maggie to go back upstairs with Beau.

He pulls away after a few moments, his forehead pressing against mine as he tries to catch his breath.

"Your kisses will be the death of me."

I smile, kissing him once more, before dragging my hands down his chest. "I wish I didn't have to go, but I promised Aiden."

"I need to go into work too. I want to follow up a few other leads."

"Do you think you'll find something?" I ask quietly.

He waits a beat, probably wondering how to answer, but then he does with a resigned sigh. "I don't know. Everything we've followed up on has been a dead end. My gut is telling me the guy he was staying with knows more than he's letting on. I've got a friend of mine, who is good at hacking, looking into it for me."

"Isn't that illegal?"

He grins. "Yeah, but I don't care. He hurt you, Faith. I'll do everything in my power to find this scumbag."

I run my fingers over his cheek gently. My big bear of a man is really overprotective, but he's also going to let this eat away at him if he keeps on. "Beau, I don't doubt you for a moment, but you need to take a step back. You can't run yourself ragged over this or get yourself into trouble. You can't. I don't know what I'd do if you got into trouble because of me."

My eyes start to sting, and a few tears fall free.

"Hey, don't get upset and don't worry. I'll be fine. He's just pissing me off. He's been getting away with this for too long. I can't let him get away, especially now."

If I didn't already know he had a big heart, I would certainly know now. But his big heart might get him into trouble.

The urge to tell him I love him is on the tip of my tongue. It catches me by surprise, and before Beau can ask about it, I kiss him.

"What time will you be back?" he whispers against my lips, just as affected as I am.

I'm still reeling over my near slip of the tongue. "What?"

He chuckles. "I'm glad our kisses affect you like they do me. What time will you be back from looking at the kittens?"

Oh.

Shaking my head, I try to give him my best smile, but my nerves are skyrocketing over the notion that I think I'm in love with Beau Johnson. I have to be. It nearly slipped past my lips so easily, but the feeling behind those words would have been one hundred percent real.

"I'll take them to the surgery to give them a health check and go from there. If they aren't old enough then they can't be parted from their mother. It's up to Maggie to decide what she wants to do with them. For some reason, the mother feels they are safe there as she didn't try to move or hide them anywhere else."

"Give me a text when you're finished. I'm hoping to be a few hours at most but if not, I'll meet you back here at six to take you out. Sound good?"

"Sounds perfect."

We lean in close, like we can't get enough of each other, which is true enough. His kisses are addictive, and I'm hooked.

After saying goodbye, I get in the car and head over to the address Aiden gave me last night. From what I know about the area, it's one of the most expensive. The houses are quite big and worth over half a million.

It still surprises me she has agreed to let Aiden stay there. My brother would never hurt her, or let anyone else, but first glance at him and you expect trouble.

He's the most laid back of my family, but it doesn't mean he hasn't been in scraps over the years. In fact, he's been in more than I count, but he's not a bad person, and he doesn't hit someone unless they start it. It's something our parents drummed into us. They didn't raise us to be bullies.

But for an old lady living on her own, I'm surprised she didn't go for someone different.

However, I do know my brother will take care of her if she needs it, so in part, I'm glad he'll be there. And although I don't know the lady, it's nice to know she won't be getting ripped off again. Aiden wouldn't do that to anyone.

I just hope she knows what she's getting herself into, because Aiden can be a little boisterous; blaring his music until early hours of the morning and coming home drunk. From what he explained about the layout, the garage is attached to the main house. Hopefully, her walls are thick, and she won't hear the stuff he gets up to.

As I pull into the road, I glance at each number, marvelling over the size of some of the houses. Some have even got gates at the end of their drives, like they are royalty or something.

I could never picture myself living in something so extreme. I think you have to be born into that kind of life to fit into it. You have to have a certain look. Hell, if I wore something glamourous, I'd feel like a drag queen, so living in a house this size would make me feel like a squatter.

Noticing the house number of Aiden's soon to be new home, I pull into the curved driveway, noticing it's not as nice as the others on the street. In fact, even their neighbour's house looks a little unkept. The garden needs cutting, the weeds removing, and a lick of paint on the door would work wonders.

Maggie's house is just the same, except a few of her windows are cracked and filthy. You can see she hasn't lived there for a while.

I park in front of the garage, surprised at how big it is. When I look up, I see the extension on top, with stairs to the side leading up to a door.

I'm still reeling over how my brother managed to snag this place when the front door opens and an elderly lady steps out. She's wearing a pair of black leggings and a white T-shirt with 'Do not disturb' written in black letters.

She's nothing how I imagined. I was picturing a frail old lady who needed taking care of, but from the looks of it, this woman is as healthy as a horse and fit as a fiddle.

I get out of the car as she's removing her yellow dish-washing gloves. I wave hello and give her a smile before grabbing my bag and cat basket out of the back seat.

"Hi, I'm Faith, Aiden's big sister."

She beams at me. "I'm Margaret, but please, call me Maggie. It's lovely to meet you. Your brother said you're the best vet around."

I'm so going to tease Aiden with that when I see him tomorrow.

"I wouldn't say that, but I know what I'm doing. It's nice of you to let Aiden come live here."

She opens the door and gestures me in before answering, "To be honest with you, I had just about given up hope when he showed up at the door. Even though I can tell he's been in trouble a few times, there was trust and kindness in his eyes. Not an ounce of hate in that boy. It didn't hurt that he looks like he can carry his own, and I need that around here. Did he tell you what happened?"

I wince. "Yeah. I'm sorry it happened to you."

She nods. "This home has been in my family for generations. But when my daughter moved to Cyprus to live with her husband, it felt too empty. I moved over there a year later, so I've been gone for four years. It's bad because the man I hired to housekeep never put the alarm back in. Most of my belongings were in storage anyway, but what was left here has been taken or trashed."

"And you've been staying here?" I ask, completely shocked.

"I was staying in a hotel until a month ago. I arranged for a plumber and electrician to be here and fix everything while I was there, then worked on getting the bedroom done up. After that, I've been slowly trying to clean the place up. There's a lot of work and painting to be done. After painting my bedroom, I knew I'd never be able to do it alone. Your brother should be here soon to start fixing up the guest house. It's not as bad as the main house but it still needs cleaning. He told me he'd bring along some family to help out."

I give her a warm smile. "I'm sure he did. He didn't like the fact someone did this to you. Plus, he's moving out of our parents' home, he'd do anything."

She laughs at that. "Follow me upstairs. They are good cats, not once hissed or scratched. After spending some time with them, I think I might keep them all. It will be nice to have the company."

Now I love this lady a little bit more. "It would be great if you did. Homing animals is harder than people realise."

She gives me a cheeky grin. "I just don't want to pull them away from their mama."

Ah, so flipping adorable.

For the first time since arriving, I take my eyes away from the older lady to look around what once was a lavish home, and gulp back a gasp.

The walls are covered in graffiti, the wallpaper peeling away, and stains cover what used to be cream carpet.

"They really did a number on your home. I'm so sorry this happened to you," I tell Maggie when we reach the top of the stairs.

She gives me a small smile, her eyes filled with sadness. "I'm just glad anything of value or meaningful to me was either brought with me or kept in a storage compartment not far from here. It was my sister who suggested it, since I didn't want anyone living here. I'm glad I listened."

"Me too."

Her smile brightens as she heads down the hallway, coming to the boiler. The door is no longer intact, so the kittens and mother are the first things I see.

The mother looks up at me warily, moving to sit further on her babies so I can't see them. I let out a tiny chuckle and bend down to the dirty floor, not caring about my jeans.

"Hello, I'm Faith. I'm here to check you and your babies over," I tell her gently, reaching out so she can stiff my hand. She sniffs, curious as to who I am, before flopping her head back down. She moves a little, so I can see the three tiny kittens, enough for me to tell they are far too young to be separated.

I gaze up at Maggie who is smiling down at them. Yep, she's totally keeping them. I see this all the time in my line of work.

"I can tell you they are too young to be moved, Maggie. If I were to guess, I'd say they were only three weeks old, if that. I'm not going to mess with them as the mother seems protective, which is normal. They seem to be healthy and feeding right."

"Is there anything I can do or should be doing? The mother seems so skinny."

"It's because of the birth and feeding her young. If you can get some kitten milk, not cat milk, it will help her enormously. It has vitamins in that will help Mummy." My gaze turns to the right to find a litter tray and food. She already has the basics covered. "Add some wet food to her biscuits."

I finish checking Mummy's gums and pupils before getting up.

"They're okay then?"

I smile at her worry. "Yes, Mummy is doing beautifully. If she were having trouble feeding, she wouldn't be letting them suckle. Letting them whilst she was dry would only cause her pain and discomfort."

"Thank you so much for coming out of your way to check on them. Your brother seemed to think they were ready to be rehomed."

I scoff, looking down at the beautiful sight. I'm about to answer when the door opens downstairs.

"Maggie, I'm here. I've brought some people for you to meet," Aiden shouts.

"We're up here," she yells down, turning back to me.

I bend down when Mummy moves to let the kittens have better access, and quickly look them over, making sure to keep a safe distance.

Loud footsteps stomp up the stairs as I stand back up, and then Aiden, my uncle Max, Mark and Liam are walking towards us.

"Hey." I wave at my uncle.

"Maggie, this is my uncle Max, my brother Mark and cousin Liam. My sister and other cousins are here too. The girls are in the room above the garage getting a start on the cleaning whilst we get rid of the carpet and other stuff. We've brought two skips."

Maggie looks startled and close to crying. I rub her shoulder, hoping she's okay with us all being in her home.

"Oh, Aiden, you are such a good boy."

"You won't be saying that after spending more than an hour in his presence. I'm Max, the better uncle." Max winks as he holds his hand out to Maggie.

She gasps, one hand going to her chest and one to shake his hand. "My, are you all good-looking?"

I laugh at her abruptness. She's my kind of people.

"No, just me," Max laughs. "Um, what the hell is that?"

He steps back, looking over to Mummy and her kittens, making me laugh. "What's the matter, uncle Max? Afraid your allergies will play up?"

"Oh, my, I'm sorry. I didn't know anyone would be allergic," Maggie gasps.

I roll my eyes. "Don't worry, Maggie, my uncle is a big fat fibber."

Max holds his hands up. "Look, you don't understand."

"Understand? What, that you've been lying to me for years? You could have taken in stray animals, Max."

"I have nightmares!" he yells, throwing his hands up in the air. "That cat, that animal—it was, it was… It was the devil," he whispers, turning pale. I'd laugh at his expression, but he'd probably throttle me.

"It was a cat, Max."

He shakes his head in denial. "No, it wasn't. That thing was possessed. I tried every day of its life for him to like me. He'd act all sweet and innocent when the girls were around, even approachable. But I learnt my lesson after the first time. He bit me." He points to his chest hard, and I bite back a laugh.

"It still doesn't give you the right to lie to me."

He looks down at his hands, most likely picturing scratches from a cat in the past. "My college teachers thought I was self-harming. I'd walk into college each day and have fresh cuts on my wrists. When I told her, it was my girlfriend's cat, she didn't believe me. She even referred me to the college councillor."

"Oh, God," I groan. He is unbelievable. He's making the cat sound like a psychotic killer. I've seen pictures of him; he's adorable.

"I'm not lying. One night—god… One night, I was asleep and felt something crawling up my body. At first, I thought your aunt Lake was just copping a feel, but then I noticed his paws. I screamed, ready for his attack, and tried to block him. He slit my bloody throat. I'm surprised I don't have scars."

"Dad, you're being dramatic again. Mum said you scared him and he reacted. He was only after a fuss." Hayden walks to join our group, rolling her eyes at her dad before turning to Maggie. "Hi, I'm Hayden. Pleased to meet you."

"Maggie." Maggie's voice is still stunned, and she's looking at my uncle in horror. She's probably regretting letting Aiden move in now she knows how crazy our family is.

I don't blame her.

"Ignore his dramatics. You have to get used to the men in our family, otherwise they'll drive you insane."

"No, the girls are the nutty ones," Liam grunts, eyeing his sister.

She narrows her eyes at Liam before turning to her dad. "Why did you have to give me a brother?"

"Why did you have to give me a sister?" Liam bites back.

"Because I didn't have any condoms?" Max answers.

Maggie giggles at that, whereas I bite back a groan of embarrassment. "Since there are so many of you here, I'll pop out and go and get everyone some breakfast sandwiches."

"You don't need to do that," Hayden and I say.

"Sounds awesome, we're starved," comes from the boys.

"So, go yourself," Hayden tells him.

"Well then, I'll go do that. I need to pick up some more cleaning supplies anyway. I ran out last night."

"Last night?" Aiden asks.

"I tried to finish cleaning the bathroom but I'm afraid it will all need replacing. I couldn't get the graffiti off it. Plus, I have to admit, I'm apprehensive about using it when strangers have done gods know what in here."

"Tell you what, my nephew owns a construction business and my brother fixes houses up. I bet, between the two of them, we can get you a great deal on a new bathroom set. In fact, I'm pretty sure they had someone over order on bathroom items. Want me to call him?"

Her eyes light up as her shoulders sag. "Would you mind?"

"Not at all. They can help is install them too. They're good at that stuff."

As I eye Maggie, I notice she looks a little pink in the cheeks and hesitant about something, so I speak up before Max pushes himself further into everything.

"Are you sure that's okay with you?"

She nods, but bites her lip. "Yes, but, um, are you sure they won't mind? It's going to cost a fortune to replace everything."

Ah, seeing where this is going, my uncle steps forwards. "What happened to you, Maggie, was unfair and wrong. You have—well, had—a beautiful home. We would be helping you even if you weren't taking this one off our hands." He ruffles Aiden's hair like a little kid, grinning. "And as for cost, don't worry about it. My brother is good at getting good prices and he'll probably give you the bathroom stuff for free, just to get rid of it. They won't mind, I swear."

Her eyes water as she looks at the group of us. "I knew as soon as I met you you'd be good to have here. Thank you, all of you, from the bottom of my heart."

"Ah, don't go making me cry." Max sighs dramatically, wiping under his eye.

She giggles. "Let's get to business then."

"Sounds like a plan."

"I'm going to pop to the surgery and grab a house bed for the cats. With all the noise and people, it might startle the mum. Do you have a door you can pop on it until everyone has gone?"

Maggie seems to think about it for a moment. "If we can clear the room at the end today, we can put their bed in the walk-in wardrobe. It's bigger than where they are and still dark. Plus, we could shut the door to the room after so they won't be sleeping on top of the litter tray."

She really was listening when I spoke to her. I beam at her for thinking of something fantastic. "Okay, that's sounds awesome." I turn to my brother. "Can you clear that room first and be quiet walking past them?"

"Yeah, sure."

"And stay away from them, uncle Max."

He gives me a 'are you kidding' look. "I'm not going anywhere near them. If there's anything I've learned from mothers, it's that you never mess with their young. Trust me, your aunt Lake just about had my balls when I tried to take the kids to give her a rest."

Laughing, I shake my head and start down the stairs, Maggie on my heels. "Would you like me to take you on your errands?" I ask her.

"I'm sure you have other things you'd like to be doing."

"Not until tonight."

Her eyes sparkle with interest. "And what happens tonight, Faith?"

This time, it's my turn to beam as I fill her in on everything that is Beau.

SIXTEEN

BUTTERFLIES SWIRL IN MY STOMACH AS I wait for Beau to pick me up. I'd decided to dress in black, metallic leggings, which look like they've been painted to my skin, paired with a black, long-sleeved top that has a half-open back. My red blazer with gold buckles completes the outfit. It matches my red stilettos with gold beads around the ankle strap.

I've left my hair down for once, letting the natural wave give it volume and character. I look hot, even if I do say so myself.

My makeup, as always, has been left simple. It's something I'll never get used to. I hate the feel of it on my face. A little concealer, blush and lipstick, and I'm ready.

He texted me a little while ago to say he was going to shower and change round his, then meet me at mine.

I'm not going to lie, I've been a nervous wreck all day. I want tonight to be special. Life is too short to sit around and wait for things to happen, and I've waited long enough. I want Beau, more than I've ever wanted anything in my life.

"Do you think this will seduce him?" I ask Buster and Roxy, doing a twirl. Sat side by side, they both bark and stare up at me. "Yeah, I hope so too."

I'm not nervous about the act itself; my heart is made up on the matter. Speaking with Maggie about Beau today just made me realise we were waiting for nothing. I already know how I feel, and I'm ready. No more waiting around.

But the thought of rejection and *him* not being ready plagues my mind. I want this with him, badly. He drives me wild with every touch, every kiss and caress. He lights something inside me that burns brighter every time we're together.

I'm also worried I won't be good enough for him. If he doesn't enjoy it and then decides to break up with me, I'll be devastated. More than that, I'll be broken-hearted.

I nearly jump out of my skin when there's a knock on the door.

"Oh, my God, he's here," I whisper yell, looking around the room frantically. My gaze continues to dart around until another knock raps at the door, and I wonder what the hell I'm searching for.

I shake my head with a nervous laugh and head towards the door. I practically skipping I'm that giddy.

I greet Beau with a bright smile. "Hey."

In a pair of dark jeans, and blue shirt, Beau looks picture perfect. His tattoos creep out his short sleeves, giving him a badass vibe. He looks hot. So hot, in fact, I'm wondering if we should forgo dinner and go straight to dessert.

"Faith," Beau says, amusement in his voice.

I shake out of my ogling, and my gaze reaches his eyes. "Sorry, did you say something?"

He laughs, pulling me against him. "You look sexy as hell."

My cheeks heat as I wrap my arms around his neck. "Thank you, you don't look so bad yourself."

His eyes twinkle as his head descends. "Yeah?"

A giggle escapes as I move in closer. "Definitely."

His lips meet mine softly. I'm getting lost in the kiss when he pulls away, smiling at me. "I have a surprise for you."

"What's the surprise?"

He raises his eyebrow. "Um, you do know the meaning of a surprise, right?"

I giggle, leaning my head back. "Of course, I do. Am I wearing the appropriate clothes?"

His gaze runs down my body, slowly, appraisingly, making me tingle all over. "Oh, yeah."

I smack his chest with a laugh when he grabs my arse. "Be serious. I thought we were going for dinner and a movie."

He throws his hands up in front of him, still giving me that sexy as hell grin. "Okay, okay. You need to pack an overnight bag and grab a coat."

Now my interest is more than piqued, it's intrigued. With a giddy squeal, I wrap my arms around his neck and peck him on the lips.

"Wait, what about the dogs? I can't leave them here alone."

"Already sorted. Aiden is coming over to watch them."

"You are the best."

I run to my bedroom, my smile hurting my cheeks. I never expected a night away, but with what I have planned, the timing couldn't be more perfect.

HALF AN HOUR later we're driving uphill, on a spiralling road. We're near the beach; I can smell the salt in the air. It's beautiful, refreshing.

"We're staying here?" I ask in awe when we pull up to a hotel.

It's huge, the white building standing out in the dark of night. People are milling around, laughing and enjoying themselves.

I turn back to Beau in astonishment. "You did this, for me?"

He tucks my hair behind my ear, gazing into my eyes. "I'd do anything for you. You deserve to be spoilt, to be cherished, Faith. I feel like a dick for not taking you out sooner."

"We've gone on dates before," I remind him, taking his hand in mine.

He shakes his head at me. "No, not like this. Even though I knew you were special, we were just friends. This is different. Tonight, I want to show you how much you mean to me."

"As much as I love that you've done this, you didn't need to do any of it to show me how much you care. I feel it and see it every time we're together, Beau. You show me every time you run me a bath, watch One Tree Hill with me, and cook me dinner. I see it in the way you look at me."

"And how do I look at you?" he asks, his voice hoarse.

I lean forwards, my lips a breath away from his. "Like you can't breathe without me. Like I'm the only girl in the world."

"That, Faith Carter, is because you are the only girl in the world for me. You are the air I breathe, the reason I feel alive each morning."

I love you is on the tip of my tongue once again, but before the words can reach my lips, Beau's door is opening.

"Sir, can we get your bags?"

Beau startles away from me, eyeing the porter with confusion. "Um, yeah." He turns the engine off, steps out of the car and hands the keys to the porter. A steward walks over, and they exchange a few words before he heads back into the building.

Beau walks around to my door and opens it, before taking my hand. "Come, this is only the first surprise."

I grin, my thoughts of killing the porter for ruining our moment gone, and take his hand. "Well, who am I to hold us up."

He laughs, pulling me into his arms as soon as I step out of the car. "God, you're amazing."

I tilt my head to the side. "I know, right?"

He chuckles once more, before leaning down and kissing me, stealing my breath away with the intensity of it. The feel of his fingers running through my hair and his body pressed against mine is all I can take.

I want him.

Now.

"Sir, we have your table ready for you."

And I'm thinking of murdering the porter again.

I try not to pout, I do, but when Beau releases me from his kiss, it's all I can do to stop myself from stomping my feet and demanding Beau take me right here, right now.

The porter takes our bags around the side of the building, following a stoned path, while the steward leads us down another leading to the shore.

The breeze from the sea blows my hair around my face, and I soak in the salt air. Being near the sea is the best feeling ever. It makes you feel refreshed, free.

When we reach the bottom, tables, under parasol heaters, line the beach. I gasp at the beauty. The flames of candles flicker on each table, and outside lights brighten the surrounding area. Couples, families and friends are busy eating, but the atmosphere is still romantic. The most romantic sight I've ever seen.

"Beau." I turn to him and take his hands in mine. I fight the urge to cry, even though I so desperately want to. This is incredible. "This is perfect. I can't believe you planned all this."

He grins as he pulls me against him and kisses me quickly. "Like I said, I'd do anything for you, baby."

My cheeks feel like they're going to crack I'm smiling that wide. "I love it. Thank you so much for doing all of this."

He gives me his usual 'I think you're adorable' look, causing me to melt against him. "Let's go eat. According to Travel Rate, this place cooks the best steak ever."

"I love steak." He pulls me down the platform built on the sand, to our table, where he pulls out a chair for me.

My knees buckle at the gesture, never having had another person do this for me. Ever.

I sit down, giving him a small smile as I hold myself back from clapping and giggling in my seat. I'm so overwhelmed by everything, including Beau. He's so darn perfect. Well, not completely perfect; he does snore. I can look past that though.

"Can I get you some drinks?"

Beau looks to me, his eyes heated as he gazes at me across the candlelit table. "Red wine?"

I sag into my seat. "Sounds perfect."

"Your best red wine, please," Beau tells the waiter, and he walks off to get our drinks.

"How did you find this place?"

He cheeks flush and I almost laugh. "I called my mum. I explained I didn't feel like a meal and a movie was enough. She told me about a few places my dad had taken her to. When I looked up this one, it seemed perfect. I remembered you telling me about your love for the beach."

Aww, he's so cute when he's embarrassed.

"Beau, this is the nicest thing anyone has ever done for me, but you need to know, movies and takeout? Best part of our time together. I'd have loved to do anything with you. But I'm glad you changed our plans. This place… I'll never forget our time here," I tell him, with more meaning than he knows. He has no idea what I have planned for later, or about the sexy lingerie I've packed. I couldn't wear it with this outfit, so I had planned to change into it when we got home. But now we are staying here… I'm glad I bought it to begin with.

I already knew tonight would be perfect, no matter where we were or what we did. Although, being here with him will not only make this night one I'll never forget, but a dream come true.

When I'd given up on finding Prince Charming, I really did stop searching. I'd had no hope of finding the love I'd read about in fairy tales, or the love my parents share. But the minute I met Beau, hope had blossomed. Now, it's spread through me and I'm living the dream.

"I'm glad. And I love our time together too. I have another surprise for you… Well, you and your family."

"You do?" I'm stunned. Him bringing me here was surprise enough. If he does anything else, I might have an emotional breakdown. He makes me so happy.

He grins. "I do. Me and my new partner helped a guy's daughter with something. He offered us VIP tickets to Party in the Park for you and your family this Saturday. There's enough tickets for all of you, I made sure."

"Oh, my God, are you serious?" I squeal. We'd tried to get Hayden tickets for her birthday, but they had sold out.

Even Liam and Landon would love this. I can't wait to tell them.

"Yes." He laughs at my antics.

"This is amazing. I can't wait to tell the others. They are going to love this."

He laughs. "I did hear Hayden moaning to your sister about not being able to get tickets. I think a boy she likes was going or something."

I laugh. "Yeah, someone she met at work. We can tell her tomorrow at the dinner. Thank you, Beau, so much."

"It's my pleasure. We're not meant to take anything from people we see, but I couldn't say no."

"Beau, you are the most thoughtful person I've ever met. They're all going to love this. Seriously."

"Don't go spreading that around, you'll ruin my reputation."

I laugh and grab his hand across the table. "I promise, but I can't promise not to gush to my mum and sister about all of this. Really, thank you."

"You keep saying that, but you don't need to say thank you."

The waiter walks over with our wine in a cooler and pours us both a glass. "Are you ready to order?"

Shit, we haven't even looked at the menu.

"You ready?" Beau asks me. "I'm thinking of the steak."

I lick my lips, it does sound good. I put my menu down and turn to the waiter. "We'll have two steaks."

The waiter smiles. "Good choice. We won't be long with your food."

"Thank you," Beau and I say in unison.

When he's gone, I watch as a steak is brought to the next table over, then turn to Beau. "My mouth is watering now."

He looks over to the food and chuckles. "Yeah. My belly is protesting that I feed it."

I giggle. "How was your day?"

"Long. I didn't think I'd get off in time, but Collings knew about my plans and offered to do the paperwork."

"Remind me to send him some chocolate."

"Don't, his wife is on his back to eat healthier," he chuckles.

"I bet he's hating that."

He nods. "Sneaks his Snickers' and Mars Bar's into his locker at work." I laugh at his serious expression. "What about you, how was Maggie's?"

"Surprisingly, really good. I see her becoming a part of our family. She's a really lovely woman. Her house needs a lot of work, but with Aiden rounding up my family, it won't be long till it's good as new."

"And the kittens?"

"Cute." My face lights up. "And guess what?"

"What?"

"She's going to keep them."

"That's great. I was going to call Aiden earlier, but didn't have time. I'm sure Collings will do it."

"What do you mean?" I ask. I didn't even know they were calling buddies. Colour me shocked.

"Yeah, I didn't expect your brother to call me either," he tells me, reading my thoughts. "But he wanted something done about this guy who ripped Maggie off. After he convinced her to make a statement, we looked into it. We found the guy. He'll be going before court in a month or so."

"That is brilliant. I'm glad she decided to do something. She said earlier she was unsure whether making a statement was worth it or not. She'll be thrilled you found him."

"Yeah, me too. I was worried your brother was going to take things into his own hands. He said he had Liam on it. But I didn't know Liam was into computers."

I laugh at hearing Liam's name. Not my cousin, but my uncles' friend from school. He's amazing with a computer and made a name for himself designing video games.

"He's not on about my cousin Liam. Liam is my uncles' friend from school. They all go to him when they want something done on the computer. He's a genius."

Understanding spreads across his face. "Ah, now it makes sense. He talked him up, but the Liam I met, although he can give off one serious glare, didn't seem the type to sit still long enough to check his Facebook."

Laughing, I nod in agreement. "Very true. My aunt Lake would threaten to tie him to a chair if he didn't do his homework when he was younger. Used to drive her up the wall when he wouldn't sit still."

I take a sip of my wine, the taste sweet, like nothing I've ever drank.

"Good?" Beau asks.

"Impeccable," I answer honestly, taking another sip.

"Let's make a toast," he says suddenly, holding his glass up.

I follow. "What are we toasting to?"

"How about to us? To finding us?"

I melt at his words. He couldn't have said anything better. "To us," I say, clinking my glass with his. My gaze burns into his, my heart falling harder and harder for the man in front of me.

SEVENTEEN

INNER WAS FABULOUS, AND THE dessert astounding. We had warm chocolate gateau that melted in our mouths, and the ice-cream tasted divine. I don't think I've ever had anything that good in my mouth before. When I told Beau that, he'd started choking, reaching for his wine.

"Sir, your drinks are waiting on your balcony."

The server passes a key card attached to our room number over to Beau, whispering something near his ear, before clearing our table.

"What was that?" I ask, suspicious.

He just gazes at me. "Want to take a walk along the beach?"

I'm out of my seat before he finishes. "Yeah, I do."

He laughs, taking my hand in his, before walking me back towards the path we entered from. Instead of going up, we walk down, following the spotlights that light up the path. When we reach the beach, I kneel to unstrap my shoes. Beau does the same.

"It's a lovely night," I say, wanting to fill the silence. I'm excited to get back to our room, but what girl would turn down a walk on the beach with their boyfriend.

Not me.

He takes my hand in his and holds his shoes in the other. I do the same, feeling merry as my toes sink into the soft sand.

"It is," he replies, leaning over to kiss my head.

I smile to myself, watching the waves crash against the shore, the noise soothing. Little cottages line the beach, a place I wouldn't mind having as a holiday home. But the cost of living there would probably be high.

"Wonder who lives in them," I muse, pointing to the row of lit up cottages.

"Funny you should mention them, we're staying in number two-zero-one."

I stop walking, pulling on his hand to face me. "What?"

He grins at my expression, or the surprise in my voice—I'm unsure, it could be both. "Yeah. I booked us our own room on the beach."

My feet move towards the houses on their own accord, then back to Beau, my heart beating rapidly with excitement. "Please don't be joking."

He laughs. "I'm not, I swear."

When he points over my shoulder, I turn, my gaze following where his finger is aimed, and gasp when I see our number on a post at the end of a stoned path.

"Beau," I squeal, before dropping my shoes and jumping into his arms. He chuckles, dropping his own shoes as he catches me.

My legs wrap around his waist, my arms gripping the back of his neck. "You, Mr. Beau Johnson, are an amazing man. Thank you, thank you, thank you." I pepper his face with kisses before reaching his lips.

My mouth opens, sliding my tongue against his. I'll never get enough of his kisses. My body buzzes with awareness, my blood surging through my veins. His grip on my arse tightens and I moan into his mouth.

He pulls back, clearing his throat. "That was…"

"Phenomenal, breath-taking, mind-blowing?"

He laughs against my lips. "Yeah."

Slowly, he slides me down his body, my arms still around his neck. "Show me our room."

At my excitement, he presents me with a smile before bending down and grabbing both our shoes.

We walk up the pathway. In front of the window is a swing bench, and next to it is a table with a silver bucket on top and a bottle of something inside. Candlelight flickers inside its glass.

Everything looks magical. It's the perfect setting, the perfect night, with the perfect man.

If I wasn't sure before, then I am now. Girls, wait for that perfect moment and nothing, and I mean absolutely nothing, could get more perfect than this, in this very moment.

Once we reach the door, Beau places our shoes on the floor, then takes the key card out of his back pocket. I reach out, stopping him from inserting the key.

"Let's have a drink before we go inside," I tell him, having a plan already in mind.

"All right, baby. Take a seat, I'll open the champagne. They told me it's their best."

"Awesome." I smile, taking a seat. A blanket is folded next to me, so I shake it open and place it over my legs, the chill in the air getting colder.

When he walks over with two full champagne glasses, I take one with a quiet, "Thanks". I'm all kinds of nervous; the good, the terrifying, and anxious kind.

He takes a seat next to me, and I drop the other half of the blanket over his legs.

"I'm glad we came," I tell him, sinking back and watching the waves crash against the shore. A gentle breeze stirs the air and through the gaps in the clouds, I see the stars, shining bright.

"Me too. Oh, before I forget, Saturday, I might be able to finish my shift early. It all depends on what calls we have. Collings said I've been working other cases, which I'm not hired to do at the moment, so he did this for me. I don't mind though. I've really liked working for the department. The guys there are great. Collings even hinted at me getting offered a permanent job after your case is closed."

"Really? I thought you were already working there full time. What will you do if you don't get offered the permanent position?" I ask. Taking a large gulp of champagne, I wait nervously for his answer. It never occurred to me he would leave once my case was solved.

"No, I'm only temporary at the moment. If I don't, I'll go back to being a PI and doing security." He shrugs like it's no big deal, but it is. Would he move back to where he lived before all this started? Would he stay? I need to know.

"Does that mean if you don't get a permanent job, you'll be moving back to where you lived before?"

He turns to face me, raising one knee on the chair beside us. He looks at me lazily, his smile small. "Faith, nothing would make me move back there. My home is here now. With you."

My breath catches in my throat. "You really mean that?"

He runs his fingers down my cheek. "I do."

His lips are soft when he kisses me, licking the seam of my lips. With a gasp, my mouth opens, and he slides his tongue against mine.

Pressing my fingers into his biceps, I melt against him the best I can in the position we're in.

My lips are still tingling when I pull back, clearing my throat.

It's now or never.

"Can I have the key, so I can go freshen up?"

Pulling it back out of his back pocket, he hands it to me. "Go ahead."

"Won't be long." I smile, giving him one more kiss before getting up.

When I get to the door, I realise we don't have our bags. A mild panic attack is brewing as I turn back to face him, trying to keep my voice from trembling.

"Um, where are our bags?"

He turns away from the view to face me. "They put them just inside the door. Want me to come in?"

"No!" I squeak before clearing my throat. "I mean, no, stay out here. We've still got a while before the rain starts."

He looks unsure but nods anyway. "Okay. Just yell if you need me."

With the cast still on my arm, that may be a possibility. Before now he's had to tie a bag around my arm for me to shower or has run me a bath. At the beginning, when the pain had been at its worst, he even did the buttons on my jeans.

I head inside, flicking the big light on. My bag is where he said it would be and I grab it, before heading to the bathroom. I don't linger to look at the king-sized bed or the forty-two-inch TV, otherwise my nerves will get the best of me and I'll back out. I don't want it to be forced. I want it to be meaningful and romantic.

In the bathroom, I quickly splash some cold water over my face. When I look in the mirror, my cheeks are flushed and my eyes dilated. It's what he does to me.

The brush is the first thing I take out. After sitting on the beach, the wind strong, my hair is a tangled mess. Not the sexy look I was hoping for when I'd pictured tonight.

Once it's done, I leave it down, and begin removing my clothes. I fold them and, with shaking hands, take out the pink lace and dot mesh babydoll with matching thong. The top is floral, covering my boobs, but the rest is see-through, leaving nothing to the imagination. I've never worn anything like this before, but I have to admit, it feels great against my skin and I feel sexy.

I have the matching robe, but for effect, I'm going to leave it undone. I want him to want me so much he can't help himself. And this outfit is a sure way to do it.

I hope.

All my prayers are on this working. I hadn't known—and still don't know—how to seduce a man, so I'd Googled, 'How to seduce your boyfriend', and the top hit was sexy lingerie.

With a deep breath, I face the mirror, my eyes bugging out of my head when I take in my appearance. I look… I look like a siren, so different to my normal plain look.

With one last glance—and another deep breath—I open the door.

As I step out, I hear something smash on the floor, followed by a gasp. I look up, surprised to see Beau standing in the doorway.

His mouth is agape, his eyes roaming my body with so much heat behind them. I start to feel unsure, wanting to cover myself, but something deep inside me stops myself from doing it.

"Holy fuck!" he manages to croak out.

The smash I heard is the champagne glass now in shatters on the floor. I notice Beau doesn't make a move to pick it up, but instead walks towards me, his gaze predatory.

My breath leaves me in one great whoosh, and when he stands in front of me, I sway towards him.

With an inhale, I close my eyes, breathing him in. I close my mind off to the world around me and focus solely on him.

When I open them, his mouth descends, his eyes dark, penetrating. His fingers run over my shoulders. The feel of the robe falling down my arms and pooling to the floor is highly erotic.

This is it. It's really happening.

Our lips meet tentatively, his coaxing mine apart with his tongue. Kissing him is like breathing for the first time.

My hands are surprisingly steady as I reach up to wrap them around the back of his neck, and before I know it, his large hands are against my butt, hoisting me up his body. I go, clinging to him for dear life.

I moan into his mouth. "Beau, I want you. I'm ready," I whisper hoarsely.

He groans, his breath a whisper across my lips. "Are you sure?"

Without words, I nod and bring my lips back to his. He walks us backwards towards the bed. He lowers me down like I weigh nothing, managing to stay above me. His hands on my skin are sizzling, and when he pulls back to look down at my body, I squirm, the look in his eyes and across his face turning me on.

Arousal is thick in the air, and with innocent hands, I reach down to pull his top over his head. He lets me, his breathing heavy.

"You're so fucking beautiful it hurts."

His words mean more than he realises. They're true, meaningful.

"Please," I plead, trying to pull him back down to kiss me. I'm going mad inside, wanting to have him lay against me.

His eyes heat and with a half moan, half growl, he reaches for the babydoll and slowly starts to lift it up over my body. I sit up to give him access, the feel of the satin gliding along my sensitive skin pulling a moan from me. I can feel the wetness surge between my legs, my hips already grinding against him for some kind of friction.

With the babydoll removed, his eyes take on a predatory look, his fingers running down my arms, my stomach, stopping at the waistband of my thong.

"You next." The words are barely audible, I'm that turned on.

He falls to the side of me, his eyes never leaving mine. A zipper being undone echoes in the room. I'm breathless, trying to focus on him when all I want to do is look down, explore.

He is gorgeous, so completely gorgeous. It's unfair.

He kicks them to the floor, and my eyes finally look down, my fingers inching forward to run down his chest. I gulp when I notice he's completely naked, his boxers removed. His hard cock stands proudly, slapping against his stomach when I inch further down his muscled, heaving chest.

Arriving at my goal, I bravely reach out and wrap my hand around his silk hood. He growls in the back of his throat, his head falling back onto the pillow.

"Is this okay?" I whisper. My insecurities are coming out, but I needn't have worried. Beau's hand covers mine, gliding my hand up and down his hard shaft.

"More than okay. But, first, let me love you."

My mind goes straight to sex and my breathing picks up. But when he starts to move slowly down my body, trailing kisses, removing my thong, I become confused. Shouldn't he be kissing my lips?

Any thoughts of rejection are removed from my mind when his soft tongue licks through my slit.

I cry out in pleasure, my body arching from the bed. My core tightens and my clit tingles in anticipation.

With fingers running through his hair, I get lost, my orgasm building until I'm screaming out his name. Every time we've done this, he's made me lose my mind within minutes.

"One more," he whispers against my most private parts.

Just when I think it couldn't get any better, his finger enters me, swirling inside me before I feel another finger follow. It feels tight, but good.

And like my body has a mind of its own, I begin to move, my hips grinding against his hand, just as his mouth descends on my clit once more.

There's too much going on for me to concentrate on one thing. It all feels good, better than good.

My body startles with the surprise of another orgasm, my skin slicked with sweat.

Beau rises, his mouth covered in my juices. He wipes them away, his gaze smouldering as he moves up my body.

"One last chance. Are you sure?"

My fingers reach for his cheeks, my gaze searching his as I answer honestly, "I've never been surer of anyone in my life, Beau. It's you I choose. It will always be you."

Pride and love flash across his expression, his mouth opening like he's going to say something. But he shakes his head, his eyes closing.

"Faith Carter, I think I'm falling in love with you."

A startled gasp escapes and tears fill my eyes. "I'm falling too," I tell him, before slamming my lips against his.

His kisses me back with so much passion it sends me dizzy. We're all lips, tongues and hands before he pulls back, gazing at me with so much adoration it steals my breath.

"Condom."

Having planned this, I packed us a few. "In my robe."

He kisses me one more time before jumping from the bed and grabbing my robe, pulling the row of condoms from the pocket. Six to be exact.

"Was you certain about getting lucky?" he chuckles.

My face heats as I smile at him. "Totally."

At my saucy reply, he grins, slipping back on the bed and rising above me. "You make me feel like the luckiest man alive."

I run my fingers through his hair, my smile nervous. "I don't know what

I'm doing, Beau. This is as far as I got with my planning. So, please, make love to me."

"As you wish."

He makes ripping open a condom wrapper with his teeth, sexy as hell. God, just seeing his white teeth biting into the foil wrapper has me clenching my thighs together.

I watch in fascination as he slides it on. My gaze reaches his once it's done and all the excitement I felt before, evaporates. Now it's replaced with a nervous energy, but more, it's filled with want and need.

He looms above me and, instead of his large body feeling intimidating, it's hot, sexy.

I jump a little when he lines up against my entrance, his heavy breathing causing a little anxiety to bubble up. He looks like he's in pain, but when he opens his eyes, gazing down at me, all I see is his desire and arousal.

He pushes inside, his gaze never leaving mine. My fingers dig in to his shoulders, preparing for the pain I know is going to come. I'm not naive enough to think it's not going to. It's a given.

"You okay?" His jaw clenches as he pushes in a little further, stretching my walls. Sweat beads on his forehead and his arms, braced on either side of my head, are shaking.

"More than."

He brings his mouth back down to mine and I try not to squirm, but it's hard when he feels and tastes so good.

He pulls back a little, his expression one of concentration as he moves a little more inside me. I tense slightly, but when his lips move down to my neck, sizzling my skin, I relax. I arch into him, causing him to slide in a little more.

I feel full. It's a foreign feeling, but not uncomfortable enough for me to pull back and stop this. Meeting resistance, his jaw clenches, looking down at me, torn. I know he doesn't want to hurt me; I can see it in his eyes.

"Do it, please. I'll be okay."

His mouth meets mine once again in a long, languid kiss. I feel dizzy, moaning into his mouth. I'm so disoriented that I forget about the sensations down below until a sharp sting has me gasping and letting out a pathetic whimper.

It hurts, but nothing I can't handle.

"I'm sorry," he whispers, his voice hoarse against my ear.

I run my fingers through his light hair as my body and mind get used to the sensation between my legs. I can feel myself tensing around him, causing him to groan.

"Beau, what do we do next?" I ask when he still doesn't move, his breathing hot and heavy against me.

He lifts up, his face tortured. "Just give me a second."

"Did I do something wrong?"

He smiles at me, tilting his head. "Faith, I'm about to blow my load already, and I haven't done that since I was fourteen. And I'm worried I'm going to hurt you."

"Please move." I shift my hips to prove how much I want him. It burns a little as he slides out, but the friction feels amazing.

He moves slowly, allowing me to get used to the fullness of him inside of me. My mouth falls open when he pushes back in. Everything in my lower body tingles and tightens, building up to something beautiful.

He reaches between us, his fingers sliding across my already sensitive clit.

"Oh, God." I close my eyes, leaning my head back as his mouth devours my throat. He moves down, his tongue brushing along my skin.

There's too much going on.

Each thrust is deep, controlled.

Each kiss is tantalizing.

And with each moment, I am falling deeply in love with the man above me.

I cling to him, embracing his shoulders as I shift beneath him, my body demanding I move. I know I made the right judgment when Beau lifts his head from my neck and groans in pleasure.

He looks beautiful, like a god.

His movements become frantic and I whimper against him, my teeth sinking into his shoulders as my nails rake down his back.

I've never felt more loved than I do in this moment.

His fingers leave my clit and pay attention to my boobs. With one light roll of my nipple, and a quick tug, I cry out, the sensations building to become explosive.

My core tightens around him and with a few more thrusts, he's groaning, lips meeting mine in a wet kiss. I kiss him back hungrily, not caring when he collapses against me.

Something inside me breaks. Whether it's from losing my virginity or from who I lost it with—or a mixture of both—I don't know. But I feel powerful, brand-new. And it's all thanks to the man above me.

Our breathing is heavy, laboured. When he pulls away from the kiss, he looks down at me, his eyes filled with so much love it nearly chokes me. Whether he knows it or not, the man is definitely in love. There are no ifs or buts.

Because I know he's reflecting the same look I'm showing him.

It's a look I'll never get tired of.

"That was epic. When can we do it again?" I ask breathlessly. I grin up at him, running my fingers through the front of his hair.

He looks at me in disbelief, before bursting into laughter. He rolls us so I'm lying on top of him, making sure to stay inside me.

I stare down at him, my hair falling like a curtain, blanketing us, and give him my best innocent look.

"Well?"

"You, Faith Carter, are going to be the death of me."

I pretend to consider it before nodding. "It will be a good way to go."

The laughter that rolls free from him has me melting against him. "It most certainly would, but first, how about we get you in the bath, so you won't be sore in the morning?"

With that, he moves and proves himself right. A sting burns between my legs, but with what just happened between us... it was totally worth it.

I move closer until my lips are a breath away. "So, Mr. Johnson, what are you waiting for?"

His grin is blinding. Before I have a chance to move, he's sitting us both up in the bed. I squeal when he lifts me up and walks us to the bathroom.

I give him a look of wonder, of love, because with my heart, my body and soul, I'll fight to keep him and this memory for the rest of my life.

I never want to forget tonight.

Ever.

EIGHTEEN

MY BODY ACHES IN ALL THE RIGHT PLACES as I stretch out in our king-size bed. I'm a little sore between my legs, but it's worth it. Last night was phenomenal.

A grin spreads across my face as I roll to my side, my hand reaching out to run a finger down Beau's chest.

And what a marvellous chest he has.

I trace the 3D roman clock with an angel wing sprouting off on the right side of his peck, near his shoulder blade. It's a beautiful art piece on sexy canvas. The detail in the hands is outstanding.

It's just another tattoo I want to find out the meaning of, but right now, I'm okay with ogling my boyfriend.

His hand wraps around my wrist, startling me. I look up into his deep, penetrating gaze and a sigh escapes me.

How did I get so lucky?

"Morning, boyfriend."

His smile is blinding. He moves his hand to my neck, tracing the bare skin delicately. "Morning, girlfriend."

I lean over, pressing my lips to his. I don't care if I have morning breath, or if he does. Hell, he could have garlic breath and I'd still kiss him.

His hand slides to cup the back of my neck, pulling me closer. I cock one leg over his and grip his shoulders, deepening the kiss.

I hum against his mouth before pulling away a little, my eyes opening to look down at him.

God, he looks so good first thing in the morning. It's criminal.

He kisses the tip of my nose. "What would you like to do today? We have to check out at eleven, but we're still welcome on the grounds."

"Well, there goes my idea of staying in bed all day." I sigh, rolling my eyes dramatically. I'm still smiling though, not really caring what we do.

"Ah, whatever will we do."

I shrug, looking to the clock before back to him. "Well, we could use the three hours we have left in the room and make the most of it." I run my finger down his chest, giving him a coy look.

His eyes darken, and his chest rises and falls heavily. He doesn't stop me from reaching my target, and as we went to bed naked, there's nothing in my way when I wrap my hand around his hard erection.

"Oh, God." He closes his eyes with a moan. When he opens them, he looks pained. "Faith, you're sore."

"I am," I tell him, my voice husky. "But, we don't have to have sex to enjoy ourselves." I pump once more, and I'm startled when he rolls us over so he's laying over me, his hard, impressive body, pressing me into the bed.

"Well, when you put it that way…" His grin is downright devilish.

I open my mouth to ask what he means, but he slowly descends my body, his eyes never leaving mine.

Wetness pools between my legs at his heated expression. He kisses below my belly button, swirling his tongue around the sensitive skin. I break out in goose bumps as a shiver runs up my spine.

He licks lower, his eyes reaching mine once again, before he hits his target.

I cry out at the first flick of his tongue. My fingers claw at the sheets, arching a little when he sucks my clit into his mouth, flicking his tongue across it at the same time.

He knows how much it gets me going, and I can already feel my body tightening. After last night, after coming together, I want that again, but I know the soreness between my legs will just get worse if we have sex.

Then a dirty thought occurs to me. Whenever I'd heard or read about this position, I'd always cringed, wondering what kind of woman would want some hairy arse in her face. With Beau, the thought of him fucking my face is a turn on.

I close my legs and for a moment, Beau tries to pry them apart, probably thinking I'm too sensitive. When I tug at his hair, he looks up, and the face he gives me is adorable. He looks like I just took his favourite candy from him.

"I want to try something different." I begin to feel nervous, but his intrigued expression eases that anxiety a little.

"What did you have in mind, baby?"

The words tumble out of my mouth before I have a chance to think about them any further. Beau looks dumbfounded for a second, before his face breaks out in a wide grin.

"You mean you want to do a 69er?"

My whole body heats. "Um… yeah, that."

"Do you want me on top or do you want to be on top?"

"You!" I blurt out quickly, before covering my face with my hand and groaning. I clench my thighs together, feeling the stickiness between my legs.

Movement above me has my eyes opening, and in front of me, standing proudly, is Beau's erect cock. I moan embarrassingly loud and take him in my hand. He groans, and a bead of pre-cum covers the tip of his cock.

I lick him, tasting the saltiness on my tongue, and hum in appreciation. He waits until I have the tip in my mouth before covering me with his. I moan around his cock, making him twitch in my mouth and growl against my clit. The vibrations cause tingles to spread to my core.

I'd thought sex was great, but this… this is something else.

I take him deeper, swirling my tongue around his tip before licking the vein that pulses from the base to the tip of his dick. His growl shows how much he enjoys it, so I do it again. My head bobs up and down, while I use my hand to pump him into my mouth.

With the feel of his tongue and the taste of him in my mouth, I lose all sense of thought. I can't focus on anything.

When he pulls away, gasping, I cry out with displeasure, arching my hips up, hoping he gets the picture.

"I'm going to come. If you don't want me to——"

The words die on his lips when I take him even deeper, gagging a little before pulling back. His mouth, wet and warm, attacks me once more, and I moan around his cock.

It's all too much. I can hear the wet sounds of him between my legs, feel the way his body tenses every time I take him deeper.

It's all too much.

I feel it the minute he's ready to explode, because I'm about to do the same. Cum flows into my mouth, but before he can spill the entire lot, I release him, screaming through an intense orgasm. I keep pumping him all over my chest, my body twitching from the aftershocks.

"Holy fuck," he gasps, his head resting on my thigh as he catches his breath.

I flop back down on the bed, my body sated and well rested. No more do I feel the aches I had before, and even between my legs, the sting has eased.

It feels good.

He gets up from the bed, moving to come lay next to me. He sees the mess he made on my chest and chuckles, his eyes dark.

"Is it wrong that seeing my cum all over your tits is making me hard again?"

My eyes widen and gaze down at his manhood, which is rising once again. He's still chuckling at my expression.

He leans over and kisses me, licking the roof of my mouth. "We really should take a shower."

"Together?" My eyes sparkle with possible ideas of stuff we could do in the shower.

"Wouldn't want it any other way."

As he gets off the bed, his phone rings from the bedside table. He grimaces when he hears it, giving me an apologetic look.

"It's Collings, I need to answer it."

"It's fine. Go ahead. I'm enjoying the view." I grin when he smirks at me. I cover myself up with the blanket then lean back and watch as he answers his phone.

"Hello? Yeah. When did that happen? Why didn't you call me?" He listens, his eyes briefly coming to me before looking away. "I get that, but I still would have liked to have been informed. I'll be there as soon as I can. Okay. Yeah. See you soon."

He ends the call and drops his head back, closing his eyes.

"Are you okay?" I ask, pulling the blanket tighter around me.

He eyes land on me and he sighs miserably. "No. Last night they arrested Devon, Noah's friend, and brought him in for questioning. They want me to be there as soon as possible to sit in on it."

I sit up straighter, a little confused on what he has to do with it. I thought they'd cleared him. "Why have they arrested him?"

He scrubs a hand down his face. "I had someone do some digging. Something didn't sit right with him. He works from home, doing some online bullshit for other people. They clearly have something if they arrested him, but Collings didn't say why over the phone. My guess is they found something in his internet history."

"You think he's more than someone who let Noah sleep on the couch as a favour to his friend?" I ask, getting up from the bed, the sheet still wrapped around me.

"Definitely. I told you he seemed dodgy. When I went round his house, he was jumpy, nervous, and kept standing in the doorway, blocking us. We had to invite ourselves in."

"Let's get going then. If you can get him to talk then we could find Noah before he does something else."

He pulls me into his arms, rubbing his palms up and down my back. "It will be fine."

I pull back a little to meet his gaze. "I know, because I've got you."

His eyes blaze as leans down to kiss me, making me forget about the past ten minutes and his phone call.

The sheet drops to the floor and pools around my feet as he lifts me up. I smile against his mouth, gripping the back of his neck.

"The things you say to me," he growls against me, causing a shiver to run down my spine.

Lightening the mood, I kiss the corner of his mouth, before reaching the other. "But what about the things I can *do* to you?"

His grip on my arse tightens and I squeal. "Shower, now!"

He moves towards the bathroom, his expression filled with concentration. I run a finger through the crease between his eyebrows. His lips twitch as he gazes at me.

"Are you going to teach me shower sex?"

He nearly drops me for a moment, before a gleam passes through his eyes. He walks us into the shower, not caring that the water is cold when he turns it on.

I squeal, my back arching away from the cold, but it soon turns into a moan when his mouth closes around my nipple.

Yep, I could definitely get used to this.

After picking me up, Beau finally asked me about tonight's arrangement. He knew we were going out for a meal with my family, but not to what extent.

His face when I told him who would be there was priceless.

"Is every family member going to be here?" Beau asks as he pulls into a free parking space.

I struggle not to laugh at his expression. I forgot to tell him all twenty-nine of us are attending, thirty including Beau. In my defence, I'm still in the after-glow stage of sex. I haven't been able to stop smiling all day, I'm just that darn happy.

I haven't asked him about Devon and what happened today. I didn't want it to ruin our day or taint what we'd shared.

And what we'd shared was mind-blowing.

"Um, yeah, pretty much. We do it every birthday."

He raises his eyebrow at me as he shuts off the car. "What about Christmas?"

I tilt my head to the side, making him sweat. I know from his parents that it's his favourite time of year. I can only imagine what he's thinking… How to get out of being with thirty crazy people, I imagine.

"No. We stick to our houses for Christmas—"

"Thank God," he breathes, his head falling back on the headrest.

"But we get together on the evening to have drinks. Usually here at the restaurant or between my parents and great-grandparents' home."

My smile falls when I realise this will be the first Christmas without them. In a few months we will have to face the reality of our great-grandparents not being there. But as a family, we will get through it. We always do.

I just wish missing them didn't hurt so much. They were the best, the life of the party, and without them, there will always be a hole in our family.

"How are they going to fit thirty of us around a table?" He noticeably swallows, choosing to ignore my last comment. I know he's still trying to come to terms with the fact my family is so large. He'll get used to it, everyone does. Kind of. I don't have the heart to tell him most places only let a certain number of us inside at once, or that most of the boys are banned from a lot of places, which is why we have to go out of town to do stuff.

"We have a large room downstairs. It's held for larger parties."

"And it fits thirty people?"

I shrug. "It used to be a strip club, according to my mum."

His mouth falls open. "Your family owned a strip club?"

"They did. My dad and uncle Mason owned it but they all had shares. When my dad's crazy mum burnt down the club on Mason and Denny's wedding day, they revamped the whole place and decided to close the strip club permanently. They had kids to think about and wanted to be able to bring us to work if they had to."

"Their mum burnt it down?"

I check my lip-gloss in the mirror, shrugging. "Yeah, I got hurt badly, trapped under rubble or something. I don't really remember."

"You were hurt?" he asks, his voice a higher pitch.

I glance over at him and notice he's deathly pale. I place my hand on his knee, giving him a reassuring squeeze.

"It's fine. It's not as bad as some of the stuff my parents went through. My auntie Denny was kidnapped and trapped with a dead girl."

I should mention he looks a little green at this point, but his hand reaches out to mine and squeezes it. "Faith, I'm going to ask you this once, and once only: are your family safe?"

I try not to giggle. "Safe to me and everyone in our family." My lips twitch when I notice his shoulders sag with relief. "But I can't guarantee everyone else's safety. We tend to get overly protective."

"And you couldn't have told me this before you released me to a room with twenty-eight members of your family?"

I giggle, turning to face him. "Are you worried?"

"Nope, not at all. I deal with crazy every day. I can deal with a few family members."

I tap his leg again, leaning over to kiss him lightly on the corner of his mouth. "You'll be fine. Everyone who has met you, likes you. Those who haven't will learn to, whether they like it or not."

His breathing turns shallow. "We could just go back home and finish One Tree Hill, tell them you got sick."

I laugh, my forehead falling against the side of his. "They'd just come and get me. Liam had the flu one year and they dragged him out of bed to attend. There's no getting out of this."

He chuckles, tilting his head to face me. "Okay, I'll do this—for you. I know how much your family means to you. Plus, there's nothing they can do that would run me away, right?"

I choose not to answer that, because if there's one thing my family have perfected, it's running off other males.

"Just shout beach if things get too much."

He cups my cheek, leaning forward to kiss me, just as a knock on the window startles us apart. We both turn to the driver's side to find Max glaring at us.

"Personal space, buddy, personal space."

"Go away!" I yell.

I watch as he turns around, talking to someone I can't see. He gestures frantically with his arms and I snort.

"Kiss me," I whisper, moving closer to Beau.

He grins, reaching out for me. "Son of a bitch," Max yells.

We both groan and look out the window to find my aunt Lake holding him back. He glares over her shoulder, his chest puffed out.

"I know how to kill with my little finger," he yells.

I groan, my head dropping to Beau's shoulder. "Let's go before he starts embarrassing himself or makes you pass out by throwing stupid moves that aren't really karate. Trust me, the moves are enough to send anyone dizzy."

He laughs and kisses my forehead, before opening his door, eyeing my uncle. "You do know I'm a police officer and you just threatened me, right?"

Max splutters, glaring at Beau as I make my way around the car, not bothering to wait for Beau to open my door for me like he always does. "I know a thousand places to hide your body where no one will find you."

"Max!" Lake shouts, smacking his chest. "You can't talk to him like that."

He looks down at her, his face softening. "But, babe, he was in her personal space."

"You won't be getting in mine ever again if you don't start behaving."

He gasps in outrage. "You wouldn't!"

"I would. Now come on, we're late."

She pulls him by the arm towards the back entrance of the restaurant that leads to the hallway and stairs. Family are only allowed to use this entrance as it leads to both parts of the building. Staff have to enter through the side door. He glances over his shoulder, his eyes narrowing when they land on Beau's hand in mine. When he looks up, he points to his eyes before jabbing a finger at Beau and mouthing, 'I'm watching you'.

"I think he likes me," Beau whispers against my ear.

I shiver, watching as Max and Lake enter the building. Once the door starts closing, I stop short and turn, before pulling Beau's head down to meet mine and kissing him.

He growls deep in his throat, pulling me hard against his body and deepening the kiss.

"Dude! That's my fucking sister. Personal space, man, personal space."

We pull apart, breathing heavily as we both turn to glare at Aiden who is walking over to us. We haven't even entered the building and already they're showing their crazy.

I wouldn't be surprised to find out they've seated us at opposite ends of the table. I really wouldn't.

I take in a deep breath as my brother walks past us, glancing up at Beau. "I'm truly sorry."

He chuckles, kissing my forehead. "Come on, it can't get any worse."

I slap his chest and walk towards the door. "You, boyfriend, will be eating those words later."

NINETEEN

W ALKING IN HAND IN HAND, BEAU and I make our way to my parents, who are talking to my uncle Malik and aunt Harlow. If I don't greet them first, Dad will think I've got something to hide or that something is wrong with Beau.

Their logic doesn't make sense to anyone but themselves.

"Hey, guys."

Dad eyes Beau, scowling. I know he likes him—okay, he deals with him for my sake, but that's just because I'm his daughter. Secretly, I know he's happy Beau is watching over me.

If only he knew how close, I muse.

Dad kisses my cheek, giving me a brief hug. "Squirt." His expression changes, his eyes hardening a little when he faces Beau. "Beau."

"Maverick!"

Mum, being mum, steps forward, pulling me in for a hug before kissing my cheek. "Hey, Mum."

"Hey, baby," she greets, then frowns, looking at me weirdly. I try not to squirm under her appraisal, but it's hard not to when her eyes widen, like she knows I'm no longer a virgin.

Thankfully, she snaps out it and addresses Beau, pulling him for her motherly hug. "It's good to see you again, Beau."

"You too, Mrs. Carter."

Dad scoffs, but Mum and Harlow sigh, smiling sweetly at my boyfriend. It only pisses my dad and uncle off as they pull their significant others into their chests.

"Call me, Teagan, please."

Beau smiles as I excuse us. "I'm going to introduce Beau to everyone."

Aunt Harlow looks around before leaning in closer. "I wouldn't go near Jacob for a while. He's still in a mood over Myles taking the explosive candles away from him."

"Where the hell did he get those?" I shouldn't be shocked, but I am. The damn kid is only sixteen and has gotten himself into more trouble than all other family members combined. He doesn't even do half the shit intentionally. Just in the wrong place at the wrong time.

"They weren't explosives," Malik mutters, shaking his head at his wife.

"Enough to make the cake we made the triplets explode, according to his explanation," Mum argues.

"And you did get rid of them, right?" I ask, making sure to note that we don't sit anywhere near one of the triplets. Knowing our luck, he had a back-up stash hidden somewhere.

"Yeah, even his hidden stash." Dad chuckles nervously, probably wondering if Jacob had planned for that to be found too, as he looks around the room for his brother. "I'm just going to have a quick word with Myles. Be right back."

I nod before turning my attention back to the group. "We'll be back."

"Take your time," Mum tells me, giving me a creepy smile as she watches me. I squeeze Beau's hand tighter and pull him away.

"Um, Faith, your cousin really doesn't have explosives, does he?"

Glancing up, I notice his face is pale as he eyes the room with a different look. I also notice him check out the exits before nodding his head.

"Beau, he can't get real explosives. It's probably something he cooked up in science class. Nothing harmful."

"Cooked up?" he squeaks, as he nods his head at Landon, who is talking to Charlotte.

"Okay, he accidently cooked up an illegal substance once, but like the solicitor proved and the judge agreed, it had been a simple misunderstanding. He wouldn't do that again. Plus, if it's what I think it is, then he most likely got it off the internet. There's this site where you can buy loads of different prank kits."

"I see," he mumbles, pulling me away from the group where my dad is, talking to Myles and Jacob.

Seems like Beau clicked on to who Jacob is, because he takes one look to where he's standing and is then moving us in the opposite direction.

By the time we make our rounds of introductions, Max calls us to the table, where we all take our seats.

"Is that a pig roast?" Beau whispers in my ear.

Feeling his breath on my skin causes shivers to run down my spine, and when his hand lands on my thigh, I have to clench them together. He quickly glances at me, his eyes heating.

My throat is dry, so I clear it before answering, "Yep."

"Hey, Faith, Aiden said he was dog-sitting last night. Where did you go?" Hayden asks, her eyes raking over me inquisitively.

My smile turns into a wide grin as I place my hand over Beau's on my lap. "Beau took me on a romantic getaway by the beach. It was beautiful there."

"Really?" she muses, her eyes now glancing between us, calculating.

"Yep." I turn, grinning up at Beau to hide my red face. I'm not ready to share with the girls what we did last night. Lily will know as soon as I have a minute to do so, but the others… they don't need to know anything.

"Why do you look flushed?" Maddox asks, who is sitting a few seats down, opposite us.

I frown, narrowing my eyes on him when the table comes to a silent halt. "I'm not."

"You are," my dad agrees, eyes narrowed on me.

"She's glowing too," Hayden adds, grinning from ear to ear.

"And you haven't stopped making googly eyes at him," Aiden puts in—you know, being helpful and all.

That bitch. I should have known she'd guess, but to throw me under the table in front of family... She's a traitor.

"No, I'm not," I squeak out, turning to Beau. "I'm not, am I?"

He just grins, shrugging lazily. "You're even more beautiful when you're glowing."

I growl under my breath and reach over to pinch his thigh. He winces, cursing quietly.

Dad shoves his chair back and stands up. "She's not glowing."

"Uh-oh," Mum mutters, pulling my dad back down to his seat.

"Oh, my God, would you all shut up and concentrate on the triplets, who we're here to celebrate with?"

"No, not until you tell me he hasn't deflowered my angel," Dad demands, banging his fist on the table.

I want to cry, badly.

Mum rubs her hand down Dad's back. "Honey, calm down."

"No! I won't calm down. Faith, didn't you listen to me when we had *the talk?*"

"Kill me!" I beg to anyone who is listening.

"Or the labour video I got you to watch, so you could see what would happen if you did it?"

"Dad," I groan, closing my eyes.

"Nope. I refuse to believe it. Not my girl. Not my daughter. My daughters are good girls."

"Please, honey, calm down."

"He deflowered my girl. Took advantage of my sweet, beautiful girl."

I cover my face with my hands, not bothering to argue any longer. I can't believe this is happening, and in front of Beau, of all people.

"No, he hasn't. Relax, will ya. She's waiting until she's married, right, sis?"

I remove my hands and glance at Mark. He gives me a pointed look, one that tells me to agree. However, I'm too embarrassed to look at him any longer, so I turn away and face Beau.

"I'm sorry about this. Truly. I swear, they get out for a day and all hell breaks loose."

Max gasps. "You all agreed to wait until you were forty-five."

"Dad, really?" Hayden gives him a dry look, but he ignores her, his gaze on me and Beau.

Max finally turns his attention to his daughter, his face turning bright red. "You so much as look at another boy and I will ground you for the rest of your life."

"I'm nineteen, Dad. You can't tell me what to do."

"I can, I'm your dad."

"And I'm an adult," she argues, staring blankly at him.

He stutters, opening and closing his mouth, before finally snapping, "I forbid it! You will not see another male unless it's a relative. And you'll do as you're told while you're living under my roof."

She gives him a coy smile. "Bit of a good job I'm moving into Grandma's then, isn't it?"

He splutters, looking close to combusting, before he turns to his wife, demanding she do something. Lake just smiles and pats his head.

"As happy as I am that you're all protective of Faith, can you all please refrain from talking about her sex life and embarrassing her? She's a grown woman, and all you're doing is making her feel uncomfortable. Now, can you change the fucking subject?"

Every man at the table stands, and my dad flies across the table, knocking over glassware and whatever else. It's short-lived, because he's six seats down, on the opposite side of us, and doesn't reach us.

"What sex life? You don't have a sex life," Dad yells, still trying to reach Beau.

Beau and I stand up and move back from our seats, just as Trent pulls his fist back to punch Beau. I gasp, ready to move in front of him, but Beau pushes me behind him and grabs my cousin's fist, twisting it and pushing him away.

"Remember, I'm a police officer," he warns, his eyes glancing around the table.

Trent looks like he's ready to argue, but Maddison, god bless her soul, slaps the back of his head and lays into him about attacking innocent people.

"Anyone else want to assault a police officer?" Beau growls, making sure to eye everyone in the room.

"I do if you have any friends," Hayden tells him saucily, earning another scuffle from Max as he tries to reach her, looking like he wants to shake some sense into her.

Maddox sits back down, reaching for his bread roll. The other men around the table give him a look. Maddox's head lifts, and he looks around at all the scowling faces. "What? I can't get arrested again, they could send me to jail. I'm nobody's bitch," he mumbles around a mouthful of food.

I groan, rubbing the back of my neck, wondering when my family will ever act normal, for just once.

"Sit down, now!" my mum screams to the room.

When no one moves, Harlow stands up. "Do as she says, otherwise all of you can go somewhere else to eat."

"We mean it," Denny snaps, her body leaning forwards, threatening bodily harm to anyone who is willing and stupid enough to ignore them.

The men wisely sit-down, looking scorned, but I notice they're all still glaring at Beau. Max lifts his butter knife and runs it across his neck as he mouths, 'dead', to Beau.

I'm seriously worried for Hayden when she introduces someone to him. She'll have to give the police notice and have them on standby.

Beau doesn't seem fazed as he pulls me back towards the table, and to my seat. Only when I'm seated does he happily sit down.

"I'm sorry," I whisper, close to tears. "We can go if you want."

His hard expression softens when his eyes land on me. "No, it's fine, nothing I can't handle. Plus, this was bound to happen sooner or later."

Across the table, Hayden grins at me and I narrow my gaze on her, before sniffing and looking away. It becomes awkward with everyone silent, staring at us like we're under the microscope.

"This is awkward," Charlotte blurts out, making a few of us laugh. I chuckle, but it's forced.

"She's my baby." I turn to glance at the heated discussion going on between my mum and dad. He's gesturing wildly towards Beau, his face red with anger.

Beau's right though, it was bound to come out sooner or later, and as much as I hate they attacked Beau, it was better they did it in one go, so he wasn't constantly watching his back for one of them to attack.

Albeit, he may still have to watch it for a while; not leave his food or drinks unattended and make sure to check his breaks. If he does that, everything will be fine.

Lily, who is sitting on my other side, takes my hand. I glance at her, finding her smiling. She winks before leaning in close.

"I'm so happy for you. You still have to tell me everything, but not tonight. One thing I want to know though, was it really as romantic as you said?"

I open my mouth to answer but Beau leans over me and whispers, "She can't tell you everything; it's scandalous, but Lily, it was romantic, Hallmark romantic." He gives her wink before sitting back in his seat.

Lily gasps, her face going bright red from being heard. I begin to giggle when a scuffle gains my attention. Malik has Dad in a headlock on the floor.

"Let me at him!"

"Is he okay?" Beau whispers to me, nodding towards my dad.

I sigh. As much as my family want to kill him right now, I know they never would intentionally hurt him.

Kind of.

At least some of them have a brain and realise Dad hitting my boyfriend, who is a cop, would be a bad idea and ruin the triplets' birthday.

I wave him off. "He's fine. He's probably got something in his eye."

"Hmm," he murmurs, watching as Malik shoves Dad back in his chair.

Needing to distract everyone from the breakdown my dad and Max seem to be having, I get their attention. "Hey, guys, I have some great news."

"You aren't going to tell us you're pregnant, are you?" Liam announces dryly.

I can't see him since he's sitting somewhere down the table to the right of me, but I turn my glower down his way. "No!" I snap, before smiling wickedly at Hayden.

She scowls, and I can see the wheels behind her eyes turning, most likely wondering what I'm up to.

"You need to cancel tomorrow's plans. All of you."

She gasps in outrage, standing up. "No! You can't make us change plans. I have my outfit and everything. It's taken me months to find the perfect one, you bitch."

I shrug, seeming bored. "Yeah, but then you wouldn't be able to use the tickets Beau got for us all. That's if he's still kind enough to give them to you after what you guys pulled tonight."

Hayden looks adorably confused and continues to sulk.

Liam sits forward in his seat, his expression wary as he eyes Beau and me. "What tickets?"

I smile brightly. "What tickets, you ask? Well, VIP tickets to Party in the Park."

Beau chuckles against my ear. "You're cruel."

"They deserve it," I whisper back, watching Hayden's face transform from shock to excitement.

"What? Oh, my God, please don't be fucking with me. Do you know who's playing there? Dunk!" She screeches, bouncing around. "Dunk," she sighs, her face turning dreamy.

Since the new rock band released their debut single a few months ago, Hayden has been infatuated. Already they're a big hit after being number one since its release. She turns to Beau, her expression serious. "And sorry about dropping you in it. I was bored."

Beau shrugs, his lips twitching. "Don't apologise to me."

She bites her lip before turning to me. "Sorry!" She doesn't wait for me to accept her apology, instead she grabs her phone, muttering about making her friends jealous.

"For all of us?" Liam asks, practically bouncing in his seat. Beau nods, wincing when Liam starts howling and slamming his beer bottle down on the table. "Fucking aye. Can't wait. All those chicks."

"How are we going to get back? The trains stop running at eleven." Charlotte, ever the worrier, puts her phone down, waiting for us to answer.

"You can all drive up there. The manager said if you have tents you can pitch them in the VIP section. He did mention hotels were fully booked the minute they knew where the venue was being held this year."

"Cool."

I glance back down the table to the parents, finding them still arguing amongst themselves. I swear I hear Max telling my dad it's not kidnapping if it's your kid, but I can't be sure with the way they are going back and forth.

That's when things take a turn for the worse.

A waiter brings out the giant cake my mum and aunts made, and they stare at it in confusion. A look passes between the women, before they turn their attention down the table towards Jacob, who is grinning.

I take it all in, noticing not one person has questioned why they've brought the cake out before dinner and instead start singing *Happy Birthday*.

Kayla opens her mouth to warn the triplets as the cake is placed down between them, right in front of us.

My eyes widen when I notice Jacob duck under the table, just as the three-tiered cake explodes, and the sponge and icing rains down on all of us.

And just like that, chaos erupts along the table, starting with Hayden throwing cake down the table to where Jacob has now risen, taking photos with his phone.

Beau's mouth is hanging open at the eruption, but I just lick a smudge of icing off the corner of my mouth before sitting back in my chair.

This is a true Carter gathering, so it was better he saw this now rather than a couple of years down the line.

This night will either make us or break us.

Not that I will let him get away.

I'm a Carter after all.

TWENTY

SQUEALING LOUDLY, I TRY TO PUSH Beau away. His aggressive hands digging into my sides are close to making me pee myself.

If there is anything a girl hates, it's being tickled. We don't look sexy like they do in the movies. We look like deranged hillbillies having an epileptic fit.

It's not pretty.

"Please, I call mercy. Mercy, I tell you!"

He chuckles deeply as he rolls on top of me, pinning my hands above my head. "I don't negotiate with mini terrorists."

"I said I was sorry." I blow the hair out of my face while trying hard not to laugh. "Stop tickling me."

He tilts his head to the side, glancing down at me with an amused expression. "See, I would, but you promised me the cake was a misunderstanding."

I nod my head vigorously. "It was. It really was. He was only aiming for the triplets. He didn't know it would explode like *that*."

"And my car?"

I bite my lip, glancing over his shoulder. "Was an accident?"

"Are you asking me or telling me?"

"Um, telling?"

"I see," he chuckles, his one hand gripping both my wrists as the other starts to move down my body.

I squirm, already crying from laughter. "Please, no. Don't! It really was an accident."

"How is covering my car with silly-string an accident?" he asks dryly, his lips twitching.

"Jacob just wanted you to feel like one of the family?"

"He also let my tyres down."

He didn't do that part, but I'm not going to tell Beau that.

"I said I was sorry." I pout.

He chuckles deeply, leaning down to take my mouth. I try to wrap my hands around him, but he keeps my wrists pinned down securely.

Pulling away a little to look at me, he says, "What are you going to do to make it up to me?"

"Apart from clean your car and get someone to replace all four tyres?"

"No, I can sort the car out. I did most of it last night. I'm more interested in how you're going to make up for the fact you fell asleep last night, *while* I cleaned the car."

My mouth forms an O. "Oh."

"Yeah, oh," he grins.

When we got back last night, I'd been so tired from the chaos my family caused that I'd readily agreed to make it up to him in the shower, after we got the cake washed off our bodies.

But while I'd been in the shower, he'd gone downstairs to clean what he could off the car. Turns out, silly-string dries like glue.

He took too long, and the last thing I remember was my head falling to the pillow.

I give him what I hope is my saucy look and lower my lashes at him. "Well, if you let me go, I'm sure I could think of a few things."

He licks his lips. "I'm listening. What were you thinking?"

I suck my bottom lip into my mouth. "Something tasty, something mouth-watering that will keep you going for the rest of the day."

His eyes dilate, heating with passion. "Now that is what I'm talking about."

Smiling coyly, I nod my head and inwardly grin when he lets go of my hands. I run my finger down his bare chest, trying to ignore the clenching between my legs as his erection presses against my core.

"I'm glad you think so. Because if you want a cooked breakfast, I should really start it now."

He rears back, looking adorably confused as his eyes scrunch together. "What?"

I nod my head to the side where the clock is. "You have work in an hour, and if we go at it again, you'll be late."

He gasps, his gaze coming back to me, looking truly stunned. "You sneaky little woman."

I shrug, grinning widely. "I do my best."

"When I get you alone tonight, you're so going to pay."

I press a kiss against his lips, smiling. "Promises, promises."

Before he can do anything else that will result in me giving in and making love to him, I push him off. He rolls to the floor with a grunt, whilst I whistle and jump from the bed before grabbing one of his T-shirts and pulling it over my head.

"I'm going to get you back, sweetheart."

I stop at the door, looking over my shoulder. "So, you don't want breakfast?"

He gets up, his expression predatory. "Oh, I want breakfast." I squeal when he dives for me, and rush from the room.

One thing is for sure, tonight just got more interesting. I can't get enough of him.

———————————————

LILY AND I finish getting our face paints done before skipping off to join the others. The boys had gone off on their own, complaining that we were ruining their game.

We all got the same face paints; little white flowers on a stork running down the side of our faces, all covered in glitter. They look amazing as we snap another group selfie.

"Say cheese," Hayden yells, holding her selfie stick in the air. We all smile for the camera, before moving off through the large crowd.

I'll have to remember to double thank Beau when he meets up with us later. Today has been a blast, and as the evening flows on, it just keeps getting better.

Lily links her arm through mine. "You look positively happy."

I'm grinning like a mad fool, because instead of breakfast, Beau and I had sex again. It was worth being twenty minutes late to meet the others. And if the blush that had covered my cheeks was anything to go by, the others guessed what I had been up to.

"I really am. He makes me happy, Lily."

"I'm glad. Has Dad spoken to you since last night?"

I grunt, not a fan of my dad at the moment. He'd promised me he had nothing to do with helping Jacob with the prank. He'd forgotten to mention he was the one who'd let down Beau's tyres. I haven't had the heart to tell Beau, not wanting him to dislike my father.

He'd promised me last night he would make it up to Beau and to me, but I'm not holding out hope. I'm his eldest daughter and the first to have a boyfriend. I honestly don't think he'd prepared himself for this moment, praying I'd stay single forever.

With Beau not going anywhere though, he is going to have to get used to it. I wasn't giving Beau up for nobody.

"No. I'm still a little mad he went that far last night."

"At least he didn't punch him," she says.

"Yeah, it's progress, I guess. Or at least it would be if he hadn't done that dive across the table. Right now, though, it's Hayden I want to get back at."

Lily grins as we watch Hayden ahead, dancing to the music. "She really does have it coming."

I grin evilly. "She really does."

"Ewww," Lily moans, and when I glance at her, her face is scrunched up in disgust.

"What? What's wrong?" I ask, looking around, not seeing anything.

She pulls me to a stop and drags me back a few steps, before pointing to the crowd on our right. I gag when I see my brother Aiden with some scantily dressed girl in his arms, dry humping him. She's barely wearing anything and it's freezing out.

I'm wearing my puffy bomber coat, gloves, and my UGG beanie I'd got in the sale last January. How the fuck this girl can be wearing a short denim skirt, a long-sleeved T-shirt that is ripped so it ends just below her breasts, and a bomber jacket undone is beyond me. On her feet she's wearing simple boots, and by the look of the blue tinge to her legs, she's not even wearing tights.

Stupid.

"That is just gross."

Lily pulls me back and we rush to catch up with the others. "I hope he remembers the talk Dad gave them. She doesn't seem very—"

"Bothered with who she sleeps with?"

She scrunches her face up. "Yes. I was hoping he'd grow out of sleeping around by now. I don't want him to catch STD's."

"He probably already has one," I add, waving at Charlotte. "Did she really bake loads of cupcakes?" I whisper.

Lily laughs, pushing me in the shoulder. "Stop. She was being kind, thinking the boys would get hungry."

"She's just so darn cute, but her cooking really sucks."

"Yes, it really does, but I won't be the one telling her that. She's loves mothering people. It's just who she is."

"She really is one in a million. Anyway, how are you doing?"

I know coming here wasn't something Lily would normally do, but because her favourite girl band were playing, she couldn't say no. My dad even offered to chaperone, so if she wanted to leave, he would take her home. After last night though, we declined his offer, telling him we'd look after her.

We've managed to stay away from the beer tents and larger crowds. We also didn't visit the other side of the park where a different techno beat of music was playing. According to Maddox, who had scoped the place out first before letting Lily go anywhere, it was a rave over there. People were smoking, drinking and bumping all over the place.

People are still drinking from clear white cups filled with beer, but so far, she hasn't seemed too affected.

"I'm doing okay. It still pisses me off how much it can affect me, but as long as no drunken fool stumbles into me or breathes on me, I should be okay. I'm actually having loads of fun. I can't wait to go on to the fair."

"And we will, we just want to see Dunk before Hayden tracks them down again. And fairgrounds are always better when it's dark. The music is louder, and the lights are brighter."

"Speaking of Dunk, did Hayden really punch the lead singer in the nose? I thought Immy was joking."

I laugh lightly, because seeing Hayden stumble over her words in front of the star singer had been hilarious. What made it funnier was when she'd gone to get out her autograph book for him to sign. She'd ended up whacking him in the nose, causing him to bleed all over the place. It wasn't a pretty sight.

"Yeah. She's hoping she can get his attention from the crowd and say she's sorry."

Lily throws her head back, laughing uproariously. "She's still going to try and get him to sign it, isn't she?"

"Totally." I grin as we step behind our group.

"This should be a good spot," Hayden yells over her shoulder, waving her hands in the air as the band on stage finishes their set.

Madison steps towards us, worrying her bottom lip. "I don't think this is a good idea. The security bloke said she had to be on her best behaviour."

Hope, who is standing near, glances at us. "You do realise no one can tell her what to do? Not even her parents can tell her, so I doubt she's going to listen to him."

We watch as Dunk is announced on stage and Hayden goes wild. She hangs onto poor Ciara's arm, jumping up and down as she yells for his attention.

I glance to the stage briefly, wincing when I see the dark bruises under his eye and across his nose. She really did a number on him. I don't think it helped when she'd offered to ice it. She'd whacked it on, making it worse.

When I glance back, Ciara backs away, shaking her head at Hayden. I start to giggle, but soon lose it when Hayden turns to us and storms over.

"One of you put me on your shoulders. I need him to see me and those bimbos have got their boyfriends to do it. I'll never get a chance if they stay up there." She points furiously to where a couple of guys have girls on their shoulders, scowling.

"And what are you going to do, knock them down?" I ask, joking.

She sniffs. "If I have to. Now, let me on your shoulders."

"No way, I like my back in working condition, thanks."

She glares at me before looking at Lily, who wisely takes a step back. "Can't, weak knees."

When the others shake their heads, she stomps her foot before moving back over to Ciara, who is another huge fan of Dunk.

"I love you, Milo. I'm your number one fan," Hayden screams, bouncing around and waving her hands. The people in front of her turn around to glare, but she ignores them, screeching at the top of her voice.

She even goes so far as to knock one of the girls off their boyfriend's shoulders, so she can take a selfie with Dunk in the background.

The boyfriend, still scowling, says something to her, but when he doesn't get an answer, he turns to us and walks over.

"Get your friend in control. She's ruining my chance of hooking up."

My face scrunches up in disgust. Why do men think about sex every second of the day?

I smile sadly, patting his shoulder. "We'll try out best, but she only gets to leave the ward once a year."

"Ward?" he asks, looking over his shoulder quickly.

"Yeah, she accidently grabbed the balls of the man who was being cocky to her in the line at HMV. It was a terrible occurrence, so they hospitalised her. She's on meds, but once every year they let her take a break from it all."

I bite my lip to stop myself from laughing when his eyes widen, and he rushes over to the group of friends he was with, gesturing them to move away. They do, and another crowd moves in, dancing along with the music.

Hope laughs, glancing over at me. "You are looking for trouble, missy. She's going to kill you."

I hold my hands up in surrender. "It's not my fault she has crazy tendencies that have people believing my stories."

"It's the eyes," Lily agrees.

"Now what is she doing?" Charlotte asks, her expression concerned.

My eyes cast towards Hayden, finding her pushing the new crowd away so she can see the stage better.

This group look a little rougher, so messing with their heads won't work. When the biggest of them watches her, then us, we all automatically move to the side.

Even when Hayden walks towards us, we give her a wide berth. For as long as she's star struck over Dunk, we're going to pretend she doesn't belong with us.

She's at a level of crazy none of us are at, but put Theo James in front of me, and I'd definitely reach that level.

TWENTY-ONE

"C AN WE DO IT AGAIN?" LILY SQUEALS, jumping off Wipe Out to link her arm through mine.

My legs are shaking, my face pale as I turn to my sister. "We've been on it five times in a row. Don't you want to go on the tea cups? Or maybe we could do the bumper cars?"

I hope to persuade her since I don't know how much more I can handle. Even the way she bounces next to me has my tummy curdling.

She scrunches her face up adorably. "But they aren't fast, and the tea cups are for babies. What about the waltzers?"

I look to the other girls for help, but they look away, pretending they weren't listening. "How about you guys go on together? I'm going to grab a bottled water and sit this one out."

Because if I'm spun one more time, I'm going to puke up the hotdog and fries I had earlier. My stomach is in knots.

She looks unsure as she bites her lip worriedly. "Are you sure? We can wait until you're ready."

"No!" I screech, but then stop, clearing my throat as I wave her off. "It's fine. You guys go and have fun."

"But you'll be on your own."

"You have your fast track bands, so I won't be waiting forever, Lily. It's fine, now go."

She still looks unsure, her body tensing up. "Maybe we should wait."

I hug my sister, but I can still feel how tense she is. "Just go and have fun."

"I'm going to sit this one out too," Hope offers, and I watch as Lily's shoulders visibly relax. I mouth a 'thank you' to Hope for jumping in.

"Are you sure don't mind? It's going to be a lot of fun, but we'll do it again, so you can have a turn."

"I'm sure. I'm not keen on the waltzers anyway."

Satisfied, Lily grins, pulling Hope in for a hug. "You are the best." She turns to the others, smiling so wide her cheeks must hurt. "Let's go. After, we can go on the high drop."

I pale when the words leave her mouth. The high drop is a line of six seats on each side of a block that rises high in the sky. It's stops at the top, waiting until you feel safe, before dropping you like your life means nothing. Whoever thought they were brilliant for conjuring that ride up needs to die a slow and painful death.

Lily waves goodbye and heads off with the others, squealing with excitement.

Hope and I find the nearest burger van before ordering our drinks.

"I don't think there's any seats," she says as I take my change and grab my drink.

"Let's look over by the waltzers, that way we're close."

"Okay."

We find a bench close to the others and take a seat. I rub my gloved hands together, fighting off the cold. After being spun in the air on the last ride, my cheeks are frozen solid.

"You look like you're going to be sick." Hope chuckles, taking a large gulp of her water.

"I just may if she doesn't stop dragging me on so many rides that spin or go upside down. There's only so much tossing I can handle."

She giggles. "But you will if she asks because she's having the time of her life. Four drunken men have bumped into her, one even sat down next to her on the last ride, and she hasn't even blinked or noticed."

I sag against the bench. "I know. I asked if she wanted to switch seats with me when I saw him looking at her. I thought Immy was going to sit there, otherwise I would have said something before."

"A lad on the other side of us caught her attention. What did Lily say?"

"She looked at me, grinning with excitement, but also confused at my offer, saying she was fine where she was."

I have to smile because my sister has really shone bright tonight. She always does at places like this.

She went to her first fair at the age of eleven, and it had taken us hours to get her to leave. And when we did, we'd left with Dad holding every stuffed animal they had, a bunch of sweets she'd won on the penny machines, and a ton of pictures of us together on the rides.

"I'm sorry I didn't say anything last night."

I glance at her, a little confused to what she means. Her comment is abrupt, which is also confusing. "What do you mean?"

She fiddles with her hands. "When they were talking about you and Beau like you weren't there. I should have spoken up for you, for Beau, but if I'm honest, I wanted to see how they all reacted."

I giggle at that. "I think everyone did."

She laughs, her expression relaxing. "Yeah. Still, we should have stood by you. We'll be in your position one day and it will be nice to have your support."

"You've met someone?"

Her cheeks turn pink. "No. But I have been going on a few dates. I'm just worried over how the men in our family will react when they find out. We're not at school anymore; they won't hold back because my date is underage."

I feel her pain. "I hear ya. My advice?"

She glances at me, her eyes round with hope. "Anything would be good. Not that I've met anyone I want them to meet, but if I do, I want to be prepared."

"Don't introduce them until you're sure they're the person you want to spend the rest of your life with. I think, in time, Dad will see that Beau is that person and come to terms with me not being his little girl anymore."

"Your mum is already won over. I heard her say to Mum it's the uniform that decided for her."

I laugh because that sounds like my mum. "She drooled and everything when she saw him in his work attire."

"Does he look as good as she says?"

The sparkle in her eyes doesn't go unnoticed. My cousin is known for her obsession with men in uniform. "Hotter."

She grins, nudging my shoulder with hers. "Lucky bitch."

"Oh, my God, can we get some cotton candy? I saw it as we were spun."

I jump at the excited sound of Lily's voice, in awe of her skills in noticing cotton candy while enjoying the ride. She's like a little girl.

"Yeah."

Hope and I jump up from our seat and follow the group. We're just passing some game booths when a hand grabs my upper arm, pulling me away from the girls.

Hope notices me slip away, as a startled yelp escapes me. "Hey!"

"Bitch, come with me now before someone gets hurt."

My knees threaten to buckle under me as the voice that haunts me breathes in my ear. My entire body stills as he tries to pull me away.

How did he find me?

Oh, god, he can't be here.

Lily.

She'll be scared if she sees him, and it will cause her to have an episode.

My eyes glance away from Hope, even as she grabs the others' attention.

"Okay," I whisper shakily to the man holding me.

He spins me around to face him, his snarling face having me inwardly whimper. His eyes are dark, soulless, and the hardness in his expression has the hairs on the back of my neck standing on end.

Oh, my God!

It's him, the man from the restaurant the night he stood me up, the man who'd helped me pick up my purse.

Noah.

"Let her go!"

My eyes widen when he spins us again to face my sister and cousins. All of them are standing in a semi-circle around us, their arms crossed over their chests as they scowl at the man holding me.

His fingers latch on to my ponytail, pulling it sharply and making me cry out. "Or what? You going to strip for me?"

Hayden, who had been the one to speak before, swaggers forward, not even flinching at his degrading dig.

"Hayden, don't," I plead, not wanting them to get hurt.

She doesn't even glance at me, keeping her eyes on Noah. "I said let her go. If you don't, we will hurt you."

He scoffs, dismissing her threat with amusement. He spins us around again, dragging me by my hair towards a secluded area. I notice, for the first time, we're near the emergency exit.

My hope of someone seeing him handling me roughly and get me help comes crashing down when he starts dragging me towards it.

I hear a war cry before I'm jerked to the floor and away from Noah. I roll over to my side and see my sister tumble to the floor, still screaming bloody murder and drawing a crowd.

Noah gets up, his eyes cold as he steps towards her with the intent to hurt her. I can see it in his eyes, the way his hands clench into fists, and the way his jaw locks.

"No!" I scream, trying to crawl over to my sister. My legs are still trembling and weak.

Just as the words slip past my lips, I'm stunned into silence and pause my attempt to get to Lily, because Hayden rushes forwards, screaming, "This is Sparta," and does a full roundhouse kick to his stomach, knocking the breath out of his lungs. He flies backwards, landing on his back with a thud. Before he has a chance to regain his composure, she dives on him, her elbow sticking out as she lands hard on his chest.

"You son of a bitch," she screams, moving to straddle his stomach.

He grunts, shoving him off her, but the second she rolls off, she jumps to her feet, ready to attack.

That's when rushing feet gain my attention. As one, all my cousins dive on top of him, screaming at the top of their lungs, not caring there's a crowd forming behind them to watch the show.

I sit up, my eyes widening in shock when Charlotte shoves one of her muffins in his mouth. I wince a little, feeling a little sorry for him. Okay, I don't, he really does deserve the torture. He pales, gagging as he tries to fight her away at the same time as spitting the muffin out.

"Eat it," she screams, shoving another in his mouth. She looks a little deranged as she goes for yet another muffin in her trusty backpack.

What surprises me more is the little kicks Lily keeps getting in as the others keep slapping and punching him.

"You leave my sister alone, you A-hole." Another kick to the ribs.

Mouth agape, I watch as Hayden really gets into it, slapping his face almost comically. "How does it feel to get hit back, huh? How do you like it, huh? You like it?" Her slaps become harder as he shouts at them to get the fuck off him.

Security come barrelling around the corner and I sag with relief at the sight of them, though not at the sight of my brother and cousins walking past, doing a double take before rushing towards us; or the growing crowd.

With them here, things will only get worse. It's only a matter of time, not whether they will succeed in doing so.

The security blokes pull the girls away, but the one holding Hayden is having trouble restraining her.

"Tell me, are you not entertained!" she screams, throwing her hands up and looking like a mad woman on crack as she glares at Noah. She keeps trying to throw another kick towards his broken body, but the guy holding her pulls her back, lifting her off her feet so they're swinging in the air.

Another security bloke helps Noah stand, asking if he's all right.

"What? He was the one who attacked me, he fucking beat me up," I scream, stepping forward. There is no way he can get away with this again. And they can't let him go. Beau is looking for him.

"Miss, I'm going to ask you to calm down and take a step back."

I stand straighter as I hear my cousins asking the others what happened. "No. I won't. He's wanted by the police."

"Is this right, sir?"

Noah scowls angrily at me before turning to the security guy, wincing as he fakes being the victim. "No. I was walking towards the exit to take my wife and kid home when I was jumped by these group of crazy ladies."

"You liar," I scream, my temper rising as I take a step forward. The security guy puts his hand to my chest, shoving me lightly to take a step back. "He doesn't even have a wife or kids." At least, I think he doesn't. "He tried to take me away. He's woman beater."

Mark walks up beside me, his jaw clenched. "Is he the one who attacked you, Faith?"

"Yes," I bite out, my eyes narrowed on the man I should be scared of, but if anything, I'm scared for him, because I'm not letting him leave this park without being in handcuffs first.

"I see." Before I can stop him, he's swinging a punch to Noah's jaw. Two security guys come running over to restrain him, but I lose my temper.

"No, get away from my brother. He didn't do anything wrong. You're restraining the wrong person."

I'm pulled back, but with my casted arm, I hit whoever has me in the head, stunning them long enough to let me go. I jump on the back of the guy who is trying to pin Mark to the floor, pulling his hair.

"Get away!"

"Get off me," he squeals, spinning around. I grip my legs around him tighter, and from the corner of my eye, I notice Hayden and the others get free to start helping us get free.

Hopefully we can make it home before the police show up. But then I see Noah trying to slip out of the mad chaos and scream to my family. We all dive in his direction.

TWENTY-TWO

WHEN I WAS FIFTEEN I GOT CAUGHT sneaking out with Lily to meet up with the others. We had the bright idea of doing a Ouija board, in a graveyard, at midnight, to talk to my dead grandmother. Honestly, at the time, it was a great idea. I'd just wanted to know if she was okay.

We'd got caught before even entering the graveyard by a patrolling cop car. I'd been so scared I nearly peed myself. I didn't think I could ever feel like that again, until tonight.

I don't even know what Noah had had planned or what he'd wanted to do me. I don't know if that's worse than knowing.

To make matters worse, we've been arrested and put in a cell together. It's absolutely frightening not knowing what will happen. I'm also pissed that they arrested us when we didn't really do anything. It wasn't like we attempted to kidnap someone, unlike Noah.

Charlotte's sniffling has me looking in her direction. She's been rocking back and forth for the past three hours—since we've been here. Poor girl has never been in trouble in her life. Even when we snuck out at fifteen, she stayed behind, not wanting to let her parents down. And because we're family, none of us ever forced her to step over the line. She was perfect the way she was.

"I'm a criminal. I'm going to go to prison and be someone's bitch."

"You're not going to prison," Hope tells her, trying to soothe her fears.

All the girls got shoved into one cell because of the rooms being overcrowded, since a lot of people from out of town are here. I'm actually glad, because I think it would have sent me over the edge had I not had them close.

"I am. Maybe if I lied and said I just wanted him to be fed, they'd let me go?"

"I think you lying in court would be frowned upon," Hayden adds.

"And they took samples of your muffins to make sure they weren't laced with anything that could kill him," Immy says, inspecting her nails.

"Oh, god, they're going to lock me up for a very long time," she cries, sobbing into her hands. "They were just my muffins. I didn't do anything to them."

"I can't believe I hurt someone," Lily whispers from next to me. She's still trying to calm down from the panic attack she'd had when the officer who came to check on us tried to shut the door. It took us ten minutes of screaming before another officer arrived, warning the others about Lily's condition.

"I think they're more worried about Faith bashing in one of the guys' head. I heard he got taken to hospital," Hayden says, grinning.

I narrow my eyes because she's full of shit. I'd heard the paramedic tell him he had a concussion and he should go home for some rest. Only Noah and another security guy got taken to hospital, but really, that was a complete misunderstanding.

I'd thought the security guy was Noah, and when he had turned around, I'd swung. By the time I'd realised it wasn't him, it had been too late. I punched him the nose, and even over the roar of shouting, I'd heard the bone crack. I threw up not long after.

And no one could pin what happened to Noah on any of us because we're still unsure ourselves about who did what to put him in the hospital. There were too many of us. Though I think Ashton giving him a wedgie and pinning his boxers to a gate didn't help matters. People, to get out of the way of the police, had barrelled through the gate, and every time one of them slammed it open, it slammed Noah against the brick wall.

So, technically it wasn't our fault. We had just been trying to prevent him from escaping.

"Less about my part, what about your part? Where the fuck did you learn how to kick like that?"

Hayden, for the first time since we were brought in by a riot van, looks nervous. She bites her bottom lip before sagging against the brick wall. "I couldn't sleep one night so I watched some MMA. When I got into it, I started watching wrestling and other martial arts. You pick up a few things when you see hot, sweaty men slamming into each other."

If she had given me anything but that absurd answer, I wouldn't have believed her. But believe it or not, she learnt to drive by playing this car game that made you think you were really in a car.

It didn't help that she was only sixteen and got caught joyriding her dad's car.

"I want to know what was with the abuse you were shouting. The 'Are you entertained' nearly had me peeing myself with laughter," Hope says, before giggling to herself.

I have to admit, looking back now, that was actually funny.

Hayden blushes, making me giggle louder. "I was in the moment."

"Yeah right," I scoff.

"Okay, I watch a lot of movies. I just couldn't help it."

"Do you think we'll get out of here?" Charlotte asks, still sniffling.

"Oh, God." Lily pales, sitting up. "If I have an arrest record, I won't be able to keep my job. They're going to think I'm unfit to look after the children."

I rub her back. "They won't. We will vouch for you. You won't lose your job."

"Do you think they'll let us order a McDonalds?" Ciara asks, opening her eyes. She'd fallen asleep an hour ago.

Hayden is about to throw out a snarky reply, but before she can, the door to our room is pushed open.

In his work uniform, Beau stands next to Collings and another officer, grinning widely.

"Beau," I squeal happily. I'm about to get up when he holds his hand up. "What? Can we not go?"

I bite my bottom lip. I'd been praying that Beau could sort out this misunderstanding for us. I never pictured we'd be slapped with arrest charges.

When he holds his phone up, I hear the distinct click of his camera and my eyes narrow at his grinning face.

"Please tell me you didn't just take a picture of us?"

He shrugs, nodding his head to the officer, who leaves. "I really did. I want this moment framed."

I don't buy it and neither do the others.

"Our parents asked you to take a picture, didn't they?" Ciara asks dryly.

He nods, still looking smug. "Yep."

"I hate you," Hayden grumbles.

"Are they going to take me to prison now?" Charlotte asks, getting to her feet.

His eyes soften as he takes in her swollen red eyes. "No, Charlotte, they aren't. You're all free to go. Once we explained everything, they decided to speak to the security team you attacked. They chose to drop the charges."

"They were going to charge us?" I squeak.

"Pussies," Hayden hisses, getting up and dusting off her jeans.

"Yes, apparently one of you kneed one in the balls and he's still recovering with an icepack and painkillers, one has a broken nose in three places and will need surgery, and others are in for a couple of bruised ribs."

I bite my bottom lip worriedly. "That must have happened by accident when we were helping the others."

He nods his head, his lips twitching. "I see."

"They'll be fine." I grab my coat, as the others pile out of the room, and meet Beau at the door. He throws his arm over my shoulder, smiling down at me.

"Oh, and you've been banned from any and all concerts involving Party in the Park."

"No way!" I gasp, turning to face him. "It really wasn't our fault. We were getting cotton candy when Noah grabbed me. He pulled my *hair*, Beau. We did what we had to do."

"Which was call for help?" he asks, looking at me expectantly.

I look away, sniffing. "No. It happened too fast."

"Right."

Nervously, I chance to ask the question I've been wanting to ask the other officers. "Did you arrest Noah?"

He pulls me tighter against him. "We did. They are still at the hospital with him. We were on our way over to you when we heard the call over the radio about a disturbance." He pauses, looking down at me until I nervously look away. "I knew it was you."

"How?"

"His friend? He told us everything. After all the dirt we found on his computer, we were going to pin it all on him. Once he believed it, he sang like a canary."

"So, it's over?"

"Yep, it's over. That bastard will not be bothering you again."

"What about my cousins and brother? They got pulled into the other van. Are they free to leave too?"

"Yeah. They're fine. I left them finishing pizza with a couple of female officers. I swear, even busted up and in a cell, they can act like butter doesn't melt. They had one officer really believing they were innocent bystanders throughout the whole incident."

"Oh, my God, they got fed?" My stomach grumbles as if it's protesting over not having food.

He laughs as we step into the waiting room where all our family are waiting. Dad sees me and rushes over, before pulling me into his arms.

"Don't ever scare me like that again," he whispers against my neck. I breath him in, safety surrounding me like a warm blanket. When he pulls back, he's scowling. "I was told you were the one who broke the nose. You didn't knee them in the balls?"

"No, Dad. It was an accident," I tell him, emphasizing the word accident in case the officers are listening in.

Beau snorts behind me while Dad grins. "Good girl."

"Hey, we're all over Youtube," Hayden shouts, grinning like a fool as she watches her screen.

I groan when I hear, 'This is Sparta' shouted from the screen.

Dad, who is still holding me in his arms, looks over to Max. "Get Liam on it."

"No way. We have over fifty thousand hits already," Hayden sulks. Everyone looks over her shoulder, watching it, wincing every now and then and laughing.

"You really showed him, sweetie," Myles tells his daughter, pulling her tighter.

Charlotte stands straighter, looking like she hadn't been crying her eyes out only five minutes ago. "I'm a rebel."

Myles laughs, kissing his daughter's forehead. "That you are, baby girl."

"Where's Aiden?" I ask out loud. As I look around, everyone goes silent, frowning at one another.

"Shit!" Mark hisses, grabbing his phone off the counter where the officer is giving us our belongings and turning it on. "Shit!"

"What?" Mum asks, still fussing over the cut above Mark's eye.

"We left him. He was bang——talking to some girl. He said to call him in an hour for us to meet up with him."

"What time was that?" Mum asks.

Mark bites his bottom lip, wisely stepping away from Mum. "Four hours ago."

"What?" she screeches, just as I grab my phone, turning it on.

Four missed calls and a few messages from Aiden asking where we were. I feel bad, but in all fairness, I'm glad he's not here. We wouldn't have made it to the waiting room without being arrested again if he were.

"Sweetheart, we can go pick him and their stuff up when we get the cars."

"We can't stay there?" I ask.

Beau pinches my side and I elbow him in the stomach. "You know you're banned. You're allowed to get your cars and belongings, but then you have to leave the property immediately."

I sag, disappointed. "Oh, okay."

"Seriously, sis, you shoved a muffin down his throat?" Everyone stops their exit to glance at Charlotte. She's biting her lip, blushing.

"He pulled her hair. I didn't know what else to do."

Myles and Kayla smile as they pull their daughter into their arms. "It's okay, sweetie. He won't mess with any of you again."

"Very true," Beau whispers close to me, pulling me against him.

"They won't let him get away with it, will they?" I ask, sucking my bottom lip into my mouth.

He shakes his head, running a finger down my cheek. "No, baby, they won't. I promise."

"Good. Take me home, please?"

His eyes flutter. "Yeah, baby, let's go home."

TWENTY-THREE

BEAU
THREE WEEKS LATER

WHEN WE GOT THE COURT DATE LETTER two weeks ago, I knew today, I would have to do something to cheer up my woman.

She's been acting like it's no big deal, putting on a brave face, but I know she's been fearing Noah getting away with it, even if she doesn't say it. I've seen it in the way she bites her nails, how she checks her emails for updates from her lawyer, and how she will ask Collings if everything is okay.

The past week has been hard on her. She's hardly eaten or slept, and a few times I've woken up to her in a cold sweat.

When we were informed other victims were being called forward, she started to relax. She admitted one night, after we'd finished in bed, how she was glad they were coming. She didn't feel as alone with them standing by her side.

Faith became friends with Carol—my old next-door neighbour—when

I introduced them to one another a week ago. She'd come down for the court case, and to catch up with me before. We had kept in touch via texting, but other than that, I've only seen her once since I moved out to find who had victimised her.

Her son Mathew, who had also come down to testify against Noah, was here. He may not have seen him clearly the night he was attacked, but he'd had glimpses and heard him speak. For that, Carol wanted her son to feel comfortable before taking the stand.

After meeting up with him and taking him out for a game of football, I can see the difference in him. He's not the boy he was before the attack, but he isn't the boy he he'd been after either. He's been through a lot, but he seems to be doing much better.

I testified last week; telling the jury about the information I had found out about Noah from the time I took on the case to the very end.

I'd had to fight not to jump over the barrier separating him from us and knocking the fucker out. He was cold, calculating, his eyes always assessing the room. He tried to intimidate the women, glaring their way, but none of them paid him attention.

When Faith went to the stand this morning, I was there for her, but not long after, I left, getting ready for her surprise. It was hard when all I'd wanted to do was wrap her in my arms and protect her from that monster. He's no longer a threat to her, but the rage still simmering inside me feels fresh. I don't think I'll ever not be protective of her.

Over the past few months, since meeting Faith, my life has changed for the better. I'd never expected to be in a serious relationship with anyone, but for some reason, she pulled me in from the very first time she'd screamed in my face. I knew just looking into her mesmerising eyes that I'd never be the same again. She's surprised me at every turn, her nutty side coming out the more we hung out. I wouldn't change who she is for the world, not even her family. It's what makes Faith, Faith, and I can accept that with no problems.

After Noah was released from hospital and taken into custody, my excuse as to why I was staying with Faith was up.

My excuse had been valid at first, but the real reason I pushed to stay with her while she recovered after her attack was so I could be close to her all the time. I couldn't get enough of the girl who had wormed her way under my skin.

Our time spent together was something I deeply treasured and never took for granted.

My clothes and shit were still lying around her flat, so when she didn't move them or broach the subject of when I was leaving, I hadn't either. I was a coward. I didn't want her to tell me she wanted her space back, especially after finding out from her sister that her flat was her haven away from the family.

So instead of pulling on my big girl pants, I did the only respectable thing a man can do; I moved all my stuff into her flat.

When she noticed, her eyes seemed to light up, all the tension over the court case leaving her. She'd asked me if I had moved in while she was out, and I answered yes before going back to cooking us dinner. From the corner of my eye I'd watched her smile, her eyes filling up with tears.

I'd had to hide my face, so she didn't see me grinning like a damn maniac. I was just too fucking pleased she didn't argue and ask me to take my stuff back.

The group of women and the entire Carter family come walking out of the court house, shaking my thoughts from my mind. They're smiling, so I take that as a good sign as my eyes glance to Faith and Carol. They're crying, pulling each other into a hug before stepping back and smiling.

I immediately relax. For a second, I'd contemplated going into the courthouse to find the fucker and end him.

Faith notices me at the bottom of the court steps and grins widely before running at me. I brace for her impact, clinging to her when she throws herself at me, wrapping her legs around my waist.

God, she feels so fucking good my cock stirs. It always does when she's around.

"Baby," I whisper, her smile infectious.

"He's going away for a very long time."

I laugh at the pure joy on her face. "Good."

She bites her lip. "We're going out to celebrate. Are you coming, or do you still have work to do?"

The flash of hurt nearly has me confessing where I've been all morning, but there's no way I'm fucking this surprise up.

I glance over her shoulder to where her mum and dad are standing, wrapped in each other's arms. Her dad gives me a chin lift, which I return before glancing back at Faith.

Fuck, she's beautiful. Her eyes are red from where she's been crying. My woman has a big heart and no doubt got affected by everyone's own accounts of Noah's misgivings today.

"No, I have a surprise for you."

"You do?" she asks, doing that cute head tilt that I love so much.

"Yeah, come on."

"What about the others?"

"Your mum and dad will inform them. They know all about it. Even helped me."

That has her smiling and giving a quick glance towards her parents. "They did, huh?"

"Yep, now come on, before it gets even colder."

"YOU'RE BRINGING ME to the cemetery?" she asks in disbelief. The way her eyes lower in disappointment has me biting back a grin. "You're not going to turn into a serial killer now, are ya? I kind of like having you around."

I laugh, throwing my head back. My woman is sassy and can bounce back from anything—even a date in a cemetery. "Your mum said this was your favourite place to be when you want to forget everything."

Her eyes mist and pain flashes behind them. "Yeah. Both my great-grandma's and great-grandpa are buried here. They're in plots next to each other."

I rub her back as we walk down the footpath to where they are buried. Her mum had brought me here a few days ago. And then this morning, after Faith gave her statement, I came to set everything up.

I am worried about it raining. It's getting colder, wetter, and darker earlier with Christmas a month away. Luckily, the rain has stayed away, but the sky is still dark with the promise.

We're only a few graves down when I hear her gasp. "Oh, my God, you did this?" she asks, turning to look at me.

Feeling a little uncomfortable, I nod, hoping I did the right thing by bringing her here. When her mum suggested it to me I had been a bit wary, wondering if she was pulling my chain. Turns out, she wasn't. Her sister, Lily, confirmed it, saying Faith would come out here all the time to talk to them.

If this doesn't go as planned, I do have another surprise up my sleeve. I was going to wait until Christmas, but when I got the phone call I had been waiting for, I decided I couldn't wait.

"Yeah, it's why I left court this morning after you gave your statement."

I light the candles that are already on their graves and add some battery-operated star lights to cover the ground and stone, wanting to give us more light. I wasn't sure how long we'd be here, and I didn't want to sit in the dark, at night, in a graveyard.

I'm a chicken shit when it comes to the supernatural, and I'm supposed to be a badass policeman.

"It's beautiful. Did you make us dinner too?" she asks, surprised when she sees the basket I had waiting for us.

I shrug, feeling my cheeks heat. "It's just some baguettes and cake until we get home. I also got you some WKD. I knew you'd need a drink after today."

"This is beautiful and just what I needed. Thank you."

"Hold on," I tell her, grabbing the plastic tarp out of the bag and placing it on the ground. Once it's done, I grab the blanket, doing the same before getting the two others for us to wrap around each other.

"You thought of everything."

I laugh. "This is okay?"

"Yeah," she whispers, before turning to the two graves. Her one pair of great-grandparents were buried together, wanting it that way. Her other great-grandma is on the other side, her stone just as beautiful. "Hey Grandma, Nan, Grandpa. I want you to meet Beau, my boyfriend, the guy I told you about."

I cuddle her against my chest, resting my chin on the top of her head as I listen to her fill them in on everything they've missed. My heart feels heavy at knowing she's spoken about me here before. It's something special to her, and for her to welcome me into it, just makes everything we have more spectacular.

Once she's finished telling them about the case, I hear her breath hitch and know she's crying.

"Hey, don't cry, baby, it's over." I kiss her forehead before moving to the corner of her eye, sucking the tear into my mouth.

"I can't help it. It's really over."

"It will be, baby. I want you to get me the cake out of the basket. We'll have the baguettes later."

She doesn't question my sudden change in subject. She never does. She's trusts blindly, and I know I'll spend the rest of my life proving to her that she made the right choice.

"Beau!" she gasps, a sob tearing from her throat.

Okay, so not the reaction I'd been hoping for.

Shit.

"Faith, I—I—I'm sorry. I thought—"

"Shut up!" she chokes out, her pained eyes finding mine. God, she takes my breath away. "How?"

I take the chain out of her dainty fingers and unclasp it to place it around her neck. "I called in a favour with Collings to get it out of evidence quicker. I knew how much this meant to you. You've been trying to keep your pain hidden over not getting it back, so I got it for you."

Her tears fall silently down her cheeks as she continues to hold the heart pendant in her fingers. "Thank you. Thank you so much, Beau. I can't—thank you. I didn't even know they had recovered it."

And the moment I've been waiting for, the moment I've made myself sick with worry over, is about to happen.

"I love you, Faith Carter."

I've never said it to another person, other than my parents—and that was when I was a kid. Now, I only say it to my mum over the phone.

I've known for a while that my feelings for Faith were more than I'd let on. It wasn't just one thing, but a million and one things that made me fall for the sassy, caring, funny, intelligent woman. It snuck on me, knocking the breath out of me, and each time she'd do something cute, the words would be on the tip of my tongue. The first time we made love, and every time since then, has been the same, each time becoming harder and harder to not blurt those three words out.

Why I never told her until now, I don't know. It wasn't that I wasn't sure, because I knew I was. I'd spent the majority of my teens and twenties screwing around with other women, and some I even cared for. But my feelings for Faith are different. They can't be measured or explained, only felt. And when I realised that I knew, from the deepest part of me, that I loved her.

Her head snaps up, the locket falling from her fingers and resting against her chest. "You love me?"

Again, not the reaction I'd been hoping for. I had imagined her throwing her arms around me, sobbing that she loved me too, but at the minute, she looks dazed, and immediately a little confused.

Even without her reply, I know I'll never take those words back. I meant them, and she deserves to hear them, even if she doesn't love me back. "I do, so fucking much."

"You really love me?"

She looks so fucking adorable as tears pool in her eyes that I pull her towards me, placing her down in my lap. "Yes, baby."

"I love you too, Beau. So much. I've wanted to tell you before now, but I didn't want to be the first one to say it." She pauses, taking a deep breath before her round eyes find mine, never wavering. "All my life I've looked for my Prince Charming. I was taught good things didn't come to those who wait, but to those who worked their arses off, so I promised myself I wouldn't give up until I found him. I wanted a man who was protective like my dad, loyal like uncle Mason, strong like uncle Malik, kind like uncle Myles and make me laugh like uncle Max. It was my uncle Malik who gave me the idea."

Her eyes are bright, shining with happiness. "He did?"

"Yeah." She laughs, her gaze drifting like she's remembering something. "It was Denny and Mason's wedding day. I remember asking each of my uncles if they'd be my prince." I growl, making her laugh. "Each turned me down gently, but when I got to Malik, something he said made me want something more. Thinking back, I don't even remember what it was, just the feeling I felt when he said it. After that, I watched how they were with their wives, and with each of them, I knew I wanted my future partner to have a part of them inside them.

"Before I met you, I had given up believing he exited. But you've protected me, stayed by my side, and even got me out of jail. You've stayed strong when my family has tried to scare you. You've cared for me from the very second I met you and every day since then. You've made me laugh when all I've wanted to do is cry. You, Beau Johnson, are who I've been searching for my whole life."

Her words leave a lump in my throat and my eyes begin to burn. Without thought, I take her face in my hands and kiss her. I show her with our kiss how much her words mean to me. There's nothing I could say that could trump what she said—nothing.

For the rest of my life I will remember this moment. Nothing could erase what she shared today, nothing.

Pulling back, I take in a deep breath before opening my eyes to look at her. It still amazes me how much her beauty startles me.

"Fuck, I love you so much."

Her smile is breath-taking. "I love you too, Beau."

My surprise jumps into my head, and like fate was watching down on me, this is the perfect moment to tell her.

"There's something else I have to tell you."

Her eyebrow raises as she looks at me adorably. "What? That you have a wife and kids stashed in some secret lair?"

I have to raise my own eyebrow at that, even if a chuckle does slip free. She comes up with the most ridiculous shit, but it's who she is. "Um, no!"

She sags in my lap, her lips twitching while she pretends to be relieved. "Good. I would hate to cut a bitch."

I laugh at the words coming from her mouth. I swear, every time a foul word comes out of her mouth it sounds funny. She's too sweet and delicate-looking to seem serious when she's saying them. It's like hearing a toddler swear.

"We wouldn't want that."

She shakes her head, pouting. "Nope, we wouldn't. So, what is this surprise? Gimme."

I grin when she starts to smile. "I was talking with your dad——"

"Okay, I'm going to stop you right there. From now on, you, my mum and my dad can't talk. I don't know if I'm comfortable with it yet."

I laugh a little at her trying to be serious. I can tell she doesn't mean it. She's glad I'm getting along with her parents. If there's one thing I learnt about her, it's that her family mean the world to her. I don't think she would truly accept someone into her life if they didn't approve. It would tear her apart.

"Before you go placing ban notices on me, listen to what I have to say."

She tilts her head, her lips puckering. "Okay, go on. I'm listening."

"So, as I was saying. I was talking to your dad about the dogs. They're too big to be cooped up in our flat." I pause, watching as she becomes apprehensive and wary. "I asked him if he knew of any places——"

"I'm not getting rid of my babies. You can forget it," she blurts out, trying to slip off me.

"Baby, I'm not asking you to. Jesus, do you ever wait for me to finish?" I ask, smiling at her.

"Sorry."

"He explained about your dream project and I have to agree with him, it's a brilliant idea. One that would need a lot of work to start up."

"Um, okay?" Her eyes scrunch together.

"Faith, baby, I bought us a house on Barrington Fields. It's close enough you are still near your family and far enough that you won't have neighbours complaining."

"What?" Her mouth hangs open, shock clear on her pretty little face.

"You can open your own dog shelter."

She shakes her head, her hands landing on my shoulders and squeezing. "You bought us a house?"

At her rising voice, I wince. "Yeah. I want us to be together. Your flat isn't big enough for us and two dogs. And if I know you like I think I know you, those two won't be the end of it."

"You bought us a house?" Her voice is a whisper now and I begin to worry, but when her eyes find mine, there're tears rolling down her cheeks.

"Yeah."

She bursts into tears, flinging herself at me like she can't get close enough. "I take what I said back." My heart is in my throat, and I pray I didn't hear her correctly. "You can totally talk to my parents whenever you want."

I sigh, falling on my back with her on top of me, my eyes closing in relief. "God, you scared me then." I open my eyes, watching for her reaction as tears continue to fall. "How about it, are you willing to move in with me?"

Her round eyes take me in, her expression soft and full of love. "Beau Johnson, I would follow you anywhere you asked me to. I love you."

Hearing her say it again is another beat to my heart. I'll never take those words for granted, or Faith.

"I love you too, Faith Carter."

EPILOGUE

SEVEN MONTHS LATER
AIDEN

WAKING UP TO THE BUILDERS WORKING on my neighbour's house puts me in an instant bad fucking mood. My head is fucking killing me after Faith and Beau's housewarming party. Wouldn't mind, but they both moved in five months ago and waited until their animal shelter was ready for opening before throwing one.

Their house out in Barrington Fields is pretty neat. It's an area we used to use to go dirt biking, until the police started sending regular officers out to check on the place.

Anyway, after watching my sister and her boyfriend act sickly in love, me and some of the others decided to hit the town.

I don't remember much after the second bar, it's a complete blur. Everything this year has been like getting run over by a train. It just never ended.

My parents wanted me to decide what I wanted to do with my life before they decided for me. When your peers are all strong, hard-working types with masculine jobs, telling them you want to be a cook isn't something you want to discuss. So, I put it off, playing my innocent act, which is what I do best, until my dad gave me an ultimatum. I could go work for Maddox, who runs a construction business, or go to college.

My decision was made after that, because as much as I love my cousin, being bossed around by him isn't something I'm willing to let happen. Seeing the disappointment on my dad's face pushed me in the direction I wanted to go. I had just been too immature to start them.

Now cooking school is on the agenda for this coming September, since I finished half the course this past April.

The banging reminds me of why I'm lying on my bed, wishing someone would put me out of my misery.

I groan, rolling over till my hands hit a warm body. I scrub the sleep out of my eyes, glancing at the naked female lying next me.

Holy fuck!

I don't even remember picking up some chick at the bar last night, let alone the girl's name. Even with a pounding headache I want to smack my head against the wall for being so careless.

One thing my dad drilled into me was to respect women who respect themselves and not to have time for those who don't.

It's easier said than done when you're a hormonal teenager with a constant boner. But I always made sure I knew something about the chick I banged— unless I get drunk, like I did last night, and don't bother even remembering how we met.

As if not knowing her name wasn't bad enough, she isn't even my type. For one, she's too fucking skinny, all bone and skin. It's fucking gross, and I cringe a little at the sight of her.

I like my women with meat on them, something I can grab hold of when I'm fucking them. I'm also a cuddlier, even if I don't fuck the same girl twice— unless she's lucky. And when I cuddle, I like to actually have something to cuddle, and a little bit of meat and soft skin goes a long fucking way. It also makes me hard as a rock.

The woman rolls over and I bite back a string of curses when I see she's probably the same age as my fucking mum.

Seriously gross, dude.

The lads are going to fucking rip into me when they see me. I can see it. There's no way they didn't see me leave with her or take pictures of my shameful one-night stand.

The builders next door start hammering away again, and I glance at the clock, my anger fuelling. Not only is it fucking Sunday, but it's seven in the goddamn morning.

Pissed that I have to spend another weekend listening to them fix her roof and whatever else the pile of rubble needs doing, I poke the old lady in the shoulder.

"Get up, you need to go," I bark out, pretending to be panicked.

I'm usually the happy, approachable one, but for some reason, my neighbour is getting to me. And it's not because of anything she's done directly.

It's because I've never fucking met her. I've only ever managed to get glimpses of her through the windows. It's like she's a vampire, because I've never seen her once come out in the day, not even to answer the door.

For the past eight months of living here, she has never, not once, answered her door to me, and I'm fucking awesome. Everybody loves me. I wouldn't even know she *was* a she if it weren't for Maggie. She still speaks to the owners and they filled her in on their granddaughter moving in.

Maggie also explained that her grandparents haven't lived in the house for years. They moved to a remote location, needing to get away to somewhere quiet with no neighbours.

I've left notes for her, even offered to mow her overgrown lawn and put up a fence between her and Maggie's property.

Not once has she answered any of them. Not even a thank you, or baked goods as a gesture of goodwill for even offering.

I'd thought maybe she was shy, so I went over again with some pasta bake and left it on her doorstep. But I found it there three days later when I got back from a trip with my family. That was the end for me. No one turns down my cooking, I'm a fucking master at it. She hadn't even taken the pot inside or cleaned the dish—which I had to soak for half the day to get the dried food off.

But that's not even why she's annoyed me—not entirely anyway.

I'm pissed because I love my sleep. A lot of it. I don't do well without it, never have done. It would take my mum hours to get me up and ready for school, and even then I was guaranteed to turn up late. It was such a given that even the teachers gave up trying to tell me to get up earlier to be on time.

"Excuse me?"

I glance back down at the woman sharing my bed and cringe once again, forgetting all about her as my mind drifted. Not only is she older, but she has the most nasally voice I've ever heard. I'd rather hear a fork on a plate than keep listening to that in my bed.

"I need you to get dressed and leave. My mum will be back any minute with Dad."

"Your mum?" she squeaks, getting up with the sheet still around her.

I shrug. "Yeah. She goes out of town for the night with my dad, so I get to do what I want. They come back early because they miss me and want to make sure I've done my homework for school." The lie easily rolls off my tongue, having been in similar situations before.

Her eyes widen. and her mouth falls open. "What?"

I should feel bad for the look of horror on her face, but I don't. I'm eighteen, basically a kid still, and she willingly slept with me. Not that I look eighteen, I don't. I look a lot older, always have.

I wink, getting up from the bed to pull my boxers on, even as I wince at the sound coming from next door.

"Don't worry, Mummy will love you. I can't wait to tell her we're getting married, but I think it's best I do it alone. She can be real protective of me."

It didn't escape my notice she's already married, and it's another thing I'm kicking myself for. I don't fuck around with someone who is in a relationship, no matter what this town thinks of me. I may like sex, but not enough to do that.

It seems last night I got more drunk than usual.

I hear her rushing to pull her clothes back on as I grab a pair of jogging bottoms off the chair.

"Look, I didn't know you were a kid. Last night was a drunken mistake. My husband forgot our anniversary and I just wanted to forget about it."

I spin around, feigning hurt. "What? You don't love me?"

She looks around the room for a means of escape, finding my door. "I'm going to go. I'll call a taxi from outside."

As soon as she's gone, I pull on my shoes, grab my phone and then run down the stairs, ignoring her squeak of surprise when she hears me coming. I ignore her as she runs down the path, her shoes in her hand and her shirt still untucked.

I rush over to next door, banging on the door so loud I instantly regret it. The pounding in my head just gets worse.

As usual, no one answers, but I didn't expect her to.

"Open the door!" I yell, looking up at the windows for any movements. I see the curtain twitch from the corner of my eye and growl, walking over to the window.

I knock on it, hearing a hiss behind the curtain.

"Go away," a soft voice says with a bite. She sounds young, which surprises me. I thought because her grandparents had basically given her a house, she'd be older.

"No, not until you tell those fucking builders to go away so I can get some fucking sleep."

When I get no reply, I growl. I hate rude and inconsiderate people.

My phone starts to ring in my hand, and seeing a number I don't recognise, I immediately answer, my tone sharper than usual.

"Hello?"

"Is this Mr. Aiden Carter?"

"It is," I answer, relaxing immediately when I realise it's just someone from college.

"I'm Doctor Howard calling from Hillsborough General hospital. I'm sorry to inform you, but last night Miss Giles died giving birth to a baby girl. She wrote her wishes down in case anything was to happen to her, as she knew the pregnancy was high risk. With her family no longer with us, custody will go to you, her father."

I pull the phone away from my ear, blood rushing from my face as I look at the screen. It has to be a family member fucking with me. It has to be.

"I'm sorry, but I think you've got the wrong person."

"You are Aiden Carter, correct?"

"Yes," I tell him, no longer recognising my own voice.

"We have DNA proof that you are the father."

"And I'm telling you, I have no idea what you are talking about. What DNA test?"

"Casey Giles took a paternity test to confirm the father. You are listed as the baby's biological father."

I feel my face drain at hearing Casey's name.

Casey was a chick I hooked up with last year at Party in the Park. It had been the triplets' birthday and we'd got free tickets from my sister's boyfriend, Beau.

Anyway, I got so wasted I hooked up with a girl I met there, and in the midst of fucking her, the condom split and got stuck somewhere up inside her.

I'd panicked, calling everyone in my family to come and help with the situation. But the girl had fucked off the minute I shot my load, tapping me on the shoulder and thanking me for a good time. Before I had a chance to tell her the condom wasn't around my dick, she was gone.

She also took my wallet, keys and everything else with her.

The only thing I had at the time was my phone.

A few months after it happened, she turned up at my doorstep with my wallet and a sheepish look on her face. I hadn't recognised her at first, until she refreshed my memory and showed me the small rounded bump she was sporting.

Even though I knew there was a possibility—okay, a strong one—I didn't believe her. The chick had fucked me, thanked me, then run off. She'd treated me like a slab of meat. It was degrading as hell and if I'm honest, I was pissed she didn't want to cuddle.

She'd started crying and left after using the toilet, saying she'd be back to get a DNA test done once the baby was born.

I'd pushed the whole thing from my memory because, even though I knew there was a chance, I didn't want to believe it, not with the way things went down with us. How was I meant to know she didn't fuck other guys that night? It wasn't like she stuck around to ask me what my favourite colour was.

"Aiden, are you there?"

I clear my throat, moving away from the window, no longer caring about the builders or my mysterious neighbour. "Yeah."

"We will need you to come to the hospital. To be cleared to take the baby home she will need a safely fitted car seat. Will you have that?"

"Yeah," I rasp out.

"See you soon."

He hangs up and I can do nothing but stare at the phone.

I'm a father.

At eighteen.

The heavy weight of what's just been handed to me forces me to my knees in the overgrown grass of my neighbour's front garden.

Stinging nettles burn into the palm of my hands and my bare chest, but I ignore the pain, once again reaching for my phone and dialling the one person on Earth who can help me.

"Hey."

"Mum, I need you."

TO BE CONTINUED

Look out for Aiden's book coming 2018

AUTHOR'S NOTE

I want to thank all my readers for being patient with me while they waited for me to get this book out. They kept me motivated through the entire writing process, and if it wasn't for them, it wouldn't have been finished.

I'm itching to start on Aiden's book straight away, but I do have other projects that I'm currently working on, so as much as I'd like to give a release date, I can't.

The Next Generation series was something I wanted to do whilst writing Max's book. It was hard knowing I only had one more book left to write before I had to say goodbye. It got to a point during Maverick's book that I knew I couldn't let these characters go. Fans of the series had hinted that they would like to see more Carter books, and I knew this would be perfect.

I hope you enjoyed reading Faith's book as much as I enjoyed writing it.

I would also like to give a massive thank you to my three children. Towards the end of writing Faith, something happened that nearly delayed publication, but my three beautiful, caring children did something amazing.

My daughter, Ellie-Mai, broke her wrist and had to go through surgery for it to be repaired. For the first few days, I couldn't even get my laptop out. Nothing could have pulled me away from her.

Then one night, when she couldn't sleep, she asked me why I wasn't working. I told her I didn't want to be distracted, in case she needed me.

My brave little girl got into my bed, curled up beside me and told me she'd sleep there so I would know she was okay.

It warmed my heart.

Not only that, but my other two children did everything they could to help her and give me more time to finish Faith. So instead of cleaning up any mess they left behind, I got to finish her book.

Also, Stephanie Farrant, you are a godsend. Even busy with other edits, your course and home life, you still managed to fit me in. I want to thank you, from the bottom of my heart, for completing another book of mine. Your work is amazing.

OTHER TITLES BY LISA HELEN GRAY

ABOUT THE AUTHOR

Lisa Helen Gray is Amazon's best-selling author of the Forgotten Series and the Carter Brothers series.

She loves hanging out, but most of all, curling up with a good book or watching movies. When she's not being a mum, she's a writer and a blogger.

She loves writing romance novels with a HEA and has a thing for alpha males.

I mean, who doesn't!

Just an ordinary girl surrounded by extraordinary books.

Printed in Great Britain
by Amazon

41497046R00158